Praise for To Catch a Husband

"More addictive than *Desperate Housewives*."

—Hilary De Vries, author of *The Gift Bag Chronicles*

"A wonderfully observed glimpse into the fabulous world of billion-dollar divorcées. The shoes, the lunches, the fillers, the whiff of desperation barely masked by Chanel No. 5. I loved it!"

—Claire Naylor, author of *Dog Handling* and *The Second Assistant*

"Lindsay Graves makes her rich heroines sympathetic, vulnerable, and charming, skewering the Colina Linda ladies with affection and humor. A wicked and delightful novel!"

—Christie Mellor, author of *The Three-Martini Playdate*

ALSO BY LINDSAY GRAVES

(Published by The Random House Publishing Group)

To Catch a Husband

To
KEEP
a Husband

AN EX-WIVES NOVEL

LINDSAY GRAVES

A Ballantine Books Trade Paperback Original

Published in the United States by Ballantine Books, an imprint of The Random House Publishing Group, a division of Random House, Inc., New York.

BALLANTINE and colophon are registered trademarks of Random House, Inc.

This book contains an excerpt from the forthcoming book *To Kill a Husband* by Lindsay Graves. This excerpt has been set for this edition only and may not reflect the final content of the forthcoming edition.

ISBN 978-0-345-48549-6

Printed in the United States of America

www.ballantinebooks.com

9 8 7 6 5 4 3 2 1

To catch a husband is an art;

To keep him is a job.

— Simone de Beauvoir

To
KEEP
a Husband

CHAPTER one

Are You Going to the Clementes'?

*L*ally Chandler Clemente had come back to San Carlino with magnificent style.

"Lally's back!" The word spread like canyon fire through salons and spas and the ecru-toned waiting rooms of the city's high-end dermatologists. It crackled over cell phones and ricocheted across thirty-two-dollar luncheon entrées. San Carlino society, which had begun settling in for the more relaxed pace of summer, began primping itself for a second social whirl.

Fabulous Lally! She'd been a Bond girl in her twenties (opposite Roger Moore in one of the late eighties flicks), then married to a succession of famous men—a rock star! a cinematographer! a game show host!—before waltzing off with local billionaire David Clemente (CEO of the Clemente Group International and currently tied for number 163 on the *Forbes* "400 Richest in America" list). The couple had married in mid-March, then embarked on a lavish honeymoon trip, the details of which had preceded the newlyweds back to town—a trek around the world via the Clemente private jet and an oceangoing ketch once owned by the late prince Rainier of Monaco, as well as by more exotic forms of transportation: camels through the Draa Valley; some sort of customized junk to navigate the tricky backwaters of the Yangtze. They had toured the Pyramids and the Parthenon and gazed with wonder at Angkor Wat, and they'd been wined and dined in the villas and palazzos of wealthy acquaintances on three continents.

And knowing Lally, her old friends sniggered, they were sure she had managed to shop up a storm—a speculation confirmed by the blizzard of boxes and baggage that had been FedExed back in advance.

The Clementes arrived home in the middle of June—the time of year on the California coast when thick fog billows in from the Pacific each day at dawn, stoppering the sky with a gray cottony quilt, retreating for only a few hours of sickly sunshine in the late afternoon. June gloom! But there was no gloom on the Clemente estate. Within a week after settling in, Lally and David threw open the doors of their baronial mansion and began to entertain. Select little dinners and butt-up-against-butt crushes. Coffees and cocktails and elegant high teas. The invitations flew and flurried onto the city like New Year's Eve confetti. "Are you going to that thingy of the Clementes'?" became the first question on every Zyderm-plumped pair of lips.

But, as everyone quickly came to realize, all these "thingies"—the dinners and crushes and high teas—were actually in the service of a higher purpose. David Clemente also presided over the Clemente Foundation, which was endowed with a billion dollars (give or take a few hundred million), and he'd appointed his new bride executive director. Word had it that the couple had combined their honeymoon with a humanitarian mission and that the new, *serious* Lally had inspected sub-Saharan irrigation projects with the same verve she used to apply to picking out the perfect Hermès handbag; that she now courted Carmelite nuns working for famine relief as assiduously as she'd once pursued A-list actors for her dinner table.

So everyone who attended an affair at the Clementes' knew to bring along a checkbook, because by the end of the morning, afternoon, or evening, they'd be hit up for a serious donation.

Caitlin Latch arrived at the Clemente estate with her checkbook securely tucked into the bottom of her bag, a knockoff Louis Vuitton monogram tote.

It was just after seven on a Thursday evening. The affair she was attending was a largish wine-and-finger-foods bash "in honor of Suraya Burab, founder of the Afghan Female Literacy Project." Caitlin considered this a marvelous cause. Educating oppressed women was something she supported wholeheartedly. She would love to contribute generously to it.

Problem was, her checking balance currently stood at minus seventy-six dollars and eleven cents, and her savings account was zilch. Meaning sometime during the speeches, after the elaborate thank-yous, and just before the appeal to cough up an additional donation, she'd have to try to melt inconspicuously away.

The Clemente estate occupied nineteen breathtaking ocean-view acres in Colina Linda, the swanky village nestled like a crown jewel on San Carlino's northern crest. Caitlin snaked up the long, crushed pink stone drive, her rattletrap Volvo wagon sandwiched between a Mercedes sedan and a Range Rover. She surrendered her car to one of the pack of mauve-jacketed valets who swarmed it and then she entered the foyer of the enormous main house.

It had been nearly eight months since she'd last been here, and she was immediately struck by a sense of both familiarity and strangeness. Nothing much had changed—nothing, that is, except her relationship to it all, and that had changed decisively. And there was that awful Clemente butler, a terrifyingly haughty man named Eduardo. For one dreadful moment, she was certain he was going to stop her:

You've got no business being here! I'll have to ask you to leave! But if he even recognized her, he gave no indication: His heavy-lidded gaze slid past her without even a flicker.

Another mauve-jacketed functionary checked her name from a digital list. "Follow the arrows," he barked.

Fluorescent orange arrows were taped to the walls, pointing the way down a spacious hall. Kind of tacky, Caitlin thought. Not quite what she'd expected from the haut stylish Lally.

She followed them dutifully into a cavernous room she'd never been in before—the ballroom, she guessed you'd call it—all butterscotch and rose, with high, coffered ceilings and soaring rectangular multipaned windows, the walls hung with the huge contemporary canvases David famously collected. It was already packed, people spilling out the tall French doors into the gardens. Women outnumbered men, Caitlin detected in a glance. This was almost always true in San Carlino: The city had unattached females the way Venice had pigeons—in huge, pecking, and almost identically arrayed flocks that gathered in the most advantageous places. The only singular thing about this particular flock was that a sprinkling of them sported Islamic head scarves.

Caitlin spotted Lally immediately. Hell, you couldn't miss her: Lally towered over six feet tall in the stiletto Jimmy Choos she favored. Flanked by the guests of honor, a gaunt elderly lady in a sari and a blooming young woman in a scarf, she was constantly in motion: She kissed, waved, laughed, hugged, vigorously pumped hands. Her husky voice blared like a train station announcement above the social babble: *"Nice to see you! So very nice to see you! It's so very good of you to come!"*

Caitlin hesitated. When you were attempting to move in social circles superior to your own, it was crucial never to give the impression that you were in over your head. This, she had discovered, was rule number one. Look and act as though you belonged, and you could pretty much soar along with the current. But one slipup and chances were you'd be savagely pecked apart.

So okay, she was pretty confident in the way she looked. Her teal blue DKNY pants suit (eighty percent off retail at the outlet in Camarillo!) was properly understated and deemphasized her spectacular figure. The Vuitton bag might be a fake, but it was a really good one—only the sleazy vomit green lining would give away its counterfeit status, and no one was likely to get a look at that.

But here was her real dilemma: What was the proper etiquette for attending a function at the home of newlyweds when several months before the wedding you'd been sleeping with the groom?

She pretended to examine a massive painting that looked like Chinese writing—slashes of black on a white background—while she puzzled the problem. She'd had a brief fling with David Clemente the previous autumn, shortly after he'd separated from his first wife and before he'd astonished the entire town by taking up with Lally—so it wasn't as if she'd gone behind Lally's back or anything. Really, it was no big deal. And Lally obviously didn't hold it against her—she'd even invited her to the wedding. True, there'd been seven hundred other guests, but it still indicated Lally harbored no hard feelings.

And, Caitlin reflected, nobody else would even remember that she and David had ever met.

"I suppose you're thinking all of this might've been yours," cackled a voice at her ear.

She whirled. *Shit!* It was Janey Martinez.

In a city that teemed with moneyed and snobbish divorcées, Caitlin considered Janey about the worst. Hers was the type of snobbery that arose from old wealth—the sort that made her take it for granted she was superior to you, despite her thunder thighs, and a grate-on-your-sinuses personality, and an ex-husband serving time in minimum security for some kind of Internet fraud.

"The big fish that got away," Janey added with an unpleasant smirk.

Caitlin forced a breezy laugh. "Oh, Janey, of course not. David and I were never anything more than friends."

Janey's smirk stretched wider. "Oh yeah, I'm sure. The very best of friends." She tugged at the hem of her Chanel jacket, which had the effect of widening the V opening, exposing a bit of disconcertingly prodigious cleavage. Janey had been a grade A frump, all oatmeal-colored cardigans and eyebrows that scraggled into a unibrow, until Lally had taken her under her wing and performed some radical makeover action. She was now waxed and streaked and Botoxed into what would be a semblance of chic, except for one peculiar thing—in the process, Janey seemed to have acquired a gargantuan new pair of tits. D cup at least. Possibly double D.

Could Lally really have suggested those? Caitlin wondered. Almost impossible to believe.

"So are you still working at that college rape place?" Janey pursued.

"The Rape Crisis Center? No, the university consolidated it with another department, and my job was cut."

"What a shame. And yet here you are generously supporting one of Lally's pet causes. Good for you. It must be quite a sacrifice."

"Not really," Caitlin said crisply. "I give to a lot of charities."

"Well, we all know you support thrift shops." Janey gave a nasty giggle.

Caitlin reddened. She knew precisely what Janey was referring to: Caitlin had worn to Lally's wedding a practically new Prada chiffon she'd scored at the Pioneer Daughters Resale Shoppe on Village Road, only to have Janey gleefully point out it was one of Lally's own cast-offs. It had been one of the most humiliating moments of her life.

Janey's attention suddenly flicked to the center of the room. "There he is!" she muttered, wheeling abruptly, and made a dash to a man emerging through the milling crowd, two overfilled glasses of wine balanced precariously in his hands.

A remarkably good-looking man, Caitlin noticed, tall and lean, with bronzy hair flopping into thick-lashed eyes and the kind of humorous, long-cornered mouth that made you think irresistibly about kissing. He glanced at Caitlin and gave a quizzical smile, causing a flutter kick of excitement in the pit of her stomach.

Then Janey snatched up one of the glasses he was holding, linked a proprietary arm through his, and steered him efficiently out of sight.

Who was he? Caitlin wondered. And why in heaven's name was he with someone as singularly unappetizing as Jane Kern Martinez?

But of course she knew why. They belonged to the same tribe. The boarding school and sailing club and never-think-twice-about-price tribe. The bottom line was, it didn't matter if you looked like one of your purebred Shar-Peis or you possessed the personality of one of your Rottweilers, being a member of the tribe was the principal thing that counted.

She was suddenly swept by a bitter feeling of rejection—the geeky girl left on the sidelines at the high school dance. There was a trick she'd picked up some years ago from an article in *Cosmo:* When you were feeling insecure, you repeated to yourself, "I'm glad I'm here, I'm *glad.*" Not only did it act like a bit of self-hypnotism, reinforcing your confidence, but when you ended with a stress on the word *glad,* it left your lips curved in exactly the right pleased-to-be-here smile. She mouthed it now: "I'm glad I'm here, I'm *glad*"; and then she threw back her shoulders and arched her back, and plunged into the fray.

The milling crowd propelled her out into a garden that formed a crescent around a water lily–strewn reflecting pool. She fought her way through the crush at a bar positioned under a bower of old-growth olives. "Chardonnay, please!" she shouted.

A glass of red wine was thrust into her hand. "Excuse me, I asked for white," she called to the retreating bartender. A pink-faced man muscled in front of her, roaring for a Glenfiddich on the rocks. With a sigh, Caitlin turned with the glass of red and began edging back through the packed bodies.

Thank God, a friend! Or at least someone she had a friendly acquaintance with—Jessica DiSantini, who used to be a lawyer, was divorced from a brain surgeon and was now romantically involved with a world-famous composer. No question of whether or not *she* fit in with the tribe, Caitlin thought wryly.

She lifted her free hand to wave. Someone jostled her from behind, and wine from her glass splashed onto the silk shantung sleeve of a woman beside her.

"You clumsy idiot, look what you did!" the woman snarled. "This is brand-new Saint Laurent!"

"I'm so sorry!" Caitlin exclaimed.

"You've ruined it!" The woman glared at her. Others were gawking with contempt or grins of snide amusement.

"I'm really very, very sorry," Caitlin muttered again. *I'm glad I'm here, I'm glad!* Her lips gelled in a pleasant curve, and she slunk quickly back into the house.

Jessica DiSantini, who had just stepped away from the bar with the San Pellegrino water she'd virtuously asked for instead of the merlot she craved, observed this little mishap with a great deal of delight—not over poor Caitlin Latch's embarrassment, but because the spoiled shantung sleeve belonged to Kiki Morrison, and Kiki was (a) the wife of Stu Morrison, a kill-the-earth shopping mall developer who'd bulldozed most of the few remaining orange groves in the county; (b) the bossy and officious chairwoman of half the charities-that-counted committees in town; and (c) a bony-assed slut whom, several years back at a yacht club Christmas party, Jessica had stumbled upon vigorously tongue-kissing Jessica's then husband, Michael, in the staff ladies' room.

Of course, that had been just a sneak preview of what the bastard louse Michael would later do. But it hadn't left Jessica with any residual tenderness for the bossy, bony-assed Kiki Morrison.

She lingered for an enjoyable moment to observe Kiki futilely dab club soda on the purple blotch, which now roughly resembled the head of the Energizer Bunny, while a coterie of fellow socialites fluttered and simpered around her. Assured that the stain was indelible, Jessica headed back into the mobbed ballroom.

Many familiar faces. If she were still Mrs. Michael DiSantini—that is, Mrs. Lord God Chief of Neurosurgery at Mission Mercy Hospital—a lot of these faces would be lighting up with hundred-kilowatt smiles, beckoning her to approach.

But as the discarded ex-wife of the Lord God, she knew that she was the one now expected to do the approaching.

She spied Taller Kern in a huddle with the mayor, the mayor's sister, and a couple of men wearing Wealthy Guy uniforms: blue cashmere blazers, gray slacks, dopey-patterned ties. She considered barging in on them: Taller was her mixed doubles partner and (since her divorce, at least) her best friend. But he'd been oddly distant lately: For instance, instead of lingering for their customary martini after a tennis match, he'd taken to hurrying off with mumbled excuses about having to do either vaguely this or not-quite-clear that; and he'd stopped calling two or three or six times a day to swap gossip or leisurely chew over the latest details of Jessica's sex life. Not that he'd dropped her completely—nothing as drastic as that. It was just that he wasn't acting quite the Vince Vaughn to her Owen Wilson these days.

She veered in the opposite direction and through a momentary gap in the throng caught sight of Caitlin Latch's tousled copper and gold head.

"Cait! Oh, Caitlin!" she called.

Caitlin hurried over to her. Funny how she always wore that same expression, Jessica thought—the kind of pleasant little smile a surgical nurse might wear while prepping you for a particularly nasty procedure.

"Jessica, how great to see you," Caitlin burbled. "I noticed you outside by the bar, but it was such a mad scene I couldn't get to you."

"Yeah, I know. And look, I saw what happened with Kiki."

Caitlin flushed. "Oh, God, I feel terrible about it! That stunning jacket!" She hesitated slightly. "Do you think I should offer to pay for the dry cleaning?"

Jessica gave a snort. "I think it's beyond dry cleaning. And I'm pretty sure that Stu Morrison can afford to buy her another, so don't even worry about it."

"I still feel terribly bad," Caitlin muttered.

"Darlings!"

As if materializing out of the ether, Lally Chandler suddenly towered at their side. It was amazing, Jessica marveled, how Lally had managed to so instantly transform herself from a somewhat glitzy celebrity ex to the hushed-luxe personification of a tycoon's spouse. Gone was the high-spouting ponytail that had been Lally's trademark since playing the Bond girl character Priscilla Much: Now her burnt sugar–colored hair fell straight to her shoulders, lifted from her flawless forehead by a velvet headband rimmed with pearls. Her mole-colored trousers suit was both rich and subdued. In fact, the only things that flashed about her now were the megacarat diamond on her ring finger and her white, white teeth.

She double-air-kissed Jessica and Caitlin. "Thank you both so much for coming! It means so incredibly much to me to know my friends support the causes I believe in."

Was she being sarcastic? Jessica wondered. For a brief time the year before, the three of them—Lally, Jessica, and Caitlin—had been involved in a fairly intense competition for the attractive, newly separated, and dizzyingly rich David Clemente. But unless Lally had become a far superior actress than in her starlet days, she appeared to be sincere.

"It's an important issue. I'm happy to do whatever I can," Jessica said politely.

"Absolutely," Caitlin echoed. "Whatever we can do."

"Thank you, thank you! You know, I've had the chance to visit some emerging nations in the past few months, and I can't tell you how much *drastically* needs to be done! Did you know that in Afghanistan the female literacy rate is less than twenty percent?"

"That's terrible," Caitlin clucked.

"A catastrophe! But we're going to change all that, no matter what it takes. In fact, David is in New York right this moment, coordinating funds with several UN agencies. And in just a little while I'm going to shamelessly beg you all to give as generously as you can." Lally bared her white teeth. "Where's Tom?" she asked, swiveling to Jessica. "Did you bring him along, or is he globe-hopping?"

"Globe-hopping. He's at a music festival in Vienna, premiering a new woodwind concerto. Then he hits a symposium in Montreal, and after that, I get him back home for the rest of the summer."

"Fabulous! You know, I often pat myself on the back for getting the two of you together. I suppose I'll always take an interest in Tommy's well-being, probably till the day I die."

Jessica smiled thinly. The fact that Tom Bramberg, the man she was furiously in love with, had been the first of Lally's four husbands, back—way back—when he was a minor rock star and Lally still a teenager, was not something she was eager to be reminded of.

As if prompted by her thoughts of rock and roll, a tinny rendition of the Ramones' "I Wanna Be Sedated" suddenly insinuated itself into the babble of the crowd.

"That's my cell," Caitlin said sheepishly. She opened her bag just a crack, Jessica observed, as if she had something embarrassing inside she didn't want anybody to see. She dug out her phone.

Lally leaned intimately toward Jessica. "Listen," she said in a low voice, "I really, *desperately* need to talk to you. Not now, sometime in private. Could we do lunch tomorrow?"

Jessica glanced at her, startled. What in the world could Lally Clemente need to really and desperately discuss with her?

Before she could reply, she was distracted by Caitlin, who was flipping her phone closed. Her face had paled, and for once her surgical nurse smile had disappeared.

"What's wrong?" Jessica asked.

"I've got to go," Caitlin said. "My son has just fallen out of a window."

CHAPTER two

All This Could Have Been Yours

aitlin's car screeched into the driveway of her little house and she leapt out, her heart pounding. The report had not been actually quite as dramatic as she'd made it seem to Lally and Jessica: The window Aiden had tumbled out of was in the kitchen and only about six feet off the ground, with an untended patch of rosemary below it to cushion his landing. But even a short fall could be serious. He could easily have fractured a bone or cracked his head severely enough to cause a concussion.

"Aidey?" she shouted, bursting through the front door.

She galloped upstairs and into his bedroom, and then she breathed a sigh of relief. He was sitting up in his messy bed, slurping a Fresca through a straw. The baby-sitter, Maria Reynaldo, straddled a corner of the bed, calmly eating Froot Loops from the box. They were watching *Meet the Fockers,* one of Aiden's favorite DVDs, even though he wasn't supposed to watch PG13, and they were both cracking up at Ben Stiller's mugging.

"Aidey, are you okay?" Caitlin said breathlessly.

He glanced up at her, and his expression changed instantly to one of pain and grievance. "No, I'm not. I hurt my leg and my arm."

"He just got a little scraped up," Maria said. "I washed it all up and put on some of that Neosporin cream you've got. And I was gonna put on some Band-Aids, but I wanted you to see first." Maria had thick, glossy black hair that swished provocatively down to her fanny, and she favored skintight clothing in loud animal prints, but she was actually a sensible girl studying to be a nurse's aide at a community college down in Oxnard.

"Let me see, sweetie," Caitlin said.

Aiden gingerly pushed off the sheet. He was wearing just underpants, and one of his somewhat pudgy legs displayed a raw, skinned knee. He thrust out his right arm to display his scraped elbow.

Nothing too serious, Caitlin saw with increased relief. "Does anything hurt when you move?"

"Nah, he's okay," Maria said cheerfully. "I wasn't sure whether to even call you."

"No, you did the right thing. Let's put the Band-Aids on."

She and Maria began ripping open Band-Aid patches and placing them gently over the scraped skin.

"Ow, that hurts." Aiden shot another look at Caitlin—the one she thought of as his "aggrieved middle-aged guy" expression.

"I'm sorry, sweetie, I'm trying to be gentle. So how did this happen?"

"I don't know. It just *happened*."

"We were hanging out downstairs in the living room playing Mario Kart, and then he went into the kitchen to get a Fresca, and then I heard him yelling," Maria elaborated.

"Sweetheart, you just don't go tumbling out of windows for no reason at all," Caitlin said.

"I was trying to look at something. What's the big deal? I didn't do it on *purpose*."

Something in the way he pronounced this made Caitlin glance at him sharply. It occurred to her that a number of times lately she'd had plans disrupted because of some problem with Aiden: the date she'd had to cancel with that sixtyish-but-cute tax attorney she'd met at Single Parents for Choice because Aiden began complaining about a sore throat just as she was heading out the door (the guy never called back); the "meet the town council candidates" tea she'd missed because Aidey forgot his clarinet case at the allergist's and she'd had to slog through rush-hour traffic back to the Mission District medical building to retrieve it . . .

Could he be doing these things on purpose?

"Do you want me to stay around, Caitlin, or should I take off?" Maria said.

"No, you might as well go." Caitlin headed back downstairs with her, scavenged her purse from the chair she'd flung it on, and counted out thirty-five dollars from her wallet—three hours' pay plus tip, even though Maria had been here less than two. Good baby-sitters were notoriously hard to come by, and she'd hate to run the risk of alienating Maria by not paying her for the promised length of time.

It pretty much depleted her cash. Funny, she'd thought she had more than that—she'd just withdrawn two hundred dollars from the ATM on Sunday. Money seemed to evaporate lately, though she couldn't figure out why. She'd pared down her expenses to the minimum: No more pit stops at the Coffee Bean; hair cut every eight weeks instead of six and no highlights until the drab brown roots were almost shockingly obvious; home facials and mini-mall pedicures instead of the luxurious ministrations of La Rocha, the day spa in Colina Linda.

After Maria left, Caitlin went into the kitchen and examined the window Aiden had fallen out of—a slightly warped casement window above the sink that opened only three-quarters of the way. He'd have had to climb up and stand in the sink basin and then shimmy himself through the smallish opening. Even if he hadn't jumped out deliberately, it still wasn't exactly a normal thing for a kid to do.

Her stomach clenched. Normal wasn't something that ran high with the male members of either side of Aiden's family. To begin with, her father, who'd been a court bailiff in Watkins Springs, Colorado, and who, when Caitlin was seven, had got up in the middle of the night, fixed himself a mug of instant cocoa, drunk it, and then gone into the garage and asphyxiated himself in his car with the radio tuned to a Spanish-language hip-hop station. And then her brother, Ken, a middle-aged virgin who collected bottle tops and still lived with their mom and her second husband in a senior citizen suburb of Albuquerque.

But the most alarming in this all-star lineup of the non-normal was Aiden's father, Caitlin's ex-husband, Ravi. Diagnosed five years ago with bipolarism—what they used to call manic depression: a chemical imbalance—sometimes too many chemicals and sometimes not enough being transmitted to the brain. But any way you wanted to put it, it still meant bonkers.

The funny thing was, what had first attracted her to Ravi Latch was that he'd seemed so completely normal. It was true that he was just a bit exotic—he was half East Indian, his mother being from a well-to-do family in Calcutta—but his father was an ordinary Protestant American who worked an ordinary nine-to-five writing life insurance policies for a firm up in Walnut Creek. Ravi, when she met him, was as down-to-earth as could be, all cheeseburgers and faded Levi's and rooting for the Giants and catching the latest Tom Cruise flick on Saturday night. And so damn smart! He'd been a rising star in the bonds analysis division of the San Francisco branch of Smith Barney. Caitlin, whose degree in communications from a mediocre small college in Oregon had so far afforded her no greater career opportunity than managing a floundering day spa, had scarcely been able to believe her luck.

They met at a pot-and-tequila party in the Haight at which neither of them had known the host. She was attracted to him right away—he was about the handsomest boy she'd ever seen, lanky and loose-jointed, with long-lashed caramel eyes and a quick, sunny grin that lit up the world around him. Within weeks, she was head over heels in love. Five months later, he proposed: It was at Candlestick Park, the Giants had just scored a winning run, the crowd was screaming, and Ravi shouted in her ear: "Do you think you might want to marry me?" To Caitlin, it suddenly seemed that the entire stadium was cheering exclusively for them.

They married under a blue-and-white-striped tent at a Sonoma winery and set up housekeeping in a second-floor flat in the foggy Richmond district of San Francisco. Ten months later, she found herself pregnant. Her future appeared securely mapped out. She'd work another few years while Ravi continued to climb the ranks at Smith Barney. They'd move to a bedroom community up in Marin, perhaps have another child, and she'd settle into the role of affluent suburban housewife, volunteering for school activities, taking up tennis, learning to cook with such exotic ingredients as green peppercorns and juniper berries.

It would all be wonderful and prosperous and, above all, normal.

So, okay, it hadn't turned out that way, to say the least. Ravi had flipped out, and their marriage had exploded. But she had bounced back. She considered her ability to bounce back—from a disastrous marriage, the loss of jobs, a hundred social slights and snubs, you name it—to be one of her greatest assets. She retained a deep optimism that each time she bounced back she rose a bit higher and that at some point she'd land on some fabulous peak, where she'd be content to stay put forever.

The thought now lifted her spirits. She began cleaning up the dishes from the hamburger and frozen peas dinner she'd bolted down with Aiden before rushing off to Lally's shindig. She scraped ketchup-bloodied remnants of meat into the disposal and then turned on the dishwasher, an ancient Kenmore that usually gave up the ghost before the final rinse cycle. Caitlin rented the house from a gay couple who'd moved up (in both the geographic and economic senses) to the cliffside neighborhood of San Carlino known as the Portofino, and every appliance was either on the fritz or totally kaput; but the rent she paid was significantly below market, so she didn't dare complain.

But it was a far cry from the stunning place she'd just come from. She filled a kettle—a battered Michael Graves, missing its little bird whistle—and set it on the stove, reflecting on the Clemente mansion. The profusion of large and light-washed rooms, exquisitely appointed with a museum's worth of art and antiques. The lush green lawns and flowering gardens rolling out to the sapphire expanse of the sea. The retinue of servants at your beck and call.

And she flashed on Janey Martinez's snide remark: "All this could have been yours."

Freaking right it could have. If things had played out just a little differently, she might well have snared David Clemente; and then it would have been *her* honeymoon tooling through the great ports of Europe, Africa, and Asia, and *she* would now be the one playing the part of Lady Bountiful, tossing brilliant fund-raisers and dispensing largesse to the needy of the world.

A thought streaked jaggedly through her mind—Aiden had been responsible for breaking things up between herself and David.

By accident, she reminded herself sternly.

It had not been his fault. And face it—she probably would have struck out with David anyway. So what kind of crappy mother was she to be blaming her son, even for a second, for something that hadn't been his fault?

Water boiling. She poured it into a glazed mug and dunked a bag of lemon myrtle tea. While it steeped, she perused a stack of parcel post boxes that had accumulated beside the kitchen door, new inventory for what used to be a sideline occupation but was currently her main source of income—selling vintage accessories on the Internet. She'd launched it several years ago, at first with just hats, scouring yard sales and flea markets for vintage items to resell on eBay and other auction sites. Lately she'd expanded to costume jewelry, which had a much higher profit margin: sparkling marcasite clips from the twenties; Bakelite brooches and bangles from the Depression years; fifties' vintage rhinestone pins in the kitschy-fashionable shapes of poodles and seahorses and pink flamingos.

The income from this online business combined with the salary and benefits from her job at the university Rape Crisis Center had made her flush enough to at least peripherally join in the social swim with some comfort. "Keeping up with the exes," as she thought of it—the divorcées with cushy alimony checks who were the true power behind San Carlino society. But it was becoming clear that unless something broke financially for her soon, she was going to have to drop out of the swim altogether.

Not that she'd ever had any illusions about it—she knew they all thought of her as a climber. A gold digger. And okay, so maybe she was. Who the hell wouldn't want to be rich?

But her real motivation was Aiden. If he was ever going to have a chance to be normal, he needed stability and security. And that, in turn, meant being raised in a pleasant and secure environment—and yeah, having the money to go along with it. Which was exactly why, five years ago, she had chosen to move to San Carlino, with its historic Spanish mission and picturesque red-tiled roofs and fabulously high number of millionaires per capita.

Blug-a-glug. A gurgling in the sluggish plumbing meant Aiden was flushing the upstairs john. He had what his pediatrician called a nervous bladder, meaning he had to pee what sometimes seemed like nineteen times an hour. Dr. Kittredge had said he'd grow out of it. *Please, please, God, let him grow out of it!*

Because really and truly, she didn't blame Aidey for anything wrong with her life. She blamed herself for not being able to make him happy.

And for the tiny but resilient dread she harbored that he was never, ever going to be normal.

She finished her tea and went back upstairs to check on him. Still in his underpants, he was sitting at his computer, typing intently away at the keyboard.

"Aidey?" she said.

He let out a little "Awp!" of surprise and spun in his chair. Then he tapped the computer mouse, and the display dissolved to the haunted graveyard images of his screen saver.

"What was that you were doing?" Caitlin asked.

"Nothing."

"It looked like you were instant messaging."

"No. I mean, yeah, I was. With Jonathan."

"Jonathan Lazaris?" This was a boy who'd been Aiden's only real friend until he'd moved with his family to Scottsdale, Arizona, the previous July. "I thought you never heard from him anymore."

"Yeah, I do. Sometimes. I mean, he changed his screen name, so at first I didn't know it was him."

"Then why did you turn it off when I came in?"

" 'Cause we were done. He had to go because his mom was calling him." Aiden squirmed in his chair. "What's the big deal?"

He was concealing something, that was obvious. But Caitlin maintained strict parental controls on his AOL account—limited access to the Net, stringent porn filters, e-mail only from names on his buddy list—so it couldn't be anything too alarming. Maybe he and Jonathan were trading fart jokes or penis-and-vagina stuff, the way ten-year-old boys did. Or maybe Aiden was just getting to that stage where he didn't want his mom nosing around in anything he did.

"It's no big deal, I'm just interested." She shrugged. "How do your scratches feel?"

"They sting."

"I'll put some more stuff on them."

"No," he said, pulling away.

"Okay, then, I think you should get into bed. I'm sure they'll feel a whole lot better in the morning."

With suspicious compliance, he slid off his chair and hauled himself back on top of his bed. She kissed his loamy-smelling head and stroked his hair, which was the same mouse-drab brown as her own color would be in the inconceivable event she stopped adding highlights. "Love you."

"Me too," he said automatically.

But the dreadful feeling still nagged her that whatever he was hiding was something more than just some smutty jokes.

CHAPTER *three*

A Walking Compendium of Clichés

*L*ally Chandler Clemente felt like the wrath of god. Early menopause. What a freaking bitch!

She was going through it all. The whole shebang. Hot flashes scorching her, inevitably at the most important or elegant occasions. They'd plagued her continuously during the honeymoon: She'd been flushing and dripping when she and David trooped backstage to meet the singers at La Scala; and while they were conferring with the head of the WHO in Geneva, her complexion had flambéed to the red hot hue of a habanero chile. Oh, and *worst* of all, the royal reception in Bangkok where that Thai princess had been so incredibly solicitous of her, because, as it turned out, she'd thought Lally had contracted malaria.

It was all just too humiliating!

Not to mention the violent mood swings, practically humming "Zippity Doo Dah" one moment and then feeling ready and willing to commit murder the next. Plus the night sweats that soaked her Anichini hand-loomed sheets. And of course constantly forgetting where she'd put down her Mont Blanc, her cell phone, her Cartier sapphire bracelet, whatever, so that she spent half her life bellowing for an assistant to help her locate the blasted things.

She was a walking, talking compendium of menopausal clichés!

Darling David was supportive, at least as far as he knew what she was going through. Not that she was exactly keeping it a secret. There *were* certain things she hid from him: for instance, the fact that she dyed her pubic hair because it had gone prematurely gray; or that the reason she had put off sleeping with him for several weeks after they'd started dating was not maidenly reluctance, but to have time to have an embarrassing tattoo (of a sea anemone—the result of a misguided madcap moment on her fortieth birthday) lasered off her upper thigh before he caught sight of it.

But Lally did scramble to hide the bulk of the beastly menopausal symptoms from him. She was forty-seven years old, but except in the strongest sunlight, she could (and usually did) pass for mid-thirties; still, David could have easily scooped himself up a twenty-five-year-old trophy—God knew there were always plenty of lovely young things slithering around him with visions of billion-dollar sugar plums dancing in their dewy heads. So why remind him he'd married a woman fourteen months older than him?

But now, grabbing a quick breakfast on the sea-breezy Hibiscus Patio of the old Broadmore Hotel with her new closest confidant Taller Kern, she felt the familiar flame rising from the base of her throat and surging toward her temples.

"Oh God, I'm turning into the Human Torch again," she moaned.

Taller tilted his elegant head and examined her dispassionately. "You know, don't you, that stress is an enormous factor in change-of-life symptoms? It interferes with the working of the adrenal glands, which are crucial in producing estrogen. And believe me, Lall, my dear, you need all the natural estrogen you can get right now."

"Since when did you become an expert in gynecology?" Lally said petulantly.

"I've been reading up. I just acquired the library of a sweet old couple over on the east side. The Harold Wellovers, do you know them?"

Lally shook her head.

"They're downsizing from a five-thousand-square-foot Craftsman to a two-bed condo, so I got the books. Mostly junk, but some interesting midcentury firsts. An extremely fine *Gravity's Rainbow* and a *Rabbit, Run* signed by Updike—"

"What the hell does this have to do with hot flashes?"

"Oh, well, for some peculiar reason that I won't even *begin* to speculate on, Mrs. W had also collected every edition of *Our Bodies, Ourselves*, starting with the original in 1973 right up to the latest one. For some equally peculiar reason, I find them very compelling reading. So go ahead, ask me anything about menopause. I know all about it."

J'en suis sûre, Lally was about to say. Her habit of tossing French words and phrases into her conversation dated to a sojourn in Paris post her Bond girl fame; but she had noticed that David looked vaguely pained when she did, and so she'd been making a concentrated effort to cut it out. "I'll bet you do," she said instead.

"And my consultation fees are extremely reasonable," he added smoothly. "Just the pleasure of your company."

Smiling, Lally let out a luxurious sigh. She'd spent the past several days shepherding the Afghani activist around town, constantly straining to understand the woman's thick accent. Taller's glibness was like slipping into a warm bath after a particularly long and arduous hike.

She regarded him now almost affectionately. He was one of that enormous clan of Kerns who had been socially prominent in San Carlino for about a million generations, a second or third cousin of Lally's *ex*-closest confidante, Janey Kern Martinez. Like most of his relatives, Taller lived off the income of some form of trust fund, while dabbling in a genteel "cachet" occupation—in his case, a cubbyhole of a rare books shop on Manzanita Street called Ex Libris, where he logged in a nontaxing three or four hours a day. He was the first man (the *only* man, now that Lally thought of it) she'd ever heard refer to himself as a "metrosexual." The term certainly fit: He was a straight guy who was fastidious about his wardrobe, had an almost preternatural appetite for gossip, and waxed his eyebrows.

He and Lally had almost come to blows over a nasty trick he'd pulled on her last year; but after she'd returned from her wedding trip, he had presented himself at her service, penitent, charming, and ever available at the press of a speed dial. Naturally, she was no idiot. She was acutely aware that if she hadn't snagged David Alderson Clemente, Taller would not be sitting here now, kowtowing to her over his one percent double latte and cranberry brioche.

Never trust a scorpion: Wasn't that what they said? Sooner or later, it *had* to sting you—that was simply and inexorably its nature. But for the time being, Taller provided for her a necessary—and, frankly, highly amusing—outlet.

"So *are* you stressed out?" he pursued.

"Well, of course I am. Just look at how complex my life has become. It's like running a small country. Do you have the faintest idea how many people we have working for us?" She paused for a sip of her fruit, herbal, and amino acids supplement shake, as prescribed by a Beverly Hills homeopathic gynecologist. The ingredients were sent over by Lally's kitchen staff, and the hotel kitchen obligingly whipped it up for her. It was the color of squashed bugs but surprisingly tasty. "Just for the Colina Linda house, it's dozens and dozens," she continued. "And then there's the Barbados compound, the London flat, and of course that doesn't even begin to include our personal staff. And everyone connected with the foundation—"

"Oh, the miseries of the super-rich! We poor peasants just don't realize how good we've got it."

Lally pulled a face. "I'm sure I sound ridiculous. And I'm not complaining. What I mean is, it's just been sort of overwhelming. And David is such a dynamo, the way he throws himself so completely into so many different things. . . . I mean, I adore him for it, but trying to keep up is staggering."

"Want my opinion? I don't really see you as Mother Teresa walking among the lepers."

"Oh, please! I never claimed to be."

"What I'm saying is, all this scooting around to emerging nations and hanging out with health ministers and Mother Superiors and what have you . . . Leave that to your husband, who loves it. You should just relax and do what you do best."

"Which I suppose you think is having my nails wrapped and going to lunch?"

"Actually, yes. Though the way I'd put it is being your fabulously glamorous self and coaxing people to give you enormous amounts of money. For the lepers, of course."

He smiled suavely and fingered his tie, a relic of the forties, extra-wide, with an abstract jacquard pattern. Taller affected a sort of living-in-another-time style; and this morning, sporting a natty windowpane-check jacket and that tie, his thinning, pale brown hair slicked back from his temples with a water-based gel, he was vaguely William Powell in *The Thin Man*—an illusion temporarily enhanced by a pencil mustache etched in foam on his lip after another sip of latte.

He dabbed away the mustache with a corner of his napkin. "To change the subject, how is the enchanting Chiara? Have you seen her lately?"

The mention of her granddaughter—the one Lally hadn't even known existed until just last fall—made something bright burst inside her. The little girl had rocked her world: Lally had never suspected she could feel anything as pure and as powerful as what she'd felt from the first second she'd laid eyes on Chiara.

"No, not since Christmas. I don't know—" Lally caught herself. It would be lethal to give Taller even a hint of the truth that, at the moment, she didn't know where the little girl was. "I mean, I hope to see her very soon," she amended. "She's got a birthday coming up. Four years old!"

"And her mother?"

"Sienna? Off on one of her jaunts. We haven't really been in close communication." To put an end to this dangerous conversation, Lally reached for her bag, plucked out a pair of sunglasses, and slipped them over her eyes.

"Great shades," Taller cooed. "Morgenthal-Frederics?"

"Yes, as a matter of fact, they are. I'm going to have to run, darling. I'm putting my old house on the market, and Rhonda's probably already there waiting for me. Oh, by the way," she added casually, "who was the man Janey brought to my Suraya Burab fund-raiser? They disappeared before I could get around to them."

"That was our cousin Evan. Jane and I are both related to him through our great-grandparents. But I thought you knew him. He's the architect designing the new building for your foundation. He's popped down from Seattle to oversee the groundbreaking."

"Oh, so he's J. Evanson Kern! I've seen his name on the plans, but they were finalized before I got involved."

Taller grinned—a Big Bad Wolf grin. "Good-looking guy, isn't he?"

"I suppose," Lally murmured. "I hadn't really thought about it."

"Yeah, right." Taller raised an arm and signaled for the waiter. "This is my treat."

Naturally, Lally thought. Taller always snapped up small checks. It was when the big ones arrived that he was conveniently preoccupied.

Lally's car, a Bentley the translucent silver gray of San Carlino fog, glided up to the Broadmore entrance the moment she stepped out the door. Her driver, an almost loonily cheerful, stubbly-chinned, short-on-English young man named Stefan, who was from the Czech Republic, God knew where David had picked him up, shot out of the car as if from an ejector seat. He snapped open the back door, practically clicking his heels as Lally ducked into the backseat.

"Polite Child Lane," she told him and settled herself into the bisque-colored leather.

She'd thought she would adore having a driver. She had pictured herself nestled in a sort of mini-office, catching up on calls, dictating mail, and getting scads of work done while tooling efficiently around town. But Stefan seemed constitutionally unable to exceed the speed limit; plus he had an almost uncanny knack for making wrong turns. So she spent most of her time in the car redirecting him or fruitlessly urging him to step on it.

Besides, she missed zipping around in her Mercedes convertible, a phone cradled under her chin and the sea breeze whipping her ponytail. It had made her feel young and carefree and slightly reckless. Being chauffeured, on the other hand, made her feel like some ancient dowager—as if she should have flannel blankets spread over her knees.

The Bentley swooshed in slow state through the eucalyptus-bowered lanes of Colina Linda. Lally opened her phone and spoke the name of her personal assistant, Perla, into it, and within seconds Perla responded. A decided perk of being a billionaire's wife—never any waiting. They spent several minutes weeding out Lally's crammed schedule. "Set up a meeting with everyone involved with the foundation headquarters groundbreaking," she directed. "I feel like I've been kept out of the loop."

"I'm on it," Perla said.

"Any word from Jessica DiSantini?"

"I've left three messages. No call back."

"Well, try again." Lally glanced up from the phone. "Left here," she snapped at Stefan. "A left, not right." To Perla, she said, "I'm almost at the house now. I'll check back in twenty minutes."

Stefan executed a leisurely left and inched up to Lally's former home. It was a meandering pink neo-Mediterranean with a four-story campanile modeled after the one on the church of San Michele in Lucca. Lally had purchased it with her third husband, Artie Willman, former host of the eighties' hit game show *Have I Got a Deal for You!*, and then had doubled the square footage and added the campanile with the settlement from their divorce. *Darling Artie!* Thirty years her senior and plagued with an array of old-guy ailments: arthritis, acid reflux, and some intractable foot fungus that required him to wear thick black woolen socks 24/7. But he'd also been kind-hearted and more than generous, and no one could ever make her laugh the way he did.

She still kept in touch with him. Artie was living in North Vegas now, remarried to a zaftig, sixtyish redhead who mother-henned him, and cooked him latkes and lasagna, and made sure he always had ample pairs of his special socks nesting in his bureau drawers. Pulling back up to the house they had shared always brought him vividly back to Lally's mind.

The spiky iron gates were ajar. Stefan turned the Bentley into the brick driveway and parked behind a dark green Lexus sedan. It belonged to Rhonda Kluge, Realtor to the Rich—wouldn't sully herself with any listing under three million. Lally had been dragging her heels about putting the house on the market, even though it had been just sitting there with most of her furnishings still in it since her marriage to David. Rhonda had been begging her to list it—she had half a dozen potential buyers just *aching* for such a property in Colina Linda, where the market was tight, tight, tight! Finally, Lally had capitulated. They were meeting here now to finalize the price.

As Lally slid out of her car, Rhonda emerged from a side gate. "Hullo-o, Lally!" she yodeled. She approached briskly, that typical real estate agent's pace meant to steer clients from point A to point B with no time to inspect a discolored baseboard or warped closet door.

"What are you doing out here?" Lally demanded. "Why didn't you go inside?"

Rhonda held up a ring of keys and jangled it like a cowbell. "I can't get in. I've tried every single door. Nothing will open."

"That's ridiculous." Lally snatched the key ring. Perhaps in some menopausal amnesiac fog she'd had the wrong set sent over to Rhonda. But no, this was definitely the right one—a sterling silver Tiffany horseshoe strung with eight high-security Schlage keys.

She marched up to the front door and aimed one of the keys at the lock. She froze in mid-aim: The lock face on the door was not made of antiqued brass, as it should be, but was now a garish shiny mock gold. She tried the key anyway. "It doesn't fit!"

"Told you." Rhonda brandished the automatic garage door opener that she held in her other hand. "Your clicker still opens the gates and the garage, but the door going inside from the garage is locked, and none of those keys work on that one, either."

"Well, obviously all the locks have been changed."

"Without your authorizing it?" Rhonda's voice squeaked with outrage. "What are you saying, Lally? Did somebody break into your home? Do you think we ought to call the police?"

Lally took a step back from the door and gazed upward at the pink expanse of the façade. There was a faint glow in the second-story windows—lights left carelessly burning in the middle of the day. She felt a hot flash of rage as she noticed most of the ground-floor windows were also blazing with light.

"No police," she said sharply. "I know who's here."

"Who?" said Rhonda.

"Who do you think?" Lally stared back at the illuminated house, taking the measure of all that squandered electricity. "It's Sienna."

"Your daughter? What the heck is she up to?"

"Don't know," Lally said. But with Sienna, it couldn't possibly be anything good.

CHAPTER four

OH OH OH OH OH OH OH

REASONS TO BREAK UP WITH TOM BRAMBERG:

*A*fter typing this, Jessica paused a second and examined the look of the letters. She'd chosen a font called Baskerville Old Face because it had a foggy, Sherlock Holmes–ian sound to it—a direct contrast to the shrill California sun that bleached the room she was working in. She was hoping it would help her apply a ruthlessly Holmes-like objectivity to her list. Now she got up and closed the filmy, pale green curtains, creating, if not quite a Victorian gloom, at least a more filtered light. She returned to her cluttered pine desk.

She was painfully aware that making this list smacked of the adolescent: She might as well fill up the margins with "Jessie + Tommy" entwined in hearts. She felt compelled to do it, though. It was the lawyer in her: only by stating the facts in cold print could she possibly sort out her emotions. She resumed typing:

REASONS TO BREAK UP WITH TOM BRAMBERG:

1. ALWAYS TRAVELING. LEAVING ME IN THE WORST OF BOTH WORLDS—ALONE BUT NOT FREE TO DATE.
2. EVEN WHEN HE'S HERE HE SOMETIMES ISN'T. EMOTIONALLY UNAVAILABLE!!!
3. STILL GRIEVING FOR HIS DEAD FAMILY. BUT REFUSES TO DISCUSS IT.

She paused. How do you compete with the ghosts of a wife and a young son killed in a car crash on a rainy New Hampshire road some eight years ago, if you couldn't even talk about it? These first three items alone should be enough to make any reasonable woman run shrieking for the emotional exit. But there was more. Oh yeah, there was lots more.

4. SMOKES!! PROMISES TO QUIT, BUT FAT CHANCE!
5. DOESN'T CARE WHAT HE WEARS. USUALLY LOOKS LIKE HE'S BEEN OUT ON THE STREETS BEGGING FOR SMALL CHANGE.

After a brief reflection, she deleted the last item. Her ex-husband, Michael, had cared about what he wore. Very much cared. Fussed and fretted over his wardrobe as if he customarily paraded down a red carpet lined with paparazzi on the way to his surgical theater. She could still hear his petulant baritone seeping down from the bedroom: "Hey, Jess? Where are my Ralph Lauren silk knot cuff links? The burgundies, not the navy-burgundy combo." Or, "Jessica, I specifically requested you to pick up my charcoal Paul Stuart slacks from the dry cleaners so I could have them for today."

If she had to choose between the two extremes, she'd go with Tom's scruffy indifference any day. She substituted another item:

5. DOESN'T CARE WHAT HE EATS.

Now that was a true flaw, particularly to Jessica, who was a skilled and impassioned cook. The last time he was here, she had spent the better part of a day preparing an authentic bouillabaisse from scratch, complete with homemade rouille, and he had scarfed it down with hardly a comment.

For a second, she couldn't think of anything else. Oh, come on, there had to be something else. What about that his ears were too big, his mouth too wide? That he really wasn't particularly handsome—some people even thought he was ugly. Nah. The whole world could think he was hideous, a dead ringer for Quasimodo, but it wouldn't matter—to Jessica, he was quite simply one of the most desirable men she'd ever met.

Well, okay, then . . .

6. ONCE UPON A TIME MARRIED TO LALLY CHANDLER. HOW WEIRD IS THAT?

It was a pretty formidable set of charges, she reflected. The conclusion seemed pretty cut-and-dried. But lawyer that she was, she needed to present a defense. And for the defense, she needed a new font.

She scrolled through the choices and selected Lucida Sans, a name that suggested "lucid" and "without nonsense."

REASONS NOT TO BREAK UP WITH TOM BRAMBERG:

She paused reflectively once again. Face it, there were no reasons. Okay, so maybe he was brilliantly talented and famous, at least in the rarefied world of high culture, but those were attributes existing outside of their relationship and really didn't count pro or con.

Clearly, she should get a grip on herself and move on.

Then suddenly she thought of his hands, with their broad, flat palms and musician's long, tapered fingers. She imagined the touch of them on her body, soft yet contradictorily sure. She began typing compulsively: OH OH OH OH OH OH OH

"Mom, are you okay?" Rowan's voice called through the shut door.

Oh, good Lord, she must have been saying it out loud. She hurriedly closed the breakup list file. The computer screen returned to the court filing she'd been working on earlier in the morning—her client, the owner of a sedate, old school–style antiques shop, was suing the raucous hair salon that had opened next to him on a noise complaint.

"I'm fine, honey," she called to Rowan.

Rowan cracked open the door. She was hugging Wally, the oldest of their three cats, a fat white creature with a tail permanently crooked like a question mark.

"Come in, it's okay," Jessica said.

Rowan dumped Wally on the floor and edged tentatively into the room. It was the ground-floor library room that Michael had used as his study and that Jessica had appropriated for her new legal practice until she could find a more suitable office. The tangerine-painted walls were checkered with faded squares where Michael had hung his memorabilia: college and med school diplomas; photos of the kids and his deceased Irish setter, McGill; his prized eight-by-ten of the 1998 Padres, signed by the team. It struck Jessica suddenly that there'd been no picture of herself anywhere in the room—or at least none that she could remember seeing.

She presented a cheerful face to her daughter. "What's up, kiddo?"

"I thought you were, like, maybe crying again."

"Oh hey, no! I was just talking to myself. You know how I tend to do that when I'm working."

"So why is it so dark in here?"

"Do you think it's dark? I find it kind of cozy. Sometimes I just get tired of another perfect sunny day."

Rowan peered dubiously at her. Why should Rowan believe her? After Michael had dumped her for a thirty-year-old patient, Jessica had spent a solid two months shedding tears. Sobbing in the small hours of the night with a pillow bunched over her face. Misting up in tandem with the sizzle of French toast in the morning. Blubbering on the way back from car pool. She had cried over sad endings in books, and over happy endings, and over endings that were neither one thing nor the other; and even a cartoon smooch between Marge and Homer Simpson could start the waterworks flowing again.

"I promise you, honey, the crying thing is totally over and done with," she said. "I'm perfectly okay."

"Yeah, okay. Good." Rowan shifted her weight uneasily and flipped a strand of her long hair behind her ear. The gold-and-silver-link bracelet on her wrist coruscated in the diffused sunlight. It was a Medic Alert bracelet: a single silver charm dangled from the links, engraved with the word *EPILEPSY* and an emergency number to call. "Um. Amanda's waiting outside. If we don't go now, we're gonna be late picking up Alex from the karate place."

"Oh, okay."

Amanda. Uh-man-duh. One year and ten and a half months ago, Michael had drilled into this person's head to remove a walnut-size nonmalignant tumor and had apparently found her brain so irresistibly adorable, he'd had no choice but to leave his wife of nineteen years for it.

The phone rang. *Tom?* In spite of herself, Jessica glanced hopefully at the caller ID. Just Lally. Or rather, Lally's social secretary—Lally didn't place her own calls these days, or at least not to a mere commoner such as Jessica. It was the third time the secretary had called in as many days, and for the third time, Jessica let it ring.

She rose from behind her desk to give Rowan a hug. "Got everything you need? Homework and computer and whatever?"

"Mom. It's just a few streets away. You always make it sound like I'm going to New Zealand or something."

"I know, I know, I'm sorry. It's just that I miss you guys when you're not here."

"Miss you, too. See ya tomorrow night."

Jessica waited several moments after Rowan had left the room, then walked quickly to a window in the hallway that afforded a view of the driveway. A dust-spattered blue Lexus SUV purred quietly on the asphalt, Amanda behind the wheel. Jessica could make out her sharpish profile and almost clownish profusion of tight brown curls.

Rowan appeared outside, said something to Amanda, then waggled her fingers at the backseat. So the babies must be back there, Jessica thought. Cozily swaddled in their infant seats. Three months ago, Michael and Amanda had become the proud parents of bouncing twin girls. They had somewhat ridiculous names—Fox and Fiona— undoubtedly selected by Amanda, who had a near genius for combining the precious with the pretentious.

Jessica supposed she could do the gracious thing and go down and say hello. Congratulate Amanda the Irresistible Brain on her blessed event. Coo over the little bundles of joy. During the late stages of Amanda's pregnancy, Jessica had, in fact, managed to pop out now and then and exchange a few vacuous pleasantries. But those had been times when Tommy had been in town and she'd been relatively fresh from his bed, and Amanda could have been about to give birth to gold-plated sextuplets, Jessica would not have cared less.

But Tommy Bramberg was currently six thousand miles and nine time zones away; and now here she was, spying at her ex-husband's new wife from a dim window, like some spiteful rejectee.

Phone was ringing again! No, this time it was Booter, Rowan's mynah bird, in his cage downstairs—he often imitated a ringing phone in between squawking, *"¿Cómo se llama?"* and the first bars of "Yellow Submarine."

Get back to work! The court document had to be filed by the end of the day. Jessica yanked herself away from the window and marched purposefully back into her office. This really didn't need to be a lawsuit, she thought, peering at the computer screen. If Creative Cuts would simply turn down the volume a bit on Radiohead and her client would pipe some background Mozart into his shop, everybody would be satisfied. Of course, people didn't always behave simply and seldom rationally: She could offer herself up as Exhibit A on that count.

She could call Tom, she thought suddenly. Simple and rational— it was only a little after six o'clock in Vienna.

But if he were in the middle of a rehearsal, or revising a score, or arguing with the concertmaster, or involved in anything to do with his work—which was pretty likely, seeing as how almost a hundred percent of his waking time on these trips was devoted to work—she knew how annoyed he'd be by an interruption. Not that he'd say so to her. Anyone who overheard him talking to her would probably think he sounded devoted and attentive.

But she would be able to detect the faint note of impatience—the tiny catch in his voice, a split-second pause before answering a question—and it would destroy any pleasure she had in the conversation.

She clicked back on to her breakup list:

REASONS TO BREAK UP WITH TOM BRAMBERG:
7. LOVES HIS WORK MORE THAN HE LOVES ME.

If, she thought ruefully, he even did love her at all.

CHAPTER five

Living in a Virtual Paradise

The day had begun promisingly for Caitlin with a call at eight-thirty from the office of the general manager of Serenity Waters, inviting her to come in for an interview. Serenity Waters was a five-star spa located in a hot springs fifteen miles due east of the city where the Mojave Desert kicked off. Its chefs were recruited from the great kitchens of France and its meditation masters culled from the Himalayas. From the lengthy menu of spa treatments, you could select the Molten Wild Honey Immersion, a "Capistrano" facial, featuring the dried and pulverized droppings of the famous swallows, or a two-hour pressure-point foot massage that some people swore was better than sex.

Caitlin had spotted a want ad for coordinator of guest services in the *San Carlino Courier* (Serenity Waters was so not the type of place that advertised on Craig's List) and had dashed off a résumé, figuring she'd never stand a chance. Serenity Waters *was* the kind of place that required some kind of pull to get in the door; it was a miracle that they'd called. She scheduled an interview for the following week, feeling elated as she put down the phone.

The feeling didn't last long. The car pool that was supposed to be taking Aiden to day camp was ten minutes late. Caitlin waited another five minutes, then looked up Bettina Perkins's cell number from the St. Matthew's telephone tree she kept tacked up next to the kitchen phone.

"Oh, Caitlin." Bettina was in her car, and the reception was iffy. "Oh dear, love, I'm afraid there's been a frightful muddle. Didn't you get my e-mail?"

"No, I didn't."

"Bloody hell, I sent it last night." Bettina had been born in some posh suburb of London, and though she'd lived in America since about the age of four, she still affected a ta-ta, anyone-for-crumpets? British accent that became more or less pronounced depending on the stickiness of the social situation. At the moment, it was as thick as the queen's.

"I haven't had time to check messages this morning," Caitlin said warily.

"Oh, I'm frightfully sorry. The beastly thing is, I've had to drop out of car pool." A strident rise of children's voices in the background obviously contradicted this. Bettina gave a tinselly little laugh. "Actually, I'm doing car pool, but on a bit of a different route. The Greenbachers just decided to send Jonas to Sagebrush, and . . . well, you see, their place is rather more convenient to the rest of us . . ." The connection became garbled, then cleared briefly. ". . . we have such precious little time as it is . . ." Something unintelligible. ". . . up in the canyon, I'm afraid I'm going to lose you . . ."

More convenient, my ass, Caitlin thought bitterly, slamming down the phone. The Greenbachers lived on a bluff jutting out on a northern tip of Colina Linda—it took an extra ten minutes just to navigate the twisty neighborhood streets to their estate. The truth was obvious—Aiden had been dumped by that phony British wannabe and those other Stepfords in the car pool for a richer and more popular boy.

She scrambled to locate her car keys. Aiden was in the living room, hunkered over some bleeping game on his PlayStation. "Aidey, come on," she called.

The bleeping stopped abruptly, and he shuffled out into the hall. "We're going on our own," she told him.

"How come?"

"Because I totally forgot to confirm with the other moms that I wanted to be in the car pool, and now they're filled up. It's my fault."

He slanted a suspicious glance at her: The excuse sounded lame, even to her. But he didn't challenge it. He was probably relieved—Bettina's daughter, Madison, was your basic Mean Girl horror.

"Hey, Mom?" he said as they got into the car. "Can I have my phone back yet?"

The cell phone with the "I Wanna Be Sedated" ring tone was actually his. Caitlin had borrowed it a few weeks ago after emerging from a garage sale with her arms full of bulky purchases, fumbling everything and dropping both purchases and her own phone on the street, smashing the phone. She had meant to buy a new one and give him back his own.

But then it occurred to her that if Aiden could be concealing something with instant messaging, he could do it even easier with text messaging on a cell. "Sorry, sweetie, I need it just a little longer. I just can't afford to replace mine yet."

It wasn't a total lie—paying for a new cell would definitely take a bite out of her monthly budget. And if there was one thing Aiden never questioned, it was her ceaseless quest to economize. He let out an annoyed little grunt but didn't pursue it any further.

She drove as fast as she dared, skirting the central streets that would be clotted now with rush-hour traffic, but she still got caught in a tie-up of tour buses emptying in front of the mission. She idled through two lights, staring at the mustard-colored adobe façade. It was inscribed with the words *La Misión de San Carlos y de la Reina de los*

Carlinos. The Mission of Saint Charles and of the Queen of the Hills. This had also been the original name of the city—El Pueblo de San Carlos y de la Reina de los Colinas—but sometime in the beginning of the nineteenth century it had been contracted to the rather Italian- and posher-sounding "San Carlino."

It was actually appropriate that the city didn't have a "real" name, Caitlin reflected, since in a lot of ways, San Carlino wasn't a real city. Not like others she was familiar with: Denver, San Francisco, L.A. There were no skyscrapers—building codes prohibited anything taller than seven stories. The sidewalks were never thronged with rushing and jostling pedestrians, and there was nothing even re- motely like a skid row. It was definitely not a place like Hollywood, Wall Street, or Silicon Valley, where people hustled to make it in glamorous industries. The only real career opportunity was the sprawling University of San Carlino, whose reputation was based equally on marine biology and wild keg parties; but even that was ac- tually located in a different town, the scruffy, working-class Mar Verde five miles down the coast.

San Carlino was about lifestyle. Living in a virtual paradise.

And paradise was something that attracted women much more than men: Caitlin had discovered this to her dismay shortly after relo- cating here. Sure, a lot of wealthy guys moved here with their families to take advantage of the lifestyle, and more than a few of them even- tually got divorced. But as soon they did, the ex-husbands inevitably hightailed it back to where the action was—leaving one more divor- cée to rattle around paradise.

Which was probably why she hadn't met anyone yet. Anyone se- rious, that is, because she met men all the time. They went after her like wasps for pears, as her mother would say. At Whole Foods and at Target, on movie lines and at school functions and charity events, she'd be frequently hit on. But inevitably they'd be too old (geezers) or too young (you'd be surprised) or broke or not-in-recovery alcoholics or have some such fatal flaw, otherwise why the hell would they still be unattached and living in San Carlino?

She thought again of her close brush last year with snagging the newly separated David Clemente, and with a sigh she once again put the thought out of her mind.

She finally untangled her car from the maze of buses and began the ascent up Señorita Canyon, twisting her way up above the marine layer into crystalline air. The road dwindled to a narrow dirt lane and ended in a large and deserted clearing at the ridge of the canyon.

"We're too late," Aiden said. "Everybody's already gone."

There was a note of relief in his voice that made Caitlin's heart sink. "Doesn't matter. We'll just hike down to the camp ourselves."

They got out of the car and she examined the signs posted at the several trailheads leading out from the clearing. There were two day camps located in the canyon. One was called Sagebrush. It boasted twenty miles of sinuous bridle paths, a ceramics kiln, and an Olympic-size diving pool lined with Italian tile, and it cost nine hundred bucks a week per camper. The other camp was called Cottonwood, and it was run by the YMCA. No horses, no kiln, no diving, or even nondiving, pool, but it was a tenth of the price.

Madison Perkins and Jonas Greenbacher and the other kids in Bettina's car pool were enrolled at Sagebrush. Aiden was at Cottonwood. "They instill such great values!" Caitlin always chirped enthusiastically, as if that were her real reason for sending him there.

As if anybody were ever fooled.

She located the hand-lettered sign pointing to Cottonwood, and she and Aiden began trudging down the dusty dirt trail. This had to be the day she'd decided to break out the new Taryn Rose taupe sandals that were supposed to be the mainstay of her summer shoe wardrobe. Ten yards down the trail and already they had acquired a brown film that did not look as if it would brush off.

The trail took a switchback and then gave onto the camp, a conglomeration of rickety buildings engulfed by a swarm of kids in yellow T-shirts. Caitlin hunted up a teenage counselor and handed Aiden over to him, watching until the two had trudged out of sight. You'd almost think he was going off to his execution instead of a fun-filled day at camp. His jeans were droopy, his T-shirt was untucked, and the shoelaces of his sneakers flopped untied: It was the current preteen fashion, and on other boys it looked cool. Why, oh why, she wondered, did it look on Aiden as if he hadn't bothered to finish dressing?

For a moment, she nearly ran after him, scooped him into her arms: *You don't have to go! You can come back home if you want.*

But she couldn't protect him forever.

Besides, she needed him out of the house for what she was planning to do.

She kicked off the probably already ruined sandals. Then, shaking off the sticky little burrs of guilt that clung to her conscience, she turned and climbed barefoot back up the trail.

When she returned home from the campsite, she headed directly to her Mac. She entered Aiden's AOL password—ALOHOMORA. He'd said it was a Hogwarts spell that was used to get into things that were hard to get into. *Clever.* He really was a smart kid. His IQ and aptitude scores were always high. The mediocre report cards he brought home only meant he didn't apply himself.

But why was she checking up on him in secret? Other parents at St. Matthew's were forever discussing the need—the right!—to monitor their kids' Internet activity. There'd been an incident the year before—a group of eighth graders had been in contact with a registered sex offender—uncovered when one of the moms read her daughter's e-mail, and now parents were all being urged to keep strict tabs on what their kids were sending and receiving.

Caitlin was becoming more and more convinced that Aiden was hiding something from her. It had happened again last night—she'd caught him furtively shutting down his computer screen the moment she appeared in his room. "I was just browsing the *Superman* movie site, and then I was done with it," he insisted. She could always tell when he was lying: Instead of his nose growing longer, his voice got higher, rising higher and higher in pitch the further he strayed from the truth. Last night, he'd practically turned into an operatic soprano.

What if he was in touch with a pedophile? Some depraved monster, coaxing him with promises of toys and games and God only knew what. The idea almost made her heart stop.

She figured she had no choice but to investigate his account without him knowing. She pulled up his mail screen and clicked on his buddy list. About twenty-five screen names. A few she recognized: her own, of course, and Aiden's paternal grandparents, HLLATCH@SUPERLINK—they were not much into computer use, but once in a blue moon his grandma sent an animated greeting card. And there was her brother, Ken: NEWMEXICOGUY. Ken seemed to have nothing to do *but* fart around on the computer, bombarding Aiden with jokes and links to dopey-cute sites.

The rest of the screen names would include every kid in Aiden's class at St. Mattie's. Didn't mean he was popular. St. Matthew's School, in a desperate attempt to cram some concept of sharing and cooperation into children who, for the most part, had been catered to and indulged since they were fetuses, assigned each student a constantly rotating "homework buddy." Every other week, they'd be paired with a different classmate and assigned to complete a report together—meaning, of course, they all had to have access to one another's e-mail.

The screen names were typical of preteens: BRITTANY95; SITHLORD3442. Nothing that raised a red flag.

So just what had she been expecting to find? IMACHILD MOLESTER@PERVERT.COM?

A wave of self-disgust swept over her. She had lowered herself to snooping on her son, and for what? For nothing.

So what else could she do? How about bringing it all out in the open? Coming right out and having him account for all the names on the list. But he'd whine and moan and carry on as if he were being uniquely persecuted, and then he'd still probably lie to her anyway.

Or she could e-mail every name on his list and say, "Hi, I'm Aiden's mom, just checking that you are who you say you are...."

Yeah, right. Thereby humiliating him to his entire class.

Or maybe she could find a way to get him to identify the names without suspecting her true motive. It couldn't be that hard to come up with a convincing ruse.

That's what she'd do, she decided, shutting down his account. In the meantime, she had to set about making some desperately needed money.

CHAPTER six

Who Else Would Have the Colossal Nerve?

he Colina Linda law offices of Suarez, Appelthorpe and White were housed in a homey-looking cottage on Foxkirk Lane. Jessica had been an associate in the firm, roughly a year away from making partner, but she had quit abruptly after Rowan's first epileptic seizure. When she had told Ben Appelthorpe she was going back into practice, he had generously offered to toss some overflow clients her way.

Now, as she drove away from the offices, the backseat of her car was crammed with boxes of deposition transcripts from one of those overflow cases: A wealthy gay couple had died in a plane crash leaving no will and seventeen potential heirs to battle it out in probate. It was going to take hours and hours to plow through the depositions, she thought, as she pulled onto El Paseo.

She braked for a red light. Through her rearview mirror, she watched a car come speeding up behind her—a large, silvery-satin luxury car, the driver's face invisible behind an iridescent dazzle of sunlight refracted from the windshield. It's not going to stop! she realized with horror and braced herself for the impact.

The car came to an abrupt halt scarcely four inches from her rear bumper. "Jackass!" she muttered.

The red light switched to green. She turned off the heavily trafficked El Paseo and proceeded down Silver Creek Road, Colina Linda's main drag, with its open-air cafés and scented-soap boutiques and the old clapboard hotel where silent screen stars of the twenties used to book rooms for their extramarital trysts. The satiny car remained glued to her tail.

Jessica felt a jolt of alarm: Was she being targeted for some sort of robbery or carjacking? Did such things happen in the middle of the day, in a village as highly policed as Colina Linda, with dozens of people gawking from cafés?

And if so, were such crimes perpetrated by people driving a far swankier car than the one they were planning to steal?

She swerved left onto West Jackson, in the direction of the sheriff's station, hoping that would deter the pursuer, but the car followed smoothly behind. She stepped on the gas. The pursuing car speeded up as well and began a furious honking that only increased her alarm. Then suddenly it veered to the left and pulled abreast of her.

The rear window rolled down, and Lally Clemente's sleek head popped turtlelike from the opening.

"Yoo-oo, Jessica! Stop, I need to talk to you!"

Jessica pulled over to the curb, taking breaths to calm her racing heart. Lally's car—a Bentley, she now observed—swooshed almost soundlessly to a halt behind her. The rear door flew open, and Lally unfolded her lanky body from the seat.

Jessica emerged from her own car to meet her. "For God's sake, Lally, you scared the living daylights out of me! I thought you were a carjacker."

"Sorry, darling, I thought you'd recognize the Bentley. But you gave me no alternative. You've refused to answer my calls."

"Yeah, I know, I just haven't had time. I'm trying to set up a law practice—"

"That's exactly why I've been calling you. I want to hire you!"

"Me?" Jessica shot her a dubious look. Surely the Clementes had platoons of high-powered attorneys at their service? "Why me? I'm just getting back into practice after eight years. And in a really small way, wills and deeds and things like that—"

"Yes, yes, I know," Lally cut her off. "Listen, I'd rather not talk about this standing in the middle of traffic. I've got a lunch, but I could cancel it, and we could grab a quick bite."

"Sorry, I can't. I'll be up to my butt in depositions this afternoon. And right now I'm on my way to pick up my mother and take her to her podiatrist."

"No problem. I'll send my car to take her."

Jessica gave a short laugh. "I don't think so."

"Look, darling, I just need ten minutes. *Five*, okay?" Without waiting for an invitation, Lally opened the passenger door of Jessica's car and plunked herself in.

Jessica hesitated briefly, then slid in next to her. The towering and dazzlingly groomed Lally made her Saab wagon suddenly seem scruffy and cramped. She hastily plucked a few crumpled papers from under Lally's feet. There was a Skittles wrapper peeking from beneath her Ralph Lauren skirt. Jessica wondered if she could wriggle it out without Lally noticing it. "Sorry, my car's a bit of a mess," she muttered.

"Oh, I don't care," Lally said impatiently. "This is really important. Sienna's taken over my house!"

"What?"

"My daughter, Sienna. She's ensconced herself in my former house on Polite Child. I was just about to stick the place on the market. Rhonda lowballs it at four and a half million but really thinks I can get over five. She and I went over there to decide on the listing price, and we found all the locks had been changed. Every single one! We couldn't get in!"

Jessica giggled at the picture of Lally Clemente and Rhonda Kluge frantically tramping around the perimeter of that gaudy house, fruitlessly jiggling keys in locks.

"I don't think it's amusing," Lally said huffily. "I'm just about at my wits' end."

"Are you sure it's Sienna?"

"Positive. I mean, who else would have the colossal nerve? It's like she's stolen my house right out from under me."

"Did you try knocking or ringing the bell?"

"Of course I did, what do you think? I've gone back four times, knocking and ringing and hollering my head off. But obviously, if she wanted to have any contact with me, she wouldn't have changed the locks."

Made sense, Jessica had to agree. Sienna, she recalled, was the product of some extramarital fling Lally had had during her brief teenage marriage to Tommy Bramberg. She had seen the girl only once—Sienna had been the maid of honor in Lally's wedding to David Clemente—but Jessica recalled an exquisite creature, a shimmer of pale gold and silver.

A living moonbeam—that was the image Jessica had thought of at the time.

The moonbeam was widely rumored to be wild and unprincipled: a slut, a kleptomaniac, a pathological liar, you name it. At one point in the past, there had been a rupture between her and Lally—they didn't speak to each other for something like three or four years. Then Lally had discovered the existence of a granddaughter, and it had prompted a reconciliation; and then, as far as Jessica knew, it had all been happily ever after between them.

"I thought you and Sienna had made up," she said.

Lally compressed her apricot-glossed lips. "We did for about five seconds. She was happy to be in my wedding, particularly after I wrote her a two-hundred-thousand-dollar check."

"Wow."

"Wow is right. And then guess what? She wanted more. She wanted me to keep shelling out fifty grand every month, no questions asked. So I agreed to, because of the baby, you know. But then she parked Chiara with her other grandparents—the father's people in New Jersey—and I can only guess what Sienna was doing with the money. So I cut her off and she stopped speaking to me, and now she's pulled this stunt of taking over my house."

"Sounds to me what you really need is a locksmith," Jessica said.

"I really don't want to antagonize her. She could stop me from ever seeing Chiara again, and that would be just so awful!" Lally suddenly seemed to crumple, as if some essential mineral had been leached from her bones. "Look, I love David very much, and I do love my daughter, even if she doesn't want to believe it. But with Chiara, it's something else. It's the most powerful thing I've ever felt. From the moment I first laid eyes on her, I knew I'd give up the entire world for her in a second."

"Yes." Jessica nodded. "I can understand."

"I can look back now on what a lousy mother I was to Sienna, and I feel so staggeringly guilty about it. I had her when I was so young, you know, just a kid myself, and I made a lot of mistakes, so I can hardly blame her for turning out the way she has. But what makes me crazy is thinking that unless I do something, Chiara will turn out the same way. It's like I've been given a second chance. Maybe with Chiara I can make up for some of what I failed to give to Sienna." Lally drew herself up stiffly again. "And frankly, Jessica, this time I don't want to blow it."

"Okay, but why do you want to hire me? If I start some kind of eviction procedure against Sienna, don't you think that'll antagonize her even more?"

"I don't want you to evict her. What I want is for you to find out what she's up to."

Jessica gave a startled laugh. "What makes you think I could do that?"

"You're the perfect person. In the first place, you're with Tommy, and she adores him. He's always been a kind of father to her, even though he's not her biological one."

"Then why don't you get Tommy to talk to her?"

Lally blew a little puff of exasperation. "He always takes her side. It's like he's got this totally blind spot when it comes to Sienna. He could catch her stealing from the poor box and he'd find some way to excuse her. I mean, he'd say she was planning to pay it back with interest or something."

Jessica grinned. That sounded precisely like Tom Bramberg.

"The main reason I'm asking you," Lally went on, "is because you're somebody she could relate to. You're practically the perfect mother, everybody says so."

The perfect mother? Jessica flashed on her two-month crying jag. And how in her midnight fantasies she used to inflict on her ex-husband—the father of her children!—a pustulating and fatal skin disease. And how that had been replaced with an X-rated obsession with a tormented composer.

"That's ridiculous," she said. "I'm not that great a mom."

"Oh, but you really are. You could get Sienna to open up to you, and she wouldn't even suspect you were doing it for me."

"Oh, wait a minute! You mean you want me to *spy* on her."

"I've got to find out what she's up to," Lally said tensely. "Look . . . I haven't told anybody, not even David, but Chiara has disappeared. I mean, she's not with her other grandparents anymore. They said Sienna showed up last month and took her away with no explanation, and she wouldn't say where she was taking her. They're frantic, too. For all I know, Sienna's got her with her in my house."

"Locked up in the house? That would be pretty creepy."

"Sienna's capable of creepy, believe me."

Jessica suddenly had a vivid memory of watching Sienna glide up the aisle at Lally's wedding. Sienna had swiveled her head and, catching Jessica's eye, made a face—a gruesomely cross-eyed, gargoylish face. Jessica had been both startled and disturbed by it, and for some time afterward, she had wondered what it had meant.

"Look, Jessica," Lally went on, "I realize this is outside the usual scope of your professional services."

"You think?"

Lally ignored the sarcasm. "I'd expect you to bill above your standard rate. Let's say double. And if you're successful, I'll throw in a substantial bonus."

So typical of Lally! Thinking she could get anybody to do any damn thing she wanted if she threw enough money at them. Jessica struggled to keep her temper. "Lally," she said, "I've got to go pick up my mother. You have two choices: You can either get out of my car right this minute, or you can take a spin with me out to the Sycamore Springs Independent Living Village and then to the extremely inviting office of Dr. Seymour Wiest, podiatrist."

"Okay, so don't do it as a professional thing. Do it as my friend."

Jessica turned on the ignition.

With a grumble of frustration, Lally snapped open the door and stepped out of the Saab. The Skittles wrapper she'd been sitting on clung to her bottom for a second, then fluttered lazily to the ground.

"Think about it," she said, and sashayed back to the Bentley.

Some people possessed perfect pitch or a knack for picking stocks that would triple overnight: Caitlin considered her unique talent to be the ability to root out a treasure buried under slag heaps of junk. It was as if some sort of Angel of the Thrift Shops whispered in her ear: *Check out the contents in that filthy packing crate back in the corner. No, look under the old* TV Guides *and fake fur boa!* She pictured the angel as being shaped kind of like the Mrs. Butterworth maple syrup bottle, but with fabulous taste in accessories: a chic felt hat tilting over her thick gray bun and maybe a calfskin Ricky bag dangling from her sturdy arm.

The angel Mrs. Butterworth had been whispering loud and clear at a garage sale Caitlin had cruised through down in Camarillo the week before. At first glance, the sale had looked particularly unpromising: nightmarish goose-necked lamps, stuffed animals missing eyes or tails or button noses, and sweat-stained plus-size cardigans.

Then the whispering began: *See that crappy old dressing table over there? The one that looks made out of waterlogged cardboard? All its drawers are warped and hard to open? Give 'em a good yank and search inside.*

Caitlin had directed herself obediently to this hideous piece of furniture and yanked hard on the double row of drawers. From the bottom one, she'd unearthed a shoebox crammed to the lid with costume jewelry. She'd offered twenty bucks for the box, got it for twenty-five. At home she'd sorted through it—mostly tangles of plastic beads and yellowing fake pearls. But there were also a sizable number of brooches, and when she examined these, her heart began to beat quickly. Nineteen in all, from the forties, she guessed, fashioned in the shapes of natural things—leaves and flowers, frogs and hummingbirds. They appeared to be real gold set with semiprecious stones.

She had dashed them over to a jeweler friend, a septuagenarian with a shop on Fourth Street who appraised things for her for almost nothing, unless you counted the privilege of staring at her tits. He'd confirmed her find: "Mostly eighteen-karat gold. Beautiful workmanship, real old school." He'd identified the gems: peridot, garnet, aquamarine, and a few Caitlin had never heard of—chrysoberyl and alexandrite.

She had posted the brooches on a variety of online auctions, and by this afternoon seventeen of the nineteen had sold, the lowest for two hundred and seventy-two dollars, the highest—a dragonfly of white and yellow gold set with blue zircons, fire opals, and diamonds—for just under eighteen hundred, to a bidder in Vancouver. She was eight thousand six hundred and forty-nine dollars richer!

She wrapped each pin, first in tissue and then in bubble wrap, then entombed it like a tiny mummy in a shiny white box filled with Styrofoam popcorn. Then she encased each box in brown parcel paper, double-taped it, and printed the address in black Magic Marker. It was almost four p.m. by the time she was finished. She stacked the parcels in four sturdy shopping bags, loaded them into the trunk of her Volvo, and sped off to the post office.

Like most of the city's official buildings, the San Carlino Post Office was a historic structure, heavy on charm but lousy in the efficiency department. Its parking consisted of ten narrow slots fitted into a small lot wedged between Flower Street and a service alley. All the spaces were filled. There was a parking structure five blocks away, but that would mean trekking back through a seedy section of town with over eight thousand bucks' worth of vintage jewelry in her possession.

She idled her car at the entrance to the lot and waited. Finally, someone began to back out of a space at the far end. The lot wasn't wide enough for two cars to pass: Caitlin waited for the other one to drive out before starting toward the vacated space.

Before she could get to it, a dark red SUV whipped in from the alley and pulled smoothly into the space. One of those aerodynamic German models: BMW? No, Porsche Cayenne. Asshole car.

"Shit!" she exclaimed. She gave a furious blast of her horn.

A guy leapt out of the Cayenne. A preppy asshole in a black baseball cap and royal blue windbreaker. Figured. He carried several long white tubes in the crook of his arm like a Frenchman toting baguettes.

Caitlin leaned on the horn again. He ignored it and jogged into the building.

"Goddamn bastard!" She slapped her hands on the wheel in frustration.

It was twelve minutes before another car pulled out and freed up a slot. She grabbed her four shopping bags and entered the chill, dim interior, cursing the line that snaked all the way to the door.

Preppy Asshole was standing at one of the customer writing stations, scribbling something in a daybook. Apparently he'd already concluded his business—he no longer had the cardboard tubes.

She marched angrily up to him. "You stole my space, asshole."

He glanced at her, startled. "I stole what?"

She registered dark blue eyes fringed with black lashes, bronze-colored hair flopping from beneath the brim of his cap, a long-cornered mouth. He was the guy she'd seen at Lally's thingy—the one who had appeared to be Janey Martinez's property. He was somewhat older than he'd looked in the roseate light of the Clemente ballroom. Early forties, she guessed—there were silver threads among the bronze; and he had those Robert Redford–ish crinkles that were crow's-feet on a woman but somehow attractive on a man.

"My parking space," she told him. "I was clearly sitting there in my car waiting for it, and you shot in from the alley and grabbed it."

"Jesus, I'm sorry. I guess I was in kind of a cloud. I had to have something postmarked by five o'clock or I'd have been in serious trouble." He smiled, a little-boy-sorry smile, peering at her from under his amazing lashes.

Oh yeah, he knew what kind of charm he had. Was probably used to zapping women with it and getting his own way. "I'm in something of a hurry too," she said coldly.

"Then I doubly apologize. But I've seen you before, haven't I? Wasn't it at one of these affairs my cousin Jane's been dragging me to?"

Cousin? So he was one of Janey Martinez's many relations and not necessarily her date.

"So where was it?" he went on. "That drunken debauch on the McCaffreys' boat?"

The McCaffreys' "boat" was a schooner bigger than a basketball court. Sean McCaffrey was commodore of the Colina Linda yacht club. Dixie McCaffrey adorned herself with diamonds the size of brussels sprouts just to play golf. Caitlin was hardly on their invitation list. "I don't think so," she said stiffly.

He snapped his fingers. "Franz Kline!"

"Wrong again. I don't even know him."

He laughed lightly. "No, I meant you were standing in front of the Franz Kline, the painting, at that mob scene at the Clementes'."

Caitlin flushed bright red. *Idiot.* She had taken an art history course at the lousy college she'd gone to. She was perfectly aware of Franz Kline, knew he was an important modern artist. Instead of making the connection, she had revealed herself to be a first class airhead.

"I'm really in a hurry," she said brusquely. "If you'll excuse me, I need to get on line." She turned abruptly and headed to the tail of the snaking queue.

When she emerged from the building, she found him waiting for her, leaning casually against the hood of his Cayenne. He shot up a hand and strolled over to her car.

"Look, I really want to make amends for my piggish behavior," he said. "I'd love to take you to lunch. I'm jammed up for the next few days, but next Tuesday would be good for me. Café Cygne, okay?"

Such complete and infuriating confidence in his voice. Just assumed she'd be eager to have lunch with him—couldn't possibly imagine anyone not wanting to. Particularly not anyone female.

But Café Cygne was the priciest place in town—where the ladies-who-lunch lunched—and he had just cost Caitlin a half hour of her life, so why shouldn't she soak him for an expensive meal?

"I guess I could do that . . . ," she began.

"Excellent," he said briskly. "One o'clock, okay? I'll see ya there." Without waiting for further confirmation, he turned and began that same insouciant stroll back to his car.

"Hey!" she said.

He turned back, swiveling on the heel of a loafer.

"What's your name?" Or did he think he was such totally hot shit that everyone simply knew who he was?

He grinned. "Evan. Evanson Kern." He yanked a wallet from a pocket of his windbreaker and slid out a card. "This has got all my pertinent info. And I guess you should tell me yours."

"Caitlin Latch."

"Caitlin," he repeated. "See ya Tuesday, then."

Another little-boy smile, and then he sauntered back to the Porsche, leapt in, and pulled out of the lot.

Caitlin examined the card. It was pale green with engraved-looking lettering. J. Evanson Kern, AIA. A Seattle address and phone and fax numbers.

He was a Kern. That would explain his I'm-so-goddamned-entitled aura.

But what did AIA stand for? American Incorporated Assholes?

She giggled and tucked the card in her purse. She glanced at her watch, a silly Swatch affair worlds removed from the thin-as-a-wafer gold item Evan Kern sported on his wrist. Eek, later than she'd thought! She'd have to step on it to pick up Aiden on time.

There was some sort of commotion at the camp trail-head clearing when Caitlin pulled up to it. Kids from both camps were being picked up, their camp affiliations identified by the T-shirts they wore—rich piney green for Sagebrush; plebeian stop sign yellow for Cottonwood—and both kids and parents seemed hugely upset. Some of the younger campers were crying, and one little girl was howling at the top of her lungs.

Then Caitlin noticed that it seemed to be only the Sagebrushers who were making the fuss—the yellow-shirted Cottonwooders looked, if anything, mildly entertained. A snarling trio of buffed and cashmere-hoodied moms that included Bettina Perkins had cornered a cringing Sagebrush counselor, backing her practically up against a prickly pear, and were lambasting her with a string of colorful profanities. Other parents were ushering their Sagebrush progeny into cars as gingerly as if the kids' little butts had been turned into glass.

Caitlin inched her car up beside a feral-looking black Jaguar. A wiry, dark-haired man in a pink shirt was feeding several Sagebrushers into the backseat. It was Jessica DiSantini's ex-husband, Michael, the neurosurgeon who'd run off with one of his brain surgery patients—Caitlin recognized him from the two moles above his left eyebrow that made it look arched in perpetually sarcastic surprise.

"Hey, what's going on?" she called. "What's everybody so upset about?"

"Sagebrush got swarmed by bees," Dr. DiSantini snapped back. "At least three kids got stung. It was all that blasted jasmine they planted last year—it attracts the damn things from miles around. It was just lucky that none of the kids had a reaction. Anaphylactic shock can be fatal."

"That's awful," Caitlin said. The jasmine, she recalled, was one of the big selling points in the glossy Sagebrush brochure: "The natural beauty of Señorita Canyon is enhanced by a profusion of cultivated flowering shrubs. . . ." It somehow neglected to mention the killer bees.

"Damn right it's awful. Criminal, if you ask me. We ought to sue!" Dr. DiSantini hurled himself churlishly into his Jag and slammed the door.

Caitlin scouted the yellow-shirted kids for Aiden, finally spotting him emerging up the trail. It struck her suddenly that he was becoming handsome. He had dropped some of the baby fat that had given him that almost piggy look (no wonder his jeans were so droopy). Being leaner made his pale brown eyes look larger and more lustrous and accentuated his long eyelashes.

He was starting to look more like his father, she realized with a pang. Why hadn't she noticed it this morning? Funny how kids could change sometimes right before your eyes!

Then she saw he was with a bigger, tough-looking Hispanic boy who was shoving him around. She threw open her car door, prepared to leap out and defend him; except Aiden wasn't being bullied—it was just friendly roughhousing. Both boys were giggling as they shoved and swatted at each other.

Aiden was roughhousing! She practically bounced for joy.

She tooted the horn and caught his attention. He waved good-bye to the other boy and, still laughing, came over and got into the car.

"So how did it go?" she asked.

"It was okay," he said.

Yes! She pumped a mental fist in the air. *It was okay!* Not "It sucked," or "It was terrible," or "I hate it, why do I have to go there?"

She struggled to keep the raw elation out of her voice. "So what kinds of things did you do?"

"There was a nature hike, and we had to like collect leaves to bring back so they could get identified? And this one kid brought back poison oak? And then, after that, I was like on the Badger Team, and we played the Coyote Team in this new kind of handball, and we won eight to seven."

He won! *Double yes!*

He wasn't the kid who brought back poison oak! *Yes, yes, and yes!*

She raised a hand and high-fived him. It was turning into one of those days when, for a miracle, everything clicked into place.

CHAPTER seven

That Atrocious Little Social Climber

uesdays, between eleven a.m. and two p.m., was Brokers Caravan, when the listing agents of homes for sale in the San Carlino area held open houses for the benefit of other real estate agents. A few months before, Janey Martinez had been struck with the brilliant idea that Brokers Caravan would be the key to her getting a decent night's sleep.

Actually, her first idea had been to cruise the Sunday open houses for the general public, but at these, the showing agents were too likely to stick to your heels, eager to point out the priceless Batchelder fireplace tiles or the exquisite maple flooring lurking under the ratty brown wall-to-wall. But at the brokers' opens, it was apparently professional courtesy to let you wander and poke about on your own.

So on Tuesday mornings, Janey attired herself like your basic real estate agent. Prim navy blazer. Pleated white blouse. A capacious shoulder bag that looked as stuffed as a capon with multiple listings books and closing documents and what-have-you.

Then she perused the caravan listings in the weekly Realtors magazine and picked out her destinations. She avoided listings in Colina Linda and the upper-crust sections of San Carlino, where she was likely to be ID'd by such familiar busybodies as Rhonda Kluge. Instead she targeted those in the development sprawls located in the landslide-prone foothills to the south and east of town—anonymous clusters of overbuilt "haciendas" huddled together in treeless cul-de-sacs, where she was unlikely to encounter anyone she knew.

She signed in using a variety of phony names and phony Realtor affiliations—Century City, Sotheby's, Re/Max; then, after a token cruise through the all-granite kitchen, the double-height living room, the pickled oak-paneled den (*gag me!*), she'd hike to the master bedroom. As soon as she was sure the coast was clear, she'd begin scouring the contents of the cabinets for prescription vials.

If the open house was a flop, with just one or two agents straggling in and out of rooms, she could take a bit of time examining the inventory. But in a crowded showing, with people constantly popping in and out of the master suite, she might have only ten or fifteen seconds to search before someone approached.

It wasn't a perfect system. The majority of times, she came up empty-handed. Or if she did find anything, it might just be half a tablet rattling around in the bottom of the vial or stuff that had been moldering since 1993 and lost all its potency. But by hitting four or five homes per Tuesday, she managed approximately every other week to score something good: Halcion, Xanax, Ambien (so popular now), or her favorite—good, old-fashioned, and always super-reliable Valium. Enough, anyhow, to let her get some rest, without having to go begging to some tut-tutting internist or patronizing gynecologist.

But since the middle of June, she'd been in a dry spell. She'd started to slip into her old pattern of insomnia—bolting awake at two in the morning, thinking she'd heard a footstep creaking on a stair or the sound of a door being jimmied open somewhere in the house and then not getting back to sleep until well after dawn.

But today, on her very first try, she'd had success—a nearly full little vial of lorazepam, which was the generic name for Ativan.

Darling little thing! She'd discovered it snuggled beneath a turquoise sink in the bathroom of a ghastly split-ranch on the outskirts of Mar Verde. The prescription, belonging, per the vial, to one Christine Abounader, dated from nearly a year ago—not so old as to be worthless, but old enough to indicate that Ms. Abounader wasn't hugely dependent on it or anything. Probably had forgotten it was even there. Janey had copped it without a smidgen of guilt.

She'd swallowed one immediately, rationalizing that she merited one after such a long period of going without. And almost immediately she felt its lovely, soothing effects. By the time she had driven back to Colina Linda, the world had acquired a mellow glow. How marvelous it would be to stretch out for a long and luxurious nap!

But she couldn't—she had a lunch date at Café Cygne. At home, she peeled off the pseudo-Realtor's getup and slipped into her new dusty-rose-colored Dior suit. Then it was back into the Mercedes to tool over to Silver Creek Road.

Lunch was with a new client, Tilda Lazenby. Janey designed garden rooms—designated outdoor spaces with walls, floors, sometimes even ceilings, fashioned from trellises, pavers, and vegetation. It was what Lally Chandler Clemente referred to as a "cachet job," meaning you didn't do it for the money—Janey, of course, possessed a hefty private income. But if you didn't have children to justify your existence and still wanted to be taken at least semiseriously, you had to have some sort of career. Every season she took on one or two little projects. And she was good at them—she prided herself on that.

She hoisted a little tower of photo books from the Mercedes and carried them into the café. She spied Tilda Lazenby seated at a crummy table in the Siberia behind the hostess's desk. The Lazenbys were new to Colina Linda and obviously new to money as well—everything they did was too loud, too ostentatious. Tilda, as always, was an alphabet soup of designer initials—Chanel double C's, Louis Vuitton LVs; the Dolce & Gabbana D&G—you could teach a child to read from any one of her outfits. Small wonder she'd been banished out of sight.

"I'm with Mrs. Lazenby," Janey informed the hostess, Regine.

Regine's eyes popped, and her jaw went slack with dismay. "But she didn't tell me she was meeting *you*, Mrs. Martinez! And now I'm afraid I have no other table, we're booked solid—"

"Don't worry, Regine, it's fine." Janey felt mellow as moonlight. She glided placidly behind the hostess to the crappy table and smacked the air beside Tilda Lazenby's overrouged cheek.

Tilda had already ordered a cocktail, something with a chartreuse hue in a highball glass skewered with tiny onions. *Poor gal—she simply doesn't get it at all.* "Evian, no ice," Janey murmured to the hovering server.

"So I was thinking, Jane . . . ," Tilda boomed. She always spoke at a volume that suggested she thought the neighboring tables were all dying to be in on her conversation. "Instead of that wisteria arbor we talked about on the streetward side, maybe we could do a classical colonnade. Because we're doing the marble pavers, right? And so I just thought a colonnade would go. I brought a picture from *Architectural Digest* to give you an idea."

She shoved a folded magazine across the table at Janey.

Janey glanced at the photo spread and sighed. She remembered seeing this—an aristocratically shabby sixteenth-century palazzo on the outskirts of Rome belonging to some dotty old *principessa*.

Clueless.

She pushed the magazine back at Tilda. "A colonnade is marvelous if it's real, but fake columns are just about the hokiest thing you can imagine. We might as well go with garden gnomes and a flock of fake flamingos."

"Oh. Uh, yes, I see what you mean." Chastened, Tilda reached for her silly drink.

The saving grace of these nouveau types was that they were so easy to push around. Janey smiled indulgently, then flipped open one of her picture books. "Here's that high-backed bench I wanted to show you. We could have it copied in teak. And I found an herbaceous border that I think is really lovely. . . ."

She reached for another book, and as she did, she glanced at the café entrance. Her heart did a flip-flop.

Her cousin Evan had just come in.

Second cousin twice removed, to be exact. She'd had a major crush on him since she was thirteen and he was fourteen and they had close-danced to "If I Was a Carpenter" at his big sister Kathryn's wedding in Laguna. His family had migrated to Bellingham, up by Seattle, and then he'd gone east for college, Williams and Yale Architecture, while she'd gone upstate to Mills. After that, well, they'd both married and he'd settled in Seattle, and she'd seen him only at the occasional large family baptism or funeral.

But now here he was, in San Carlino, bunking at first with their mutual cousin Taller before subletting a beach-view condo on the west side. She had invited him to Lally's Afghanistan affair the other evening because her previous escort had punked out on her; but she hadn't been with Evan for more than ten minutes when she began to have the same electric shock feeling she'd had at thirteen, crushed against him in a slow dance with his hand on the small of her back.

He was walking right toward her. Her heart pounded. She started to get up, a greeting bubbling to her lips.

But if he even noticed her, he gave no indication. Regine marched him briskly past Janey's table to one of the desirable blue leather booths on the far side.

Janey could hardly believe her eyes!

Already seated in the booth was that atrocious little social climber Caitlin Latch!

Caitlin had arrived seven minutes early, though she'd tried her hardest to be late. She had lingered in the shower and fussed over her blow-dry, then taken her sweet time selecting an outfit she hoped would look as if she'd put no thought into it at all (ivory silk DKNY twin set, grass green linen slacks, Edwardian enamel locket that she'd already auctioned off but hadn't sent to the buyer yet). And then she'd leisurely made up her face, separating and feathering each lash with mascara and meticulously painting her lips with M•A•C Crème de la Femme.

She'd spent some moments appraising the results. She wasn't a classic beauty: Her eyes were a bit too googly round, her cheekbones just a hint too broad. She didn't possess the cream-alicious Madonna looks of a Jessica DiSantini, nor was she glamorous, long-legged trophy wife material à la Lally Chandler Clemente. Basically, she was the kind of perky, pretty girl who was forever being compared with other perky, pretty girls: When *When Harry Met Sally* was a hit, people told her she resembled Meg Ryan; after *Charlie's Angels,* they said, "You know, you look a lot like Drew Barrymore." And so forth.

Her body was another story. Classic definitely being the word for it.

Spectacular being another.

Maybe now, in her mid-heading-to-late thirties, she was starting to get a teensy jiggle here, a bit of a dimpling there, particularly since, after losing her job, she'd had to drop her membership in the Colina Linda Sports Club; but all in all, she still had a knock-'em-dead shape. The irony was that she was often trying to hide it: It would be social death to show up at, say, a committee meeting for a pediatric lymphoma benefit looking like Lingerie Model Barbie.

But with the twin set and slacks, she'd felt she had struck the right balance between Barbie and tailored committee lady. Sexy without being totally va-va-voom.

Satisfied that she had dawdled long enough, she'd headed out to her car and cruised at a leisurely pace to Colina Linda. She'd shunned the freeway in favor of the backdoor route of Mordecai Road, where you often could be held up for five minutes or more at the railroad crossing. But today there had been no train and almost eerily no traffic anywhere. She had zipped down into the village in record time and found a parking space just two doors down from the café.

So she'd ended up doing exactly what she'd wanted not to—arriving early and looking too pathetically eager.

And naturally Mr. I'm-So-Entitled Preppy breezed in ten minutes late. Sank into the opposite seat of the booth with no apologies, as if he'd naturally expected to find her waiting for him.

"What a morning I've had!" he announced. "One damn crisis after another. And unfortunately I've only got about an hour, then I'll have to shoot back." He beckoned to the waiter. "A bottle of the Puligny-Montrachet." Almost as an afterthought, he glanced at Caitlin.

She had no idea what it was, but it sounded expensive. "Fine," she said.

Her original impression of him was right. Overprivileged asshole. As if he'd been conceived at Cartier's and raised in Tiffany's. She ought to just get up and ditch his privileged ass.

But the most heavenly smells were wafting in from the kitchen, and she had skipped breakfast in order to do this meal justice. Eating well was the best revenge, correct? And the wine he ordered was probably superb, so she might as well stick around to sample it.

The waiter returned quickly with the bottle, and during the fussy ritual of displaying, opening, and tasting, Caitlin regarded her companion. She had Googled him and discovered he was an architect—AIA stood for American Institute of Architects. It seemed to her a glamorous but somewhat remote profession, one she'd always associated with white-haired men in rumpled suits staring up at skyscrapers with exalted expressions.

There were photos on the Net of some of the buildings he'd designed, mostly small public structures—additions to museums, small-scale university halls, a public library in Boise. One, the McArdle Art Gallery in Sacramento, had won a flurry of seemingly prestigious awards, though to Caitlin it looked basically like a shiny box that had been punched out at random by some enraged giant.

But then what the hell did she know about modern architecture? She'd already made a fool of herself with the Franz Kline thing. With luck, maybe she could refrain from doing so again.

The waiter finished pouring, handed them menus bound in blue leather that matched the booth, and retreated. Caitlin took a sip of the chilled wine. Delicious.

"So you're an architect?" she began.

"Yep, I'm an architect. That's why I'm down here—I designed the new Clemente Foundation headquarters, and we're breaking ground next week."

"That sounds very impressive."

"It's an exciting commission. Actually my biggest so far. I started my own practice about ten years ago, and I've had some good small commissions, but this should catapult me into a higher category altogether."

"Will it look anything like the McArdle Gallery?" Caitlin ventured.

"Not really. I'm still working in a deconstructed vocabulary, but the Clemente will quote the Mission Revival style of this city. When people walk by it, I'll want them to feel a sense of continuity, but at the same time be exhilarated by something that's totally new."

"Mmm, I see," she said, not sure that she did. "Was David Clemente very involved with the design?"

"You bet he was. Working with him has been . . . well, let's just say challenging. Have you ever met him?"

Caitlin flushed. "A few times."

"Then you probably think he's this charming, easygoing guy. That's the way he comes across in public, right? But you don't get to be as rich as he is without being an autocratic son of a bitch. He wanted to control every aspect of the design. Trouble is, I don't like to be controlled. At one point I finally told him, 'Either fire me or back off.' "

"Obviously he didn't fire you."

"No, he didn't. He wants a great building. That's why he hired me."

That maddening cockiness again. Except this time she didn't mind it quite so much. In fact, it was actually kind of exciting to be with a guy who was good enough in his profession to be able to tell David Clemente to go to hell and get away with it.

"So you've visited the McArdle?" he asked her.

"Oh no. Actually, I've never been to Sacramento." She smiled sheepishly. "I looked you up on the Web."

"Yeah? I'm flattered." Dark blue eyes danced from under black lashes. "You know something? I picked you out right away at the Clemente affair. You didn't look like you belonged there."

She stiffened. "Why not?"

"I don't know. Maybe because you were one of the few women there who looked like she still had all her original body parts. And fantastic body parts, I might add." He grinned, those long kissable corners of his mouth turning up . . .

She suddenly found herself grinning back at him like a goon.

They ordered, both choosing the same entrée, roasted monkfish on a bed of saffron pearl fettuccine. Though it didn't really seem to matter what they were eating: Maybe it was the effect of the delicious wine or the heady sense of being in the quintessentially right restaurant, seated at exactly the right table, with a guy every other woman in the place couldn't take her eyes off of, but Caitlin found herself hardly tasting the food. She had always prided herself on her talent for listening—she had a way of tilting her head slightly and gazing with eyes widened and lips slightly parted that could make the most boring guy in the world feel like a scintillating raconteur. But for once she didn't have to fake interest: Architecture suddenly seemed like the most fascinating profession in the world, and Evan Kern was its most glittering practitioner.

Then he paused, twirling a strand of fettuccine on his fork, and gave a little laugh. "Okay, I've yakked on long enough. I'd like to know something about you. What do you do?"

There was something irresistible about the way he was looking at her, the expression in those deep blue eyes, teasing but at the same time telegraphing the message *Wow, you're really something!* It was just charm, she told herself—the kind of thing they teach you in dancing school or whatever.

"I have a little business, buying and selling vintage things," she said almost primly. "Jewelry. Hats. The occasional handbag or old piece of luggage." She decided to skip the tedious part about hunting for steadier work. "I spend a lot of time tramping through flea markets and garage sales, looking for buried treasure."

"You must have a really great eye."

"I've had to develop one. I've been burned a few times. Treasures that turned out to be trash."

"Still, it sounds like fun." He grinned, deepening those Redford-ish crinkles. God, he was good-looking! She had to resist the urge to simply sit and stare at him.

He took a ruminative sip of wine. "My wife is a huge fan of vintage jewelry. She's got a large collection of Victorian cameos."

Caitlin froze.

He was married?

A heads-up would have been nice. Like a ring on his finger. Or a "Hi, nice to meet you, I've got a wife."

She struggled to keep a light tone. "So how long have you been married?"

"Twenty-one years. Two daughters. Cammie's going into her junior year at Yale, and Becca's about to start at my alma mater, Williams. But Corinne and I have been virtually separated for over a year. We haven't really connected for a lot longer than that."

"Oh," Caitlin said.

"We've been staying together for the girls, but the truth is, the marriage is over. I'm thinking of relocating down here. It would make great sense for me to take advantage of all my family contacts."

Should she believe him? Married men hit on her all the time. She could usually predict the precise moment in a conversation when some hubby would start humming a variation of the old "my wife doesn't understand me" tune and then casually invite himself over to her place for a nightcap.

But what married men generally *didn't* do was ask her to lunch in a restaurant like Café Cygne, where they'd be seen by everybody in town. There was his cousin Janey, for God's sake, at a table just a few yards away. She'd been shooting them little glances the entire time they'd been here—sour glances, as if she thought Evan were slumming with someone like Caitlin. Certainly, if Evan was sneaking around on his wife, he wouldn't be doing it in plain sight of Janey Martinez.

"I hope it works out for the best," she said lamely.

"Thanks. Anyway, that's my full disclosure. What about yours?"

"Divorced four and a half years. I've got a son who's ten going on eleven. His name's Aiden." She had the urge to confide her fears about him: how he was acting strangely, crawling out of windows and furtively shutting down his computer—how she was sure he was hiding something from her.

But Evan suddenly consulted his watch. "I'll have to introduce him to my daughters someday," he murmured distractedly. "I hate to break this up, but I've got to get back to work." He made a check-scribbling gesture to the waiter. Without glancing at the check, he dropped a Platinum Amex card on the waiter's tray. "Maybe we can do this again."

"That would be nice," she said eagerly. A little too eagerly.

"Hey, why don't you come to the groundbreaking? Eleven a.m. next Tuesday. There'll be a little ceremony. I think you'll find it interesting."

"I'd like to. I mean, I'd have to make some arrangements—"

"Great. You know where the site is? On Loma Grande, adjacent to the County Art Museum."

The waiter returned to the table, his face pinched in distress. "I'm terribly sorry, sir, but the card has been refused. Do you have another one?"

Evan nonchalantly took back the card. "Yeah, of course. Or, you know what? It's the only card I brought with me. Why don't I give you a check?"

The waiter made a shuffling movement with his feet. "I'm sorry, but we don't—"

"Hey, it's okay. My cousin Jane Martinez will vouch for me." He took out a checkbook and began to write.

The waiter darted a glance at Janey's table, then looked uncertainly back at Evan. "Oh, well, Mrs. Martinez . . . Then I suppose . . ."

He accepted the check and melted away.

Evan smiled at Caitlin without a trace of embarrassment. "I should have known this would happen. Corinne's been playing these little financial games on me. It's not the first time she's canceled my cards. I guess I should take some sort of legal action to stop her, but she's been so distraught about our breaking up, I can't bring myself to do it."

"Oh, I understand." Caitlin reached over and laid a hand on his wrist. The physical contact, her skin touching his, produced in her a zap of excitement. "I've been through it," she assured him. "There's never any easy way to leave."

CHAPTER eight

The Fans Are Going Crazy

The first of the instant messages had popped up on Aiden's screen one night two weeks ago.

HEY DUDE!!! GUESS WHO THIS IS????

The IM name was weird: KCUDYFFAD. Aiden had immediately guessed it was Jonathan Lazaris, who thought it was cool to make up weird screen names. After Jonathan first moved away, they'd IM'd each other about a thousand times a day. Jonathan had told him Scottsdale sucked and he was going to come back to San Carlino in the summer and stay with Aiden till he had to go back to his lame-butt school. Then suddenly he stopped saying Scottsdale sucked and started talking about some dude named Roger and all the cool stuff they were doing together and how they were both into Dragon Quest. Then it started taking him days, sometimes weeks, to answer Aiden's messages. And then he stopped answering altogether, and finally Yahoo! said there was no such address anymore.

Aiden typed hopefully: "jonathan????"

DING!!! STRIKE UNO. TAKE ANOTHER SWING

Aiden's next thought was Kyle Lewison. Kyle was a real turd. Mean to everybody, but especially Aiden. Like last Christmas, during their school's candlelight procession, Kyle was marching right behind him, and he kept holding his candle to Aiden's hair, going, "Hey, hothead!" like it would be so funny if Aiden's hair caught on fire. Plus it was Kyle who was the one who'd first started calling him "Aidey the Lady," and now a lot of kids called him that, he heard it all the time, and it always made him want to hurl.

And another thing—Kyle was dumb. Like the dumbest kid in the class. There was this summer break assignment the two of them were supposed to be doing together, a report on the Native American tribes who used to dwell in San Carlino before the missionaries showed up, but so far Aiden hadn't had a single bit of help from the turd.

But maybe this was him now.

"kyle?" he wrote.

STRIKE DUO!! HERE COMES THE THIRD PITCH AND IT'S A SLOW CURVE RIGHT OVER HOME PLATE!

Now Aiden was really getting PO'd. He should just shut down and go tell his mom that some weirdo had hacked into his instant messaging.

But he didn't. Because suddenly he knew for total and absolute sure who it was.

For several moments he didn't do anything, just sat rigidly in his chair, staring at the IM box on the screen. One thing he also knew for sure—if he was wrong, he just totally wasn't going to be able to stand it.

Finally, with shaky hands, he touched the keyboard.

"dad?" he wrote.

HOME RUN DUDE!!!! AND THE FANS ARE GOING
CRAZEEEEEEE

And then there was nothing more.

For four days in a row after that first one, Aiden had received IMs from his dad. Almost every time he logged on, one would pop up from him. Aiden had figured out pretty quick that the IM name KCUDYFFAD was DAFFYDUCK spelled backward, which he thought was pretty hilarious.

"are you in india?" Aiden had asked the second time.

NO WAY JOSE! I'M BACK HERE IN THE USA DUDE. IN
THE GREAT STATE OF CALIFORNIA IN THE CITY BY THE
BAY!

Aiden knew that the city by the bay was San Francisco, where he'd been born. His grandparents still lived nearby and sometimes took him to visit it. His mom used to love singing that song about the little cable cars climbing halfway to the stars, though he hadn't heard her sing it in a long time.

"do u live with grandma and grandpa?" he typed.

NOPE. NO WAY! I'VE TAKEN UP RESIDENCE ON THE
TOP OF THE TRANSAMERICA BUILDING WHERE I CAN
SEE ALL!!!

"awesome!" Aiden replied.

But the next two messages had been pretty weird. They went on and on about some tree in India that ate bats and the Giants trading their best pitcher for some yo-yo from Cleveland and the words to an old-time Prince song, "1999." None of it seemed to make much sense, though Aiden figured he just wasn't smart enough to know what it all meant.

But then the last time he'd gotten a message, he had decided to ask his dad the most important question of all.

"hi dad!" he typed. "there's something i really want to ask u. are u coming back to be with us???"

He waited for what seemed like a long time. Then finally his dad answered:

THAT'S THE FIVE HUNDRED DOLLAR QUESTION!!!

Aiden knew very well that doing stuff depended mostly on having enough money. His mom was always like "You'll have to wait to buy those Nikes until they're on sale" or "You can go on the class day trip to Carmel, but we can't afford the overnight to Yosemite." So his dad probably needed five hundred dollars for the plane ticket and everything.

"is that what it costs?" Aiden wrote.

But the message popped up that his dad had signed off.

Now almost a week had gone by with no message. Aiden had become frantic that his dad had gone back to India. But then, just now, he'd been online checking out some information about stegosauruses and

DUDE!!!

had popped up in his IM box.

He felt a rush of relief.

"dad i thought u went away," he wrote. "i've got something important to tell u!!!"

He suddenly heard his mom coming upstairs. She sounded like she was barefoot and so maybe trying to sneak up on him, but the house was so rickety, with all these creaky old floors, that you could hear every step anybody took.

"cant talk now dad. gotta go," he wrote, and logged off just in time.

His mom wasn't barefoot—she was wearing that pair of bright orange socks that were coming apart at the heels and the stretchy black shorts and top she wore to do her yoga workouts. She padded up close beside him, smiling too much, holding a pad of yellow paper and one of her purple-ink pens. "Listen, Aidey, I've been thinking. How about for your birthday this year we have a party for you?"

He tensed. "I thought we were gonna go to Magic Mountain."

"We can do that, too. I just thought it would be cool to have a party and invite all your friends from school."

"You mean, like have it here?" Aiden thought of his classmates' homes: He was hardly ever invited to them, but he knew that most of them were gigantic, with their own private movie theaters and these huge backyards with swimming pools. Two kids he knew had play-houses that were actually castles—Jared Young's even had a moat around it with an electronically operated drawbridge. Lily Cavanagh was always bragging about how they had their own stable with all their own horses and a riding ring, and there was supposed to be a whole bowling alley in the bottom of Trevor Goldwater's house.

"I wasn't thinking of here," Caitlin said. "I thought maybe we could have it at JungaZone."

Aiden considered this. JungaZone was the coolest laser tag place in town. Even if kids didn't like him, they'd probably show up if it was there. "That would be okay," he said. "Can I invite that guy Nando from camp?"

"Absolutely. He'll be number one on the list. So now we need to decide which of the kids in your class you want to invite. I know some of them will be away, but there are still a lot of people in town."

Aiden hesitated. It was a strict rule of his school that anybody who had a birthday party had to invite all the other students in the same grade. But there were a few guys he'd really like to leave out, like dork-head Kyle Lewison and that stuck-up Madison Perkins, and

Zander Loh, who was the tallest kid in class and liked to punch and kick other kids when he thought no grown-ups were looking.

Then Aiden remembered that Zander was in China with his parents—he'd been bragging about what an awesome trip it was going to be practically all last year. And besides, since it was summer vacation, Aiden figured he didn't have to follow the St. Mattie's rule anyway.

"Yeah, okay," he said with mounting enthusiasm. "I guess I can decide which guys I want to come."

"Great!" Caitlin squatted beside him in front of his Mac. "What I'll do is, I'll design a really cool e-vite and send it out to the ones you want. Why don't you pull up your buddy list and let's pick them out."

Aiden felt a deep stirring of suspicion. "I'll do it later. I've got to go to the bathroom."

He popped out of his chair and trotted down the hall. For once in his life, he actually didn't have to go. He managed a little tinkle, then flushed and zipped and started back out; then he remembered he'd left the seat up and turned and dropped it down.

When he got back to his room, he found his mom still waiting for him, sitting on the floor with her legs twisted up in front of her and doodling on her pad. She was always doodling, covering notebooks and the pages of phone books with swirly shapes and daisies and mermaids and stuff.

"So I went ahead and pulled up your buddy list," she said. "We might as well go through it right now, and then I can get things rolling."

She put down her pad and lifted her arms over her head and leaned forward, like she was bowing down to the poster of Golem on his wall. But it was just one of the yoga things she did. She sat back up and lowered her arms and unpretzeled her legs, and then she knelt to be at eye level with his screen.

No way she could really know what's going on, he decided. There was nothing on the buddy list to give it away. He sat in his chair and began considering the names. "Sara Amesly. She's okay, we can invite her."

But in the back of his mind, there was only one thought—he absolutely had to get his dad to come back.

Caitlin left Aiden's room feeling somewhat reassured. He had seemed entirely comfortable identifying his buddy names, so if he was covering up his instant messaging, it was probably just as she'd speculated—he didn't want his mother nosing around in his private conversations.

Of course, now she was committed to forking out for a gang of kids at that rip-off joint JungaZone. With luck, half would be away or unable to attend: But that would still leave about a dozen, plus Aiden, which was going to set her back at least thirty dollars a head. Plus gifts—suddenly it had become mandatory for the birthday kid to not only receive presents but dole them out as well. And on top of that, there was the promised trip to Magic Mountain. Aiden's grandparents, Stan and Amrita, were paying the admission, but you could never get out of these damn parks without being socked with a ton of extras.

Amazingly, though, she wasn't obsessing about the money. Things were definitely looking up. The windfall from the jewelry auction. The interview at Serenity Waters.

And her forthcoming date with Evan Kern. If it actually was a date, seeing as how (a) he was still married; (b) the invitation was to a public event and she might not even get to talk to him there; (c) he was a Kern, meaning he came from a family that considered themselves just slightly less important than God and definitely more select; and (d) he was *still married.*

She knew she had a certain reputation in town as being on the prowl to snatch a husband—there was even a cadre of women who referred to her as Caitlin the Snatch behind her back (the nasty double entendre of the nickname didn't escape her, either). The truth was, though, she had a strict hands-off policy about married men. The way she saw it, it really wasn't even possible to steal a spouse. The notion of a femme fatale luring away a happily married man—well, that was bullshit. A wife was either going to keep her husband or lose him anyway—another woman in the mix might make it happen faster than otherwise, but most of the time you could bet it wasn't the real cause of a breakup.

And from all evidence, the current Mrs. Kern was not going to keep her husband. And if that was true, why shouldn't Caitlin be waiting front and center to snap him up, once he was truly free?

No reason at all.

She spread her yoga mat on the living room floor and slotted a DVD—the advanced *Ecstasy of Yoga*—into the player.

CHAPTER nine

The Sisterhood of the Blahniks

essica stood at the dollhouse-size stove in her mother's sunny apartment, heating up the Early Girl tomato soup she'd prepared from scratch at her own home. Without turning around, she could feel her mother's gaze fixed upon her, and she knew that in Lillian McCready's eyes, her appearance had been judged and found wanting.

Jessica adjusted the flame to a simmer beneath the saucepan. She cut two medium slices from a loaf of La Brea Bakery rustic white and popped them into the toaster oven. Then she counted slowly to five, adjusted her expression from Aggravated to Neutral, and turned to face the dinette table.

Lillian set down her coffee cup, centering it carefully in its mismatched saucer.

"Those trousers do you no favor at all, Jessica, dear," she spoke. "I know that some girls today like to emphasize their backsides, but if you're over the age of forty, I certainly can't imagine why."

"Do you think these pants make my backside look big?" Jessica said evenly.

"They do balloon back there. And you might have put on a little lipstick, even if you didn't want to bother with the rest of your face."

"I had a crazy morning, Mommy. I had to get Alex to tennis and Rowan to her riding lesson and rush back in time for the tree pruners and to finish making the soup. And all the time the phone never stopped ringing about this trust case I'm in the middle of."

"It only takes a second to apply lipstick. And not that coral shade you've been wearing lately. It makes you look like a dying fish. You have a lovely skin tone, you need to stay in the rose pink family if you want to highlight it."

Lillian's own face, still beautiful at the age of seventy-six, was meticulously and tastefully made up. Not a stray hair escaped from her short blond bob. Her ironed dandelion-colored cotton blouse co-ordinated neatly with a beige summer skirt, and her toenails, peeping out from open-toed espadrilles, were freshly painted with perhaps the very shade of rose pink she was pushing for her daughter's lips. Lillian was a former Miss Pennsylvania, and she retained the beauty queen's credo that you must at all times present yourself as fit to be judged. She persisted in believing that Jessica had "driven away" an outstanding husband by letting herself go—which in Lillian's view meant not being immaculately coiffed and painted like a porcelain doll from breakfast table to bed at night.

The soup had begun to bubble. Jessica gave it a quick stir, then re-moved the toast slices and slathered them with ersatz butter. "Did you take your medications, Mommy?"

A look of bewilderment clouded Lillian's face.

"Your Lexapro and Seroquel." Jessica pointed to the enameled pillbox on the dinette table.

"I think I did. Maybe."

She had frequent moments like this, a confusion about where she was or what she'd done or should be doing. Still, it was an enormous improvement from the year before, when she'd ricochet entirely out of the present and into some time in the past—most frequently the glittering year of 1952, when she had sported the tiara of Miss Pennsylvania. These lapses would come suddenly and without warning, in public or private. First she'd become fretful. *Where is my limo?* she'd whimper. *Has my swimsuit been altered yet? My vocal coach is late, I'm not going to be prepared!* Then she'd turn obstreperous, demanding that things be rectified immediately and throwing tantrums when she believed they weren't.

Jessica had been on the point of despair. Then serendipitously she'd served on the steering committee for a Parkinson's disease fund-raiser with a gerontologist named Cheryl Ardazian. Cheryl had enrolled Lillian in her latest study—jiggering ultralow doses of medications in combinations with one another. Miraculously, she had hit upon a combo that worked. Not a hundred percent; and, as Cheryl warned, it would probably be only temporary. But Jessica was grateful for even this small reprieve.

A rapping at the apartment door—*shave and a haircut!*—and then a diminutively built man bounded into the kitchenette. This was Lillian's beau, George Kaminski, a retired florist and one of the sparse number of widowers in the complex. He was bald except for a fringe of woolly, pinky white hair wrapped around the base of his skull, so that from the back his head looked like the kind of fancy pink grapefruit grocers displayed nestled in excelsior.

"Hello, my lovely ladies!" He picked up Lillian's hand and planted a kiss on it with formal gallantry. "What's cooking? It smells dee-licious."

"Tomato soup," Jessica told him. George seemed to keep an eye peeled for the sight of Jessica's car parked outside Lillian's apartment, knowing it would be accompanied by homemade food. "Would you like a bowl?"

"Fresh tomato?"

"And fresh-picked basil."

He slipped happily into a chair. Having a suitor helped keep her mother anchored in the here and now, so Jessica was happy to feed him. She ladled the soup into two crackleware bowls and set them on the table with the buttered toast. Lillian and George began attacking the food with gusto.

"Mommy, I've got to take off," Jessica said. "I'll call you later, and you can tell me what mass you want to go to tomorrow, okay?"

"Okay, dear." Pre–George Kaminsky, Lillian would have fretted and grumbled about Jessica leaving so soon, lacing her complaints with mutterings about the selfishness of divorced-women-who-had-household-help but still couldn't think about anyone but themselves.

Another reason, Jessica reflected, to be thankful for George.

She felt a pang of guilt anyway as she left her mother's home. Possibly because she was fleeing to the home of a man with whom she was having the kind of relationship Lillian would insist upon calling "illicit." But the feeling faded as Jessica got into her car; and as she began driving toward the coastline, it was replaced by mounting anticipation.

An equally foolish feeling, since Tommy wasn't even home. He was currently wandering the cobblestone streets of Montreal: She had spoken to him early that morning, a conversation on the run, his words muffled by the chocolate croissant he was bolting down in lieu of breakfast. For his stint as composer in residence at the University of San Carlino, he'd rented a ramshackle bungalow on Sand Dollar Lane up in the Portofino, and Jessica dropped by every day to pick up the mail (almost nonexistent since all important correspondence went through his manager), water his one plant (a spindly bamboo palm in a celadon pot she had given him), and generally make sure everything was all right (that the place hadn't burned down or slid into the ocean).

The Portofino was an entanglement of worming lanes, blind alleyways, and unpaved roads, occupying a south-side bluff with spectacular views of the Pacific. It was rapidly gentrifying, the seventy-year-old salt-rotted little shacks and bungalows being torn down and replaced by multimillion-dollar trophies. It was only a question of time before Tommy would be kicked out of his little place.

And then where would he go?

Perhaps move in with her?

She felt a wild hope leap in her chest. Then she thought of her list: "Reasons to Break Up with Tom Bramberg." Its indisputable proof that their relationship had no future.

This is just a rebound thing, she reminded herself sternly. It was about the sex and the excitement, period. Getting her sea legs back after the shipwreck of her divorce.

Do not forget it!

She parked her Saab under the gloomy ancient cedar that loomed in front of his bungalow. She plucked a few pieces of junk mail out of the rusted mailbox, unlocked the front door, and entered the tiny front room. Just being in his home sent such an intense wave of desire coursing through her that her knees almost buckled.

But something wasn't right. She sensed it immediately.

There was a pronounced scent of perfume in the room. She even knew which perfume it was—Chanel No. 5, which for some reason she associated with Lally Chandler Clemente.

Before she could totally assimilate this thought in her mind, a shimmer of gold and silver arose from the hammock strung on the seaside deck. The shimmer consolidated into a girl who resembled a living moonbeam: She gave a lazy little stretch and then turned to regard Jessica with a golden stare through the sliding glass door.

Oh shit, Jessica thought.

Caitlin and Amelie were wearing an identical pair of shoes in different shades.

It was the Manolo Blahnik whipstitched leather sandal with golden buckle and chain. The pair adorning the feet of Amelie Cushing, general manager of Serenity Waters Spa Resort, was white, and Amelie had undoubtedly paid the retail price of five hundred and eighty-five dollars for them. Caitlin's were tan; they'd been a somewhat abused display pair with a torn front strap on the left shoe, marked down to sixty-nine and change at a boutique called Arise. She'd had them buffed up and the strap restitched, and they looked just about brand-new.

Amelie's eyes had shot to them immediately. At first, Caitlin thought it was going to be the kiss of death. But Amelie's lips had twitched in a little smile of approval.

"Aren't these the most comfy shoes ever?" she burbled. "I love yours in the tan."

"The white are fantastic," Caitlin replied cozily.

And just like that, she and Amelie bonded. The Sisterhood of the Blahniks!

Amelie had warmed up further at the sight of Caitlin's Vuitton bag (the brilliant fake!) and her Cartier Tank watch (seventies vintage—had not yet met the reserve on eBay). So it was that kind of job, Caitlin reflected: You could get it only if you could afford not to need it.

The first part of the interview consisted of a tour of the facilities, Amelie whisking Caitlin around in a lime green golf cart, past the inky infinity pool, the natural stone whirlpool, the desert-rose-colored guest bungalows. They toured the three spa cuisine restaurants (sushi, Provençal, fusion) and popped into the steamy, fragrant treatment rooms. For every guest being wrapped or pummeled or guided in meditation, there appeared to be at least three employees clad in filmy white jumpsuits and wearing somewhat unfocused expressions, signifying, Caitlin thought, either beatific enlightenment or having been dazed by the unrelenting Mojave sun.

Amelie did most of the talking. Which A-list movie-star couple had been married here. How many different algae were used in the oxidating marine serum. How much it had cost to construct the blue crystal waterfall that tumbled in a sparkling ribbon into an artificially constructed lagoon.

They ended up back at the main house, which was a multistoried slab built almost invisibly into the side of a rocky outcropping. In her top-floor office, Amelie waved Caitlin into a chair and settled herself behind a Lucite desk.

"I was intrigued by your résumé," Amelie said, suddenly all crisp business.

I'm glad I'm here, I'm glad! Caitlin fixed her smile, nodded attentively.

"Your previous job at the Rape Crisis Center sounds very interesting."

"It was a fascinating experience. Helping young women who have been so traumatized was very rewarding. And it really sharpened my people skills. But the center was taken over by a larger department at the university, so unfortunately my job was eliminated."

"I see. But I notice you have previous spa experience."

"Yes, I was the manager of a day spa called Atmosphere in San Francisco for nearly four years. It was in Pacific Heights, a very upscale clientele. Because it was small, I had a hand in everything, so I'm familiar with the full range of spa activities."

"And why did you leave that job?"

"I left San Francisco. I went through a difficult divorce and wanted a fresh start. I've got sole custody of my son, so it seemed like a good idea to relocate in a smaller city like San Carlino. Safer, cleaner. Better schools."

"I'm a single parent, too!" Amelie exclaimed. "My son, Royce, is thirteen."

"Aiden's going on eleven."

"Isn't it a bear juggling a career and single parenting? I've gone through three nannies, and I can't tell you how many au pairs!"

"It's a nightmare," Caitlin commiserated.

"And don't even talk to me about baby-sitters! God, if I could only find the perfect live-in!"

"Wouldn't that be wonderful!"

"An impossible dream."

Amelie smiled sympathetically at Caitlin, and Caitlin smiled sympathetically back. The Sisterhood of the Blahniks was now augmented by the Sisterhood of the Elusive Live-in Help.

"I think you'd fit in very well here," Amelie continued. "I see that among your references you've listed Lally Clemente."

"Oh yes, Lally's a great friend," Caitlin exaggerated. "She was on the advisory board of the Rape Crisis Center, and we worked closely together." This was a bit of a gamble. It was true that Lally had briefly adopted the center as a pet cause before moving on to more global altruisms. However, would she actually give Caitlin, her former rival for David, any kind of glowing reference? But with luck, even if Amelie tried to contact Lally, she wouldn't be able to get her attention.

"Well then, I think that about covers everything," Amelie said. "I need you to meet with Martin Drucker, who's the president of the Serenity Resorts Corporation, but it's really just a formality. A meet-and-greet. I'm actually in charge of the hiring here. I'll set something up for you next week." She rose and extended an elegant hand. "It's been *such* a pleasure."

Caitlin got up and pressed her hand. "Thank you, it's been a great pleasure for me, too."

She let her eyes travel briefly around the office. It was beautifully appointed in muted shades of sandstone, ocher, and pale green. Large windows gave onto a vista of distant lavender mountains and let in a breeze intoxicatingly rich with oxygen.

These might soon be familiar surroundings, Caitlin thought, and felt a quick thrill.

She felt the need to celebrate, and back in town she decided to hit the Conquistadora Plaza. This was the most upscale mall in San Carlino, an open-air Mediterranean-style plaza, all plashing fountains and gaily painted espresso carts. A Neiman Marcus anchored one end and a Saks Fifth Avenue the other, with a graceful arcade of luxury boutiques in between.

As a rule, Caitlin ventured here only during the very end of end-of-season clearance sales—when the racks screamed "TAKE AN EXTRA 20 PERCENT OFF!" over the "70 PERCENT OFF" signs already displayed. But at the moment, she felt like doing something wild and extravagant, like buying a designer label at retail.

She passed up the stratospheric Chanel/Armani/Fendi boutiques (she hadn't totally lost her mind) and headed into Saks. She happily browsed the second floor, scooping an armful of the season's new printed wrap dresses to try on; it was a style particularly flattering to her, accentuating her full breasts, small waist, and slender hips.

The woman paying for a mountain of purchases at a register looked vaguely familiar. Caitlin hunted for the name: Tilda Lazenby. Six months ago, as volunteers on the Arthritis Association Midnight Madness Ball, Caitlin and Tilda had both been assigned to the lowly precleanup committee—Caitlin because of the meager amount of her donation, Tilda because she was a newbie and therefore low on the charity pecking order. Tilda had quickly bought her way up to chairmanships and steering committee positions and had become joined at the hip with such socially exalted people as Janey Martinez.

She probably wouldn't be overjoyed to be reminded of her precleanup committee days. But Caitlin was bursting with the triumph of her interview and dying to tell somebody.

"Tilda, hello," she called brightly. "Hi, it's Caitlin. Caitlin Latch."

Tilda clutched a purse with an oversize YSL logo to her chest like protective armor. "Oh, hello, how are you?" she said distantly. *Couldn't care less,* said her tone.

"I'm fine. Terrific, really," Caitlin replied. "I was just out at Serenity Waters, and, well, it looks like I'll be taking a fabulous job there. Director of guest services."

"How nice for you," Tilda said dimly.

"Thanks, I think it's going to be tons of fun. And of course, I'll be able to take special care of my friends when they go there. Lavish them with special treatment and all that."

A light bulb seemed to blink on above Tilda's head: Social points could be scored by having an inside connection at Serenity Waters! Caitlin could see her struggling like mad between her desire to snub a low-status person and cultivate "special treatment" at the ultra-posh spa.

The spa won out. "Well, how wonderful for you," she trilled. "I'll be sure to look you up next time I'm planning to be there. Will you be starting soon?"

"Very soon," Caitlin promised. "And by all means, look me up."

CHAPTER ten

Even a Billion Dollars Couldn't Buy Peace

The past five days had been typical of Lally's new life. She'd hopped the Clemente Group plane, a white Gulfstream V with a chocolate-and-mint interior, down to the compound in Barbados, where she was remodeling the master bedroom suite, which was actually a separate twenty-eight-hundred-square-foot bungalow connected to the main building by a thatched-roof walkway. For three wretched days she'd bickered with the decorator—a leathery-faced Brit with an overblown reputation and an almost preternatural tolerance for gin-and-bitters—over hand-printed hemp fabrics and grotto showers with tropical rain features. The contractor was a mellifluously voiced islander with the most spectacular physique since Michelangelo's *David*; and if Lally found herself gazing rather frequently at his sculpted shoulders and darling little butt, it was solely as elements of an objet d'art.

Then she popped up to New York to consult with a Park Avenue naturopath, who contemptuously dismissed everything that had been prescribed for her menopausal symptoms by the Rodeo Drive holistic gynecologist. Out with the squashed-bug shakes and in with a regimen of bark and root extracts and bitter herbal teas.

From there, a hop down to Washington, D.C., to meet David (husband, not statue) for a State Department–sponsored reception at the Kennedy Center. David had his adoptive son, Noah, in tow for the event, which made things a bit sticky. Noah was a pudgy twelve-year-old who lived most of the year with David's ex-wife, Susanna, and her art dealer–slash-gigolo new husband. God only knew Lally had twisted herself in knots trying to connect with the boy, showering him with presents and peppering him with self-esteem-enhancing comments and encouragements; and whenever he was with them in Colina Linda, she shuttled him around tirelessly to children's parties and suitable rock concerts and the kinds of movies beloved of adolescent boys in which bowel movements feature so prominently.

But try as she might, Noah continued to gawk at her with a mixture of suspicion and alarm. It was as if he were one of the von Trapp kids and she was the baroness who'd sent Julie Andrews packing.

After a somewhat trying time in the nation's capital, the Clementes flew Noah back up to his mom, and then they zipped back across the continent to home sweet home in Colina Linda.

Unfortunately, not so sweet at the moment. A man of indeterminate accent who (per the grapevine) had made a killing in hair restoration techniques had gobbled up the two neighboring estates and was in the process of demolishing all structures on both properties to erect a glass-and-titanium palace. All day long, Lally was assaulted by the *growrrrr* of bulldozers, the head-splitting racket of jackhammers, the deafening *thwomp-thwomp* of the helicopters depositing . . . what? Mature king palms? Squadrons of security commandos?

Even a billion dollars couldn't buy a bit of peace and quiet.

Lally had the impulse to leap back on the jet. East Hampton would be humming right now; or she could barge in on her pals

Serge and Louella Bourdine, who'd just reopened their stunning villa in Cap d'Antibes.

But she and David had a laundry list of commitments to keep them here for the next few weeks, the most important being the groundbreaking for David's cherished new baby, the Clemente Foundation headquarters. Scheduled to attend were the local congresswoman, a brace of state senators, and the mayors of San Carlino, Santa Barbara, and Los Angeles, and possibly the governor if he could cut short a state-promoting trip to Tokyo.

So basically it left Lally with a lot of time to hang around brooding about what Sienna was up to a quarter mile away. She'd thought that once she married David Clemente, she'd be able to do pretty much anything she wanted to, short of committing a capital crime. But if anything, it was the opposite. There were so damn many things she *couldn't* do, living in the glare of a perpetual klieg light.

Par exemple: hiring a private eye to investigate Sienna. It wasn't like in those old noir movies, where Humphrey Bogart operated under a code of honor. Hell, no! The second Lally retained an investigator, he'd be leaking the news about working for the Clementes up and down the entire coast. David would find out and be appalled.

And if Sienna caught even a whiff of a suggestion that Lally was having her investigated, she would vanish in an instant, taking all Lally's access to Chiara with her.

Lally continued to mull all this over while getting her thrice-weekly hot-stone deep-tissue massage on a padded table in her dressing room. Fluty music tootled softly, and Katya worked proficiently: Ordinarily Lally would be melting, but the thoughts about her daughter made her too agitated to enjoy it.

Katya lifted the towel, and Lally rolled onto her stomach, fitting her face into the opening in the headrest. Katya began pressing the heated black stones on various points along her spine. "Hand me my Treo, would you, please?" Lally spoke through the face hole. She stuck out her hand.

"What's the matter?" Katya fretted. "Aren't the stones hot enough?"

"No, darling, it's all superb. My mind is just on hyperdrive, that's all, and I need to check my phone. And kill the music, would you?"

Peevishly, Katya slapped the device into Lally's hand and switched off the flutes. With an awkward motion that involved wrapping an arm under the headrest and flexing her wrist like a Balinese dancer, Lally managed to position the phone more or less in front of her face. She spoke the command for her message slush pile—the dozens of junk calls she received daily from strangers and slight acquaintances and downright nut jobs, all wanting favors, endorsements, cash donations, whatever. Her longtime personal assistant, Perla, was now chief of Lally's staff of four, and these new underlings did not have Perla's faultless ability to separate the legitimate from the nuisances—among the notables who'd been banished to slush were the Park Avenue naturopath, the secretary to the president of Ghana, and Susan Sarandon. So Lally thought it prudent to occasionally check the rejects.

A week's worth had piled up, which translated to close to a hundred. A bit fuzzy without her glasses—she squinted hard at one message that had come in yesterday:

Jessie Decentiny. REGARDING: *Personal.*

"Oh, my God!" Lally bolted naked off the table. "I'll be back in a few minutes," she blurted to the startled Katya. Grabbing a robe, she strode into her bedroom and spoke Perla's name into the Treo. Perla responded instantly.

"Get me Jessica DiSantini immediately!" Lally snapped.

Jessica still couldn't figure out why she was the one who had felt like the intruder.

Sienna had stood with one hip cocked, staring at her with narrowed golden eyes, as if Jessica had just slithered in a jimmied-open window instead of walking in freely through the front door. Jessica had finally broken the ice.

"Why, hello, Sienna, remember me? I'm Jessica, I'm a friend of Tom's. We've met once before, at your mother's wedding."

For an awful moment, Jessica thought the girl wouldn't reply at all but just continue to regard her with that fishy gold stare. At last Sienna said, "Yeah, I know who you are."

Jessica decided not to tip her hand. "I didn't know you were in town. Are you planning to stay here with Tom? I've been popping by to keep an eye on things till he got back, but if you're going to be here, I guess that won't be necessary."

Sienna's exquisite lips twitched in a semi-sneer. "Well, you know, I'm not a keeping-an-eye-on-things type. So I guess you might as well keep on popping by."

Jessica no longer felt like a housebreaker: Suddenly she felt like a dowdy little hausfrau who was just itching to get her hands on a good sturdy mop. No, what she was actually itching to get her hands on was Sienna's swanlike neck so she could squeeze it until the girl's yellow eyes popped. She could not remember ever loathing anyone as instantly and as purely.

"Anyway, I'm not staying here," Sienna added. "I only came by because I thought Tom-Tom might be back by now." With an insolent swing of her hips, she turned and conveyed her slender butt into the kitchen.

Tom-Tom? Jessica's urge to strangle the girl became more intense than ever. What she ought to do was just get the hell out of Sienna's presence. But some obstinacy made her follow her into the kitchen.

Sienna had unearthed a half-empty pack of Tommy's Marlboros and was lighting one on the gas flame of the range. "Why is Tom still living in this shithole? Now that he's back to being rich and famous, he really ought to get himself something better."

"He's not that rich and only famous in certain circles. And besides, this is a sweet little house. Having a view right on the ocean like this is priceless."

"One halfway decent earthquake and it'll be right in the middle of that priceless ocean." Sienna balanced her glowing cigarette on the rim of the sink, then opened the ancient fridge and gazed disconsolately at the scant contents. She shut it, then repeated the motion with the cupboards, opening, staring, shutting. "Isn't there anything edible in this priceless real estate?"

"Well, you know Tom. He's not really concerned about what he eats."

Sienna checked out the last cupboard, absently biting the fingernail of one thumb as she surveyed the dusty dishes. It was a gesture that was shockingly familiar to Jessica—one she'd seen her own daughter make hundreds of times. "I'm hungry, too," she said impulsively. "Why don't I fix us some lunch? I'm sure I can scrounge up enough to make something good."

Sienna turned her head with a look that was almost eager. "Yeah, okay," she said.

"Macaroni and cheese?" Lally exclaimed. She was back on the massage table, talking to Jessica.

"An improvised version of it. There was a hunk of cheddar in the fridge, I just had to scrape off a section of mold. Also a can of evaporated milk and a pinch of cayenne to give it a little kick. She gobbled it down like she hadn't eaten in a week. Then I used another tin of condensed milk to make her some cocoa."

"Cocoa? Sienna drank cocoa?" Lally practically dropped the Treo in astonishment. "It must have been an act," she concluded. "Playing baby off your mommy. I'll bet she was laughing her ass off at you the whole time."

"Maybe," Jessica said. "Though I don't see how, because she almost never stopped talking. She chattered a blue streak."

"You've got to be kidding me!"

"Nope. Mostly about all the rich and famous people she knew, actresses and dukes and hot-shot artists and whatever. I pretty much let her go on without listening all that carefully."

"Mmph." Lally digested all this for a moment. "Okay, let's cut to the chase. Why is she here? Did she get around to that?"

"Sort of. She said she's been under a lot of strain lately and needed some private time to herself. She knew your house was just sitting there empty, and so she decided to kind of house-sit for you."

Lally gave a snort. "Yeah, right. Like all house-sitters change the locks. But what about the baby? Does she have Chiara with her?"

"Apparently not. Sienna said she's with her nanny."

"What nanny? Where?"

"I didn't grill her about the specifics," Jessica said. "She's not a moron, you know. I'm sure she suspects that I'm reporting all this to you."

"Oh, hell!" Lally muttered. "Ow! Jeez, Katya, take it easy!"

"What?" Jessica asked.

"Nothing. Talking to my masseuse. One of her rocks was too damn hot."

"Rocks?"

"Look, never mind. The question is, what do we do now?"

"Well, I guess the good news is that your daughter's coming over for dinner Friday night. My kids will be with Michael, so I promised I'd cook her a real meal and then maybe we'd watch a DVD. Who knows, maybe she'll open up to me a little bit more."

"Wait a minute," Lally said. "Are you telling me Sienna's coming over to your house to eat meat loaf and watch a DVD on TV?"

"Well, it probably won't be meat loaf," Jessica said crisply, "but basically, yes, that's right. She seems to be really into movies."

Lally felt her head begin to swim. It was truly mind-boggling! "Well, listen, this is all great. Just keep me posted, okay? And also, if you could fax your bill directly to Perla and make it out in her name, Perla Mueller—"

"Don't be an ass, Lally!" Jessica snapped. "I'm not billing you."

"You're not?" Lally said. "You mean you're doing this just as a friend?"

"I think," Jessica said slowly, "that I'm doing it for Chiara."

CHAPTER eleven

A Perfect Day for Shoveling Dirt

Caitlin steered her Volvo up the winding road to Señorita Canyon, with Aiden in back, plugged into his iPod. She tried to shake off her growing uneasiness about him, but she couldn't. That secretiveness of his was getting worse. Last night at about eleven o'clock, while she was in the bathroom sponging off her makeup, she'd heard the thump of the front door opening. She'd felt a jolt of fear—she had locked it before coming upstairs, she'd been certain of it. Still clutching the mascara-removal pad, she'd tiptoed out to the hall and peered down at the foyer. There was her son, whom she'd thought was in bed and asleep, standing in his PJs in front of the door.

"What are you doing?" she'd demanded.

He had jumped at the sound of her voice. "Nothing. I was just looking at something outside."

It was the same thing he'd said after he'd fallen out the kitchen window. "What were you looking at?" she'd asked sharply.

"*Nothing!* Just, I heard a dog barking, and I thought maybe he might be lost."

"Is there somebody out there?" The seductive pedophile lurking in the bushes!

"No, I told you. It was a dog."

That was his story, and he wasn't budging from it, no matter how much she grilled him. Now she needed to ask him another question. She took a deep breath and glanced at him in the rearview mirror. "Hey, Aidey?" she said loudly.

"Yeah?" He pushed back the earphones.

"Listen, sweetie. Have you borrowed any money from my purse?"

The slightest hesitation. "No," he said.

"I won't yell at you if you did. I just need to know. So I don't come up short of money while I'm out shopping."

"You always pay with your credit card."

"Not always. Yesterday I was at the farmer's market, where you can only pay with cash. I thought I had at least twenty dollars in my wallet, but I only had ten. I had to put back the cantaloupe."

"So what? Who wants cantaloupe anyway?"

"Well, I do, for one. But that's not the point. I just really want to know if you borrowed some money, that's all."

"I already told you I didn't." His voice skyrocketed to a high C. "Why don't you believe me?"

She sighed. "Okay, I believe you. Forget it."

The problem was, she didn't believe him.

Maybe she should take him back to that therapist he'd seen last year, Dr. Wintra Cohen; but it cost a hundred and twenty dollars for a measly forty-five-minute session, and just one or two sessions wouldn't do him any good. She'd have to wait till she'd definitely nailed the Serenity Waters gig before she could commit to another full round of therapy.

She didn't pursue it further as they continued to the camp-grounds. She dropped him at the clearing, then headed back to the Whole Foods at the center of town. She rarely shopped here—the huge Vons on South Delano was much cheaper—but you could park all day for free in the Whole Foods lot with any purchase. She went in, bought a roll of "green" paper towels and a small jar of organic clover honey, got her ticket stamped, and tossed the bag in her car. Then she hiked seven blocks to Loma Grande Boulevard, where the Clemente Foundation groundbreaking would be taking place.

She was early, so she grabbed a coffee at the café in the County Art Museum, which was adjacent to the site. It had to have been one of the priciest vacant lots in the country, she reflected—an entire square block situated gloriously in the middle of San Carlino's historic district, within spitting distance of the mission, three museums, and at least half a dozen restaurants of the sort that featured wild baby greens. There had once been an old brick bank there, but it had crumbled in an earthquake in 1997. Rumors had flown about what was going to replace it: a Scientology recruitment center; luxury time-share condos; a Russian Orthodox cemetery.

But until now, the only use of the site had been by Cirque du Soleil, which for several years pitched its tent there when it came to town. From the times she'd taken Aiden, Caitlin associated the location with acrobats in glittering leotards cartwheeling through the air.

At ten to eleven, she left the café and crossed the road to the lot. It was now blocked off by a high construction fence. People were streaming through a narrow opening in the fence, which was guarded by a gaggle of cops. Caitlin passed the cops' scrutiny and entered the enclosure, followed by a man in pale blue seersucker.

It was Taller Kern, she realized. He raised a what-are-*you*-doing-here? eyebrow. "Well, hello there," he said. "Are you with the bride or the groom?"

"You mean Lally or David? Neither one. It was Evan who invited me."

Taller's eyebrow shot up higher. "I didn't know you two were acquainted."

"Yeah, we are," she said crisply, and strode farther into the enclosure. Thank God, Taller veered off in another direction.

The lot, which for years had been covered with scrub brush, had now been cleared down to bare earth. A small stage was erected in the center, and a string quartet was seated on one side of it, playing some tuneful classical piece. On the other side was a large mock-up of the building-to-be. Caitlin studied it with interest. It was sort of Mission style as Evan had said—but a Mission that had been re-arranged, possibly by the same quake that had toppled the previous bank building. Its two stories jutted out in strange directions, and the red-tile roof seemed to cave in toward the middle.

Funny, though—the more she looked at it, the more she *wanted* to look at it. She supposed that's what made it brilliant.

A bank of oval-backed gilt chairs fronted the stage. Between stage and chairs, David and Lally were holding court. Lally was her usual knockout self in a wide-brimmed straw hat and a flouncy tiered skirt that you'd think would be too young for her but somehow wasn't. But Caitlin would hardly have recognized David; when she'd had her affair with him—if that's what you could call a two-night stand—he'd been a bit geeky, which she'd thought kind of suitable for a self-made billionaire: barbershop-style haircut, clunky glasses, and a fondness for high-top sneakers. Now he looked as if he had just bounded off a yacht, his brown hair razor-cut à la Tom Cruise, his clothes impeccably tailored.

But where was Evan? She finally spotted him, also down in front but half-hidden by a thick clot of his relations, the ubiquitous Kerns. Hovering particularly close to him was his cousin Janey, tossing her hair flirtatiously. Her recently acquired double-D cups were almost prodding him in the chest.

She definitely had a thing for her cousin—Caitlin was suddenly positive of it. They were only distant cousins, so there'd be nothing incestuous about it or anything. It would explain the hate rays Janey had been shooting at her at Café Cygne. Also the way she had hustled Evan off at Lally's fund-raiser, as though he were her own private property. . . .

But would Evan ever be interested in Jane Martinez? No matter how stylish she'd become, it didn't change the fact that her eyes were tiny and squinty, and even the most exquisitely cut designer jacket couldn't disguise that broad-in-the-beam shape. Of course, her money might be an attraction. . . . Janey was loaded, everybody knew that. There were always men sniffing around her just for that reason.

But Evan was a successful architect; plus, as a Kern himself, he probably also had something in the way of a trust fund. So why would he be a fortune hunter? Caitlin studied his body language. As far as she could tell, he was responding to Janey's desperate flirting in the most neutral kind of way.

No way he was into Janey. Caitlin relaxed and slipped into a chair in one of the back rows. It gave her an excellent vantage point to survey the rest of the audience. A who's who of the town's social elite. She spotted Jessica down toward the middle and considered going to join her, but then she saw Taller take the seat beside her and decided not to.

And wasn't that some famous actress—the gorgeous blond girl in a baseball cap who'd slipped into a chair several rows behind Jessica and Taller? There were always movie stars floating around San Carlino, especially in the middle of summer.

No, not an actress, Caitlin realized. It was that Eurotrashy daughter of Lally's, the one she'd had with her first husband who was now Jessica's boyfriend. Sienna—that was her name. She'd been maid of honor at Lally's wedding, which was where Caitlin had seen her before.

Caitlin leaned forward to get a better glimpse of the girl, but a woman with bushy white hair sat in front of her at that moment and obscured her view.

Like Lally, Jessica was also sporting a wide-brimmed hat, the same one, as it happened, she had worn to Lally's wedding back in March. She had opted for it today to keep the sun from beating down on her face. It was the first scorcher of the summer. The few wisps of morning fog that had managed to straggle off the ocean had been vanquished by a brutal sun shortly after dawn. It was now eighty-one degrees and climbing.

She peeked out from under the hat brim to see Taller sink into the chair beside her. He was looking very natty in pale blue seersucker with a polka-dot bow tie.

"A perfect day for shoveling dirt," he announced.

"Yeah, as long as they don't keel over from the heat," she said, grinning. She was surprisingly glad to see him: Apparently she cared more than she'd wanted to admit that he'd been neglecting her.

"Is it hot?" he said. "I really can't tell. I had a late breakfast at the Four Seasons, and the air-conditioning was positively arctic. I'm still trying to thaw out." He tilted his head toward the architectural model onstage. "So what do you think of my cousin Evan's creation?"

"I'm not sure. It's unusual. It's certainly going to stand out around here."

"You think?"

There was the squeal of a microphone: David Clemente had ascended the stage and was poised to speak. The posse of photographers below him began snapping away.

"It's showtime, folks," Taller hissed.

David delivered a brief speech welcoming everyone to this very special occasion.

"Short and sweet," Taller whispered. "I approve."

David was followed at the mike by the mayor of San Carlino, who praised David extravagantly. The mayor was succeeded by the chief of a local Indian tribe, who was dressed entirely in black like Johnny Cash and who also praised David for the foundation's largesse to tribal schools.

"I know that chief!" Taller whispered to Jessica. "I met him at a dinner party at Lally's."

"The one where the palm tree fell onto the dinner table?" she whispered back.

"Yes, exactly!" He gave a short laugh. "Good times."

After the chief, a state senator came up and praised all the people who had spoken before him as well as everybody in the audience. Then the string quartet played the adagio from Mozart's Quartet in D Major, followed by a classical rendition of "Sgt. Pepper's Lonely Hearts Club Band."

And then David again, thanking a long roster of people who had made this event possible—and especially to J. Evanson Kern, "for designing a structure that will not only brilliantly fulfill the needs of this foundation, but will be an aesthetic landmark in our beautiful city for centuries to come."

"Only centuries?" Taller whispered gleefully. "Why not millennia?"

"Just modesty, I guess," Jessica whispered back and giggled. Being with Taller was like reverting to adolescence. Maybe it was just as well things had cooled between them.

Lally had now assumed the mike in the company of a woman with a frizz of mouse-colored hair. Lally introduced her as Irene Kaplan, an expert in the art of feng shui.

"I know *her*," Jessica hissed to Taller. "She used to teach fifth grade at St. Matthew's."

"I'm guessing feng shui pays a hell of a lot better," he laughed.

"Irene is now going to burn some native grasses, in accordance with the art of feng shui," Lally went on. "This will purify the building site and direct chi, which means good energy, into it."

Taller issued a low snort. Jessica poked him in the side.

The feng shui practitioner descended the stage and strode over to a large pile of dry weeds that was assembled in an aluminum tub. She struck a match and tossed it in.

Nothing.

Two more match tosses. Still nothing.

The audience stirred uneasily. The Johnny Cash–clad chief hurried over and did some rearranging of the weeds, presumably putting the more flammable grasses on top. One more toss of a lit match and there was a little crackle of flame. After a few seconds, it bloomed into a bonfire, sending a column of gray smoke straight up into the still, hot air.

Everyone applauded.

David returned to the microphone. "And now my great friend Kazuo Arita, who is a Shinto priest, will give the traditional salt blessing of the site."

A finely built Japanese man wearing a white robe, a tall black cap, and lacquered wooden sandals rose from one of the folding chairs and began chanting loudly. He gravely traversed the perimeter of the site, sprinkling each corner with salt from small squares of rice paper.

"What next, a papal procession?" Taller asked, smirking.

Jessica didn't respond: She found the Shinto ritual moving and quite lovely, marred only by the discordant wail of fire engines out on the streets some distance away.

The Shinto priest completed his ceremony and glided back to his seat in the audience. And then David popped back to the mike and announced, "My wife, Lally, and I will now have the honor and privilege of breaking the first ground."

They climbed down from the stage. A young man with furry white blond hair scampered up to them with shovels. Beaming radiantly at each other, the Clementes struck the hard ground and each turned over a small quantity of dirt.

Everyone applauded wildly. There were some cheers, and Taller whistled.

The sirens on the streets intensified to a screaming pitch and then stopped abruptly. And then suddenly, firemen in full regalia, wielding axes and dragging hoses, came bursting into the enclosure. They began plowing roughly through the banks of chairs, sending people leaping and scattering in their wake.

Taller chuckled. "What happens when somebody yells 'Fire!' at a crowded groundbreaking?"

"I guess we're going to find out," Jessica remarked.

She glanced at the Clementes, who, still clutching their shovels, looked aghast. Lally suddenly materialized a phone and, judging by her expression, began soundly berating someone on the other end.

"In her condition, Lally must be freaking out!" Taller exclaimed.

"What condition?" Jessica inquired. "My God, is Lally pregnant?"

"Don't be ridiculous." Without further explanation, Taller bounded from his seat and scurried off.

She watched as he greeted Lally solicitously and Lally, weeping, practically collapsed on his shoulder. Jessica suddenly felt exactly as she had in the third grade when her best friend, Christie Beckner, told her she didn't like her anymore and went off to play with Maryellen Comisky, leaving Jessica flat.

Amid the confusion that followed the arrival of the fire-fighters, Caitlin decided to keep her seat. Some people were racing for the exit as if escaping a burning building; others, for more mysterious reasons, stampeded toward the stage; and more than a few trooped to the bonfire to watch as it was quickly extinguished by the high-pressure hoses. This garnered another smattering of applause, as if it were part of the show. The photographers darted everywhere, documenting it all with an enraptured frenzy.

And then the police escorted a delegation of VIPs—the Clementes, the mayor and senator, the Shinto priest, and, oddly, Taller Kern—efficiently out of the enclosure.

For a moment, Caitlin thought Evan had been among the evacuated VIPs; then she spotted him talking to the tubby fireman who appeared to be the one in charge. They exchanged a laugh, and the fireman went to join his men, leaving Evan temporarily on his own. Caitlin noticed the Kern family members begin to march his way, with Janey leading the charge.

She bounced impetuously to her feet. "Evan!" she shouted, waving. "Hi, Evan!"

He saw her, smiled broadly, and waved. Darting a glance over his shoulder at the approaching phalanx of Kerns, he turned abruptly and began wading through the disrupted rows of chairs toward Caitlin.

He grabbed her hand. "Come on, let's get out of here."

"Don't you have to go anywhere? To a lunch or anything?"

"No, all that stuff was yesterday. I'm free as the wind."

Her mind skipped to the tasks she had earmarked for the afternoon: that vintage Stetson that needed reblocking before she could sell it; the python-skin traveling case she had sent parcel post to a buyer but had never arrived and now needed to be tracked down.

But what the hell . . . She'd been working her butt off lately. She deserved a few hours of playing hooky.

CHAPTER twelve

Are You Dating That Guy?

E van bundled her into his SUV, the dark red Porsche she remembered from the post office parking lot. "I've got a great idea!" he said. "Let's go to the beach. I know one about forty minutes north of here that's practically deserted."

"Right now? In these clothes?" She was wearing one of her best summer outfits, a Chloé sundress and the Taryn Rose sandals that by some miracle had cleaned up well.

"Sure. You've got a short skirt, I can roll up my pants. We'll kick off our shoes and splash in the waves. It'll be great."

"Okay, yeah." She laughed. The way she was feeling right now, anything he had suggested—a spin through Death Valley or a climb up the side of a live volcano or just squatting right here on the side of the road—she probably would have said, "Yeah, great!"

They drove forty-five minutes up the Coast Highway, and then Evan pulled up to a scruffy-looking roadside stand. "The best milk-shakes in California," he proclaimed. He ordered two extra-large, a double chocolate for Caitlin and a strawberry for himself; they came in tall silver-and-green-striped plastic glasses filmed with frost and impaled with squiggly green straws.

Clutching her milkshake, Caitlin followed him along a path behind the stand that was strewn with litter. They ducked through a tear in a chain-link fence, teetered somewhat precariously down a pebbly, steeper path, and suddenly emerged onto a broad ocean cove.

"It's amazing!" Caitlin gasped.

"Yeah. I always feel like Balboa discovering the Pacific when I come here."

They took off their shoes and left them on a dry rock. Evan rolled up his trousers, and they began walking in the damp sand, the waves foaming around their feet. The water and the breeze were chill, but the sun was intense; and Caitlin, taking a long frosty sip of her milkshake, couldn't remember the last time she'd felt so deliriously happy.

Evan began talking about all the problems he'd had with the Clemente project, culminating the week before when Lally had sprung the feng shui lady on him. "Lally had been feeling pretty much left out of the project up till then, so bringing in this Irene person was her way of putting her own signature on the building. So suddenly I've got a schoolteacher telling me my design is full of flaws. She starts dictating all this crap about placing mirrors and fountains and aquariums, for God's sake, to deflect the bad energy, and I'm supposed to take it seriously! Luckily David stepped in and nixed the mirrors and fountains, and at the last minute there was this compromise about torching native grasses." He broke into a grin. "Unfortunately, no one thought to obtain a permit for a bonfire."

Caitlin laughed. "So who called the fire department?"

"Apparently, it was one of the friars at the mission. He saw smoke coming from what he knew was just a vacant lot and panicked. Guess he just didn't recognize good chi when he saw it."

Caitlin loved what laughing did to his face, lengthening the corners of that kissable mouth and making crescents out of the blue eyes. There was a slight gap between his front teeth, and his nose was not quite straight—it had an arch in the bridge that was more pronounced on one side than the other. But these were flaws that saved him from being too deodorant-soap-model handsome. If anything, they made him even more attractive.

They wandered for some time, fording an outcropping of black rock. A sea lion, mottled and shiny, slid off a crag and merged instantly with the dark water. They sat on a ledge below the crag and slurped up the last of their shakes.

"How long have you been living in San Carlino?" Evan asked.

"About five years. Since Aiden was six. I moved there right after I split up with my husband."

"Why did you split up?"

Caitlin hesitated. She wriggled the straw against the bottom of her empty plastic cup.

"None of my business, I know," Evan said quickly.

"No, it's okay. It's just that it always seems so strange when I tell it. Ravi, my ex-husband, was bipolar. I mean, he wasn't at first. When we got married, he was fine. Perfectly normal. He was doing great at his job at Smith Barney, and after Aiden was born, he was a terrific father."

"And then all of a sudden he changed?"

"No, not all of a sudden. It came on kind of gradually. He started to do weird things. Like, some mornings I could hardly wake him up, he'd be sleeping like he was in a coma. Then other times he'd leap out of bed at four in the morning before it was even light and go out jogging for nine or ten miles in Golden Gate Park. I used to worry that he'd get mugged. At first I just thought it was stress—I mean, his job was really high pressure, and the competition was murder. But then it started to get worse."

"Yeah? How?"

She shrugged, wondering where to start. "Well . . . he started to eat weird things. Like Wheat Chex with miniature marshmallows on top. And blue Popsicles, and jars of baby food. Frozen bread." She gave a strained laugh. "And then he just continued to get worse. He'd go on spending binges and bring home all kinds of stuff we didn't need. I found out later he'd maxed out thirteen credit cards. Then other times he'd burst into tears for no reason at all. But then sometimes he'd just seem like his normal self, and I'd feel so relieved and tell myself everything was okay, it had all been just something he was going through, and now it was over."

"But it wasn't?"

"No." She grimaced. "Oh God, this is going to sound funny. Don't laugh."

"I won't." He held up a "scout's honor" hand.

"Well, one day, out of the blue, he announced to me he had become a Buddhist. A tantric Buddhist."

"That doesn't sound so funny. I've got friends who've become Buddhists. Or at least they claim to be."

"But not like this. Rav stopped going to work and shaved his head. And then he dyed all of his clothes, even his underwear, orange. Then he found this huge statue of the Buddha somewhere in Chinatown and hauled it back to our apartment and put it up in the middle of our little living room, and then he began praying and chanting to it and leaving rice cakes and papayas and stuff as offerings to it."

Evan gave a quick chuckle. "Sorry. But it does sound a little funny."

"Yeah, I know, but believe me it wasn't. The worst part was that he started bringing strangers home—all these scruffy-looking guys and crazy women, some of them talking to themselves. They'd all sit around on the floor and steal the Buddha's food when Ravi wasn't looking. And Ravi would give them lectures about karma and emptiness and how the Buddha said that all was suffering."

"Wow," Evan said.

"Yeah." Caitlin smiled tightly. "I was working at a spa in Pacific Heights, and one evening I got off the bus coming home from work and saw one of these people—a guy who called himself Captain America. He had long greasy hair and a scraggly beard, and he wore red, white, and blue clothes and a flag wrapped around his hips, kind of like a Tahitian sarong. And there he was walking up Balboa Street with my son, Aiden, by the hand."

"Jesus. You must have freaked."

"More than freaked. I went up and kicked Ravi and all his scuzzy friends out of the apartment and threw all his stuff out the window. Everything happened pretty quickly after that, the divorce and my leaving San Francisco and moving down to San Carlino." She paused. Then she gave a little shiver, as if to throw off the memories. "Anyway, that's all in the past."

"So it seems like we both have marital horror stories," Evan said.

"Really?" She waited for him to elaborate.

But he suddenly leaned in close to her. "Damn, you're pretty!" he said, and kissed her.

She found herself eagerly kissing him back. Those lips she'd been speculating about for the past week—they were hard and soft at the same time, and warm and a little salty and absolutely thrilling.

Two black dogs came bounding from around a bend in the cliff-side, followed by several men, who silently dug fishing poles into the sand and began baiting hooks, while the dogs ran in loops, chasing waves and gulls and each other.

Evan drew back from Caitlin. "I've got another brilliant idea. There's a great little seafood place a little farther up the coast. It's got a spectacular view of the water. And they make a killer bloody bull."

"Oh, but I can't," she said ruefully. "Aiden's camp lets out at four o'clock, and I've got to get back to pick him up."

For a split second, a look of almost anger crossed Evan's face. But it vanished instantly, replaced by his easy grin. "Yeah, okay, sure. We'll do it next time."

So there will be a next time! Caitlin thought, and felt a surge of elation.

⤞⤝ The traffic had picked up considerably since the middle of the day, jamming up every few miles so that the trip which had taken forty-five minutes going out was going to be at least an hour on the return. Caitlin did some quick calculating: By the time she picked up her car at the Whole Foods parking lot and then negotiated the twisty road up Señorita Canyon, she'd be fifteen, twenty minutes late. All the other kids would be gone, Aiden would be feeling stranded, probably on the verge of panic . . .

As if reading her thoughts, Evan said, "Where is the camp? Maybe we should go directly there."

"Could we?" she said gratefully. "It's at the top of Señorita Canyon. You take Tillory Road and just keep going up. Would you really mind?"

"Of course not. My mother was forever forgetting to pick me up. I'd be the last kid left at the birthday party after even the clowns and magicians had gone home. I never got over it."

There was a mysterious easing of congestion as they entered the city, and the Cayenne efficiently maneuvered the canyon road so that they actually arrived ahead of most of the other parents. They pulled into the car park clearing just as the first Cottonwood campers appeared.

Caitlin climbed out of the car and located Aiden among them. The triumph of his first day at camp had not been repeated. The friend he had made, the stocky Mexican boy named Hernando, had a rocky home life that kept him from coming very often. She could tell at a glance this wasn't one of Hernando's days by the way Aiden was walking—his head hanging down, his shoulders slumped, as if he were dragging a grand piano behind him.

She knew he'd be mortified if she kissed him: (*Mom! Not in front of all the other guys!*), so she just greeted him with an exuberant wave. "I left our car at the place I was at this morning," she told him. "My friend Evan gave me a lift here, and he's going to take us back to it."

Aiden's pale brown eyes narrowed with suspicion. "What do you mean? How come you left your car there?"

"Remember I told you I was going to the groundbreaking ceremony? Evan is the architect who designed the building. We went out to get something to eat afterwards, and then there wasn't enough time to go back for my car." Not a total fabrication—they did have the milkshakes, which counted as something to eat. "Come on, let's not keep him waiting."

She marched him briskly back to the Cayenne. Evan jumped out. "Hey there, Aiden, I'm Evan. Glad to meet you!" He and Aiden exchanged one of those complicated basketball star hand maneuvers she'd seen other men do with boys but that she'd never mastered.

Aiden, still peering guardedly, slid into the backseat.

Please don't let him be whiny or sullen or insist that he really, really needed to take a whiz, right this minute! Caitlin prayed as they started back down the canyon.

"So what kind of stuff do you do at camp, Aiden?" Evan asked.

"Oh, just stuff," he replied.

But slowly, under careful probing from Evan, he began talking about handball and the nature hikes; and from that they segued into *Family Guy* (Aiden's favorite show) and the all-time best flavor of Baskin-Robbins, and how Superman would always beat Batman except for if Batman carried around kryptonite . . . To Caitlin's joy, the two of them rattled away nonstop until they reached the Whole Foods.

"Remember, I've got a rain check," Evan said in a low voice to Caitlin. To Aiden, he called, "See ya later, dude!"

Aiden seemed to cringe. "Yeah, okay," he mumbled.

Maybe the word *dude* was out-of-date, Caitlin speculated. He was always jumping on her when she used what he thought were old-fashioned terms: *Mom! Nobody says stuff like that anymore!*

He got into the car and remained silent, wordlessly clipping his seat belt closed, not demanding she eject the Ben Harper CD, staring out his window until they had returned.

"Are you dating that guy?" he asked as they headed into the house.

"Well, yes, kind of," she admitted. "He's nice, don't you think?"

"I don't know," he said with a shrug. "So are you going to get married to him?"

She glanced at him, startled. "Of course not, sweetie. I've only just met him. We hardly even know each other yet."

But the thought danced lightly through her mind: What if she did get married to him? *Mrs. Rich and Illustrious Architect.* Wouldn't that make the Colina Linda pack finally sit up and take notice?

CHAPTER thirteen

Something Smells Very Happy Homemaker

"You look a little tired, Jane." Tilda Lazenby, in Calvin Klein pedal pushers and saucer-shaped sunglasses that made her look like a lemur, stood with one butt cheek squashed against the rim of a chipped stone urn. "I'm afraid you've been overdoing it lately. Too much social activity."

"Yeah, I've been going out a lot. Since Lally's been back, it's been nonstop." Janey punctuated this statement with a deep yawn.

Tilda, who was not on Lally Clemente's A list, and in all likelihood not even on the B or C, let out a miffed little puff of air. "All those Clemente affairs where they soak you for every last dime—they get tedious after a while," she pronounced. "When Charlie and I accept an invitation, we don't like to feel we always have to pay for it."

How many of those freebie invitations did they receive? Janey thought acidly. The Lazenbys were hardly celebrated for their scintillating wit or brilliant conversation.

But she couldn't forget that Tilda was her client, so she murmured tactfully, "Yes, I know what you mean."

Janey was at the moment overseeing the clearance of a patch of the Lazenbys' sprawling grounds that was destined to become the freshly designed garden room. Half a dozen laborers, slightly built men who nevertheless seemed to be able to lift their entire body weight and more (Janey was always astonished by this phenomenon), were hacking down rat-infested banana trees and hauling away a collection of cement birdbaths, broken statuary, and other junk too hideous to even believe. Janey eyed the urn Tilda's buttock was resting on, a heart-stoppingly awful fake Baroque thing festooned with prancing cherubs.

"That ugly thing goes to the Dumpster, too," she ordered.

Tilda sprang off the urn as if Janey had pointed out it was contaminated with plutonium. "Yes, definitely," she agreed. "Out it goes."

"There's so much junk here!" Janey gazed at the grounds with despair. "I might have to order a second Dumpster."

She yawned again, cavernously. She was indeed feeling drowsy, but not because she was worn out from a frenetic social calendar; the truth was that she'd been popping down lorazepam rather heavily—the vial she'd swiped from the Mar Verde open house was already a third depleted. She'd start rationing it very soon, she promised herself. She absolutely would.

But if there was ever a time she needed a mood enhancer, it was right now.

Her worst fear had been confirmed: Evan was definitely involved with that ghastly, climbing little Caitlin the Snatch. The way he'd made a beeline to her after the ceremony Tuesday, so crudely turning his back on Janey, not to mention all the rest of the family . . . Well, it had just about made her livid!

She gave a savage kick to the lopped-off head of a gnome lying on the grass.

"You know what, Jane?" Tilda was contemplating her with even greater concern. "I think you should treat yourself to a nice little getaway. Maybe something like a nice long spa weekend. You could book a suite at Serenity Waters."

"Don't be insane. Nobody goes to the desert in July."

"No, no, of course not," Tilda amended hastily, "it would be scorching. Stupid suggestion. I just thought of Serenity because I could get you very special treatment there, I mean if you wanted to go sometime later in the fall. Or the winter, or whatever. I know the person who's going to be in charge of guest services."

Janey turned to watch a twelve-foot bird of paradise go toppling onto a patch of poison sumac. "Yeah? Who's that?"

"That girl Caitlin Who's-is. Hatcher, Latcher? The one who was having lunch with your cousin Evan that time at Café Cygne."

A sort of freezing sensation began at the base of Janey's spine and bifurcated icily through her shoulder blades. Caitlin Latch again? It seemed the world was suddenly conspiring to make everything fine and dandy for that nasty little climber, while she, Janey, had to swallow copious amounts of generic Ativan just to stay out of the dumps.

"So how long has she been working there?" she asked, struggling to keep a disinterested tone.

"Gee, I don't know. I'm not sure she's even started yet. I can find out if you want."

It occurred to Janey that she could find out for herself. Her ex-husband Robbie's niece Hollis had recently become the third wife of Marty Drucker, the CEO of Serenity Resorts. If memory served, the newlyweds were in Italy shopping for property in Todi but should be back momentarily. Janey had not yet entertained them—a shameful oversight that she would soon remedy.

"I can find out easily for myself," she told Tilda brusquely.

"Oh, of course, I'm sure you can." Tilda gave a self-deprecating laugh. "By the way, the board meeting tonight for the classical music festival? We're taking a final vote on the director, right?"

"I suppose."

"And we've all agreed on Thomas Bramberg, haven't we? I mean, you think he's the best choice, right?"

Janey knew almost nothing about Thomas Bramberg except that he was a modernist composer and the current boyfriend of Jessica DiSantini. Janey's resentment of Caitlin suddenly spilled over to all pretty women and their sexy lovers. "No, I don't think he's the right choice," she snapped. "His kind of modern stuff will drive away all our more conservative subscribers. Joe Meisler has done a terrific job for five years, so why should we change?"

"Yeah," said Tilda. "I see your point."

Jessica had found herself over the next few days feeling strangely nervous about her forthcoming visit from Sienna. She'd changed the menu about a dozen times, veering from a homey chicken casserole to what her daughter, Rowan, would call a fancy-shmancy recipe involving ahi tuna, esoteric Chinese vegetables, and intricate marinades. In the end, she settled on a simple summery pasta with fresh pesto sauce, a crisp salad with lettuces from her garden, and gooey homemade brownies for dessert.

Jessica had told Sienna to come at seven on Friday evening, and at five o'clock she began making the pesto, grinding three fistfuls of freshly picked basil, a generous scoop of pine nuts, and a pinch of sea salt with a marble mortar and pestle. Why in heaven's name should she be nervous about entertaining this girl? she asked herself as she worked the pestle. Nothing was at stake here. Sienna was just a silly mixed-up young woman with no real connection to herself.

No connection except Tommy—and that, of course, was huge. Maybe Sienna wasn't his actual daughter, but she was as close to him as if she were, and he loved her. And if Sienna was anywhere near as erratic and malicious as her reputation made her out to be, she could turn instantly on Jessica and blow up her relationship with Tommy.

Which, she argued to herself, might be the best thing.

REASONS TO BREAK UP WITH TOM BRAMBERG, NUMBER
WHATEVER:
He could be influenced by crazy Sienna.

She worked the cheese—part parmigiana, part Sardinian
pecorino—into the basil paste in the mortar, then stirred in a stream
of fragrant pale green olive oil. She melted dark chocolate over sim-
mering water, mixed up the brownies, and placed the pan in the oven.
Then she washed the greens—rocket, lamb's tongue, bibb, and a little
spider mustard—and threw them in the salad spinner.

At seven o'clock, she laid out plates and glasses on the pine
kitchen table and put a large pot of water on the stove to boil. She set
a selection of DVDs—*Roman Holiday, All About Eve, The Lady Van-
ishes*—on the coffee table in the family room. She wondered if Sienna
would like to have popcorn with the movie. She could microwave
some Newman's Own, which was Alex's favorite, if she did.

At seven forty-five, she reduced the boiling water to a simmer, removed the brownies from the oven, and put them on a rack to cool.

At twenty after eight, Jessica realized the girl was not going to
show up. She wasn't sure if she felt relief, disappointment, or insult.
Probably all three, she told herself. She cut a large wedge of brownie
and began stuffing it in her mouth.

The doorbell rang.

She hastily tossed the rest of the wedge into the disposal and
wiped the chocolate off her lips and chin. She took a breath and went
to the door.

Sienna wore a T-shirt advertising a band called the Dismembered
Dead, a pair of not very clean skinny-leg jeans, and metallic gold platform wedgies. " 'Lo," she said, and slouched in.

"Sienna, you were supposed to be here at seven," Jessica said
sternly.

"I guess." No attempt to justify her lateness. She tilted up her perfect nose and sniffed the air. "Something smells very happy homemaker in here."

Murderous feelings welled up in Jessica again. She must have been insane to invite this appalling creature into her house. She should tell her it was too damn late, dinner was ruined, get lost.

Then suddenly Sienna gave an almost sweet smile, and in her eyes—half-moons like Lally's—appeared a wistful and almost childlike expression. "I mean, it smells really good, like cookies being baked or something. And I'm starving. Can we eat soon? I'll help."

She's manipulative, Jessica warned herself. According to all accounts, Sienna had perfected the art of twisting people to her whims.

"Everything's almost done," she said, leading the way into the kitchen. "I've made a pesto, and it'll just take a few minutes to cook the pasta."

She turned up the flame under the pot of water and then began whisking balsamic vinegar, sea salt, and olive oil in a cherrywood salad bowl. "Do you like to cook?"

Sienna leaned indolently against a counter. "I don't know. I've never done it."

"Never? You've never fried an egg or made yourself a tuna-fish sandwich?"

Sienna thought a moment. "When I was at school in Switzerland, there was a girl who got sent all this stuff from her family to put in a toaster. Pop-Tarts and things. I was pretty good at that." She gave a snarky laugh.

"Okay, so you can make toast. It's a start. But don't you think you'd like to cook for your daughter when she gets older?"

"What for? The help does that."

There was a dismissive note in her tone that rankled Jessica. She felt like explaining to Sienna that she found cooking a pleasurable and creative outlet, not a drudgery, and that she also had full-time help, a live-in housekeeper who had weekend nights off. She might also remind Sienna that she was a professional, an attorney, and that just several hours before, she'd been at work on an extremely complex probate case ...

She could picture Sienna giving a yawn.

You don't have to justify yourself to this silly girl. The important thing, she told herself, was to find out more about Chiara.

"That nanny that Chiara's with now," she said in a casual voice. "Is she a very good cook?"

"I suppose." Sienna shimmied a pack of cigarettes out of her hip pocket, a seeming act of prestidigitation considering how tight the jeans were. She shook one out from the pack, then slouched over to the stove and tapped it on the flame to light it. Jessica started to protest, but if she tolerated Tommy's smoking, wouldn't it be hypocritical to outlaw Sienna's?

Sidestepping a plume of exhaled smoke, she removed a thick sheaf of vermicelli from the DeCecco box and tipped it into the boiling water. "You must miss Chiara a lot," she ventured after a moment.

"Yeah, sure. She's my little bunny-wunny."

"When was the last time you saw her?"

"Not too long ago."

"So she's not that far away?"

Sienna shrugged. "No place is very far away anymore. It's so easy to get around."

"Do you really think so? I find traveling to be pretty difficult these days. Especially air travel—the planes are always packed, and the security is a nightmare."

"I suppose, if you fly commercial," Sienna drawled.

Those of us who don't know a bunch of dukes and movie stars with private planes to sponge off of are pretty much stuck with commercial airlines, Jessica thought sourly. She gave the vermicelli a particularly vigorous swirl with a long wooden spoon.

"So how about your mother?" she asked bluntly. "Do you plan to see her at all while you're shacking up in her house?"

Sienna took a long, luxuriant drag on her cigarette and blew out a wobbly oval smoke ring. "Sure. I plan to spend a lot of time with both of them. The problem is Lally doesn't really want to see me."

"Why do you think that?" Jessica said.

"Because she's not once invited me to visit since she's been married. That's why."

"But it's only been four months. And they've only been home from their honeymoon a few weeks. When you're newlyweds, you need some time alone together."

"You really think those two spend a lot of time alone?" Sienna gave a snort. "And even if they did need all this bonding-togetherness time, why does Lally keep asking for Chiara to be with them?"

Jessica really didn't have an answer for that. She busied herself with removing the greens from the spinner and tossing them in the vinaigrette.

"So what's David like in bed?" Sienna said.

Jessica dropped the salad fork. It went clattering to the floor. "What?"

"You had an affair with him, didn't you? Was he any good, or did he need a lot of fluffing?"

Jessica picked up the fork and wiped it with a towel. "I did not have an affair with him, and even if I did, I wouldn't discuss it with you. Frankly, Sienna, I think it's creepy of you to even ask something like that."

"It's just a question." The half-moon eyes closed halfway. "He's a pretty good-looking guy, so naturally you wonder. And he's a lot younger than my mother."

"Maybe a year or two. Not a lot."

"For a guy as wealthy as that, it's like he's hooked up with an old hag."

"That's bullshit, and you know it!" Jessica snapped. "Your mother is a stunning and accomplished and extremely attractive woman. It's no mystery why David fell in love with her."

Sienna smiled. Lazily, she extended her long, slender arms and lifted them outward, like a golden bird taking flight. Then, just as lazily, she let them flutter down. She brought the cigarette back to her lips.

"You know what my mother always used to say?" she said, exhaling slowly. " 'To catch a husband is an art, but to keep him is a job.' Simone de Beauvoir wrote it somewhere. So I guess Lally's got her job cut out for her, doesn't she?" She gave a smug little giggle.

Jessica stared at her. A sudden and distasteful thought began taking shape in her mind. No, it was too crazy, too awful . . .

The doorbell rang three times in rapid succession. Who in the world could that be? she wondered.

"I'll go," Sienna volunteered. She squelched her cigarette in the sink and slouched out into the hall.

Jessica tested a strand of pasta and, finding it acceptably al dente, dumped the pot into a colander to drain. She heard the door open and then Sienna give a loud squeal: "Oh, my God!" followed by the rumble of a man's voice, and Jessica's heart turned over.

Several seconds later, Tom Bramberg appeared in the kitchen. He had a canvas valise hanging from one shoulder, Sienna draped over the other, and a somewhat stunned expression on his face.

"It's Tom-Tom!" Sienna said in the same squealy voice. "His boring old symposium broke off early and he's surprised us!"

Jessica stood immobile a moment, her face shiny from the pasta steam, her emotions in turmoil. She was ecstatic at Tom's sudden appearance. But she was still reeling from the fact that she was suddenly sure she knew why Sienna had come to San Carlino.

"I guess I could be wrong," Jessica said.

Snuggled in Tommy's long arms, she found it easy to believe she was wrong. Easy, in fact, to believe that there was nothing at all to worry about in the entire wonderful, delicious world.

It had been strange and awkward when he had appeared this evening. He'd been clearly astounded to find Sienna here and just as clearly unhappy about it—almost as if he suspected the two of them, Sienna and Jessica, of ganging up on him for some mysterious reason.

But he loosened up over dinner. The three of them hungrily attacked the pesto pasta and salad and drank the lovely, grassy-tasting Sancerre that Jessica brought up from the wine cellar, and after that Sienna wolfed down half the brownies. Tommy explained that a member of the panel he was supposed to be on in Montreal had been rushed to the hospital with a burst appendix, so he'd seized the opportunity to come home early. Sienna wanted to know about the Viennese festival. Who Was There?—meaning what members of royalty, recent Grand Prix winners, or hotel heiresses—and Who Were They With?

At nine forty-five, Sienna announced she had to go meet "some people" at a club in Hollywood. Jessica thought of her careful selection of DVDs all set out in the family room; Lally was right: the idea of Sienna curled up on a couch watching old Bette Davis flicks was preposterous.

"It's at least a two-hour drive to L.A.," Jessica pointed out to her. "You won't be there much before midnight."

"Yeah, probably not," Sienna said indifferently. "Good thing Lally left her Range Rover in the garage, otherwise I'd be driving some piece-of-crap rental."

Then she was gone, and Jessica was finally free to do what she'd been dying to do for the past hour and seven minutes: She entwined her arms around Tommy's neck and pressed her mouth to his and let herself dissolve completely into him. For the next rapturous hour, all thoughts of Sienna flew out of her mind.

Later, as they lay in bed murmuring to each other, Jessica filled him in on the events that had led to her cooking vermicelli with pesto sauce for the girl. "It's funny, but I don't even know her last name. Lally has had so many different ones."

"It's Bramberg," Tommy told her. "Sienna Noelle Bramberg."

"She's got your name?"

"Sure. Lally and I were technically still married when she was born."

"Oh, yeah, of course." It was disturbing that Sienna had Tommy's last name. It seemed to cement the connection between them that Jessica still didn't want to accept. "So who was her real father?"

"A guy named Reggie Lind. He was the drummer in the band I was in at the time."

"Frenzy Cat?" Jessica had never told Tommy, but she had purchased a scratchy Frenzy Cat album on eBay, and she frequently played it on her ancient turntable when she was alone in the house. She'd never been a fan of heavy metal rock—Rod Stewart and Bryan Ferry had been her teenage crushes—but she found it exciting to hear Tommy at twenty, his voice high and raw, verging on the falsetto. Exciting and deeply erotic.

"Frenzy Cat." Tommy repeated the band's name with a chuckle. "Reg was a gorgeous guy. Half Jamaican, handsome as hell, with dreadlocks down to his ass. I never held it against him—Lally and I were going to split up anyway. I just wished she had picked somebody a little steadier to make her break with. Reggie split the second he found out he'd knocked her up."

"Poor Sienna. What a strange childhood she must have had. And now poor little Chiara. Did you know Sienna has taken her away from her grandparents in New Jersey?"

"Yeah."

Jessica glanced at him. "You do? So do you know where she is?"

"Sure. Back in the flat Sienna rents in Rome. It's where they've been living for the last few years. Chiara's being taken care of by a very nice Italian lady who's been her nanny since her birth." He raised himself on one elbow. "Look . . . Sienna might not win any *Good Housekeeping* awards for mother of the year, but she's not a monster, you know. She loves her daughter."

Jessica felt simultaneously foolish and relieved. "Yeah, I'm sure she does. And it's not that I think she's a monster. It's just that right before you came, we had the strangest conversation. I got the feeling I knew why she had come here. That she had this awful plan . . ." She hesitated. "It's probably crazy."

"Yeah, what?"

"I got the distinct impression she was planning to steal David away from Lally."

"Jesus. What gave you that idea?"

"I don't know. Just the things she was saying. Implying that Lally was never going to be able to keep him."

"So? Lally has a long history of shucking off husbands and lovers." He gave a dry laugh. "Including me, once upon a time."

"But this was different. I think Sienna was hinting that she was going to seduce David away." Now that Jessica said it aloud, it sounded melodramatic and sort of silly. "But I don't know," she added weakly. "I guess I could be wrong."

Jessica's brown tabby cat, Ezra, jumped on the bed and folded itself between Tommy's feet, purring loudly. Cats were attracted to him, she had noticed. No doubt sensing a kindred feline spirit.

Tommy wriggled his feet to give Ezra more curling-up room. "You've been influenced by Lally into thinking the worst of Sienna. Those two have always had a peculiar rivalry, pretty much since Sienna spoke her first words. The problem is they're too much alike. It keeps them at constant war. But there's also an enormous bond between them, and I doubt that either of them will ever actually be able to break it."

He was right, of course, Jessica reflected. Sienna and Lally were adept at driving each other crazy, but they were alike in very basic ways. And Tommy couldn't possibly be so fond of the girl if she were anywhere near as warped as rumor made her out to be.

Jessica realized that she'd been caught up in the monster Sienna notion as well. She'd begun to picture Chiara as some sort of Victorian waif consigned to a cold garret in the charge of some Dickensian nurse. Made to sweep ashes and fed nothing but a thin gruel . . .

Get a grip, she told herself. *Stop letting your imagination run away with you.*

For the second time that night, she emptied her mind of thoughts of Sienna. Luxuriously, she curled herself against Tom's long body. "I'm so glad I've got you for the rest of the summer," she murmured.

"Well, not exactly. I've got something to tell you. I've been bumped from the Colina Linda Festival, so I've taken a job to score a film down in L.A."

Jessica went rigid. "The festival bumped you? I thought it was all set."

"We had an informal agreement, but nothing on paper. Your friend Jane seems to think my music is too avant-garde for your crowd, and she's the big honcho on their board."

That blasted cretin Janey! Jessica flushed with rage. No wonder she was on so many people's shit list. Nasty, interfering, trust fund bitch!

"Hey, it's no big deal," Tommy said, hugging her close. "I'll just be a couple of hours down the road."

A couple of hours and an entire universe away. For a moment, Jessica believed she could just murder Janey Martinez.

CHAPTER fourteen

That Shivery Feeling Deep Inside

Aiden figured he had really pissed off his dad by having to sign off so fast the last time his dad IM'd him, before they could even get to talk. There were still about a hundred things Aiden wanted to ask, starting with number one: *Are you cured?* He figured his dad had to be cured if he was back from India and living in the Transamerica Building in San Francisco, but he wanted to know for sure.

He'd checked out the building, which was called the Transamerica Pyramid Building, on the Net. It was extremely high and pointy, with what kind of looked like a pair of wings attached to it. You could see from the pictures that it was the tallest building in the city of San Francisco. The very top of it looked like the lead part of a really sharp pencil, but from what Aiden could tell, it didn't have any windows in it—so if his dad could see all, his apartment had to be in the top floor just below that pointy part. Aiden wondered just how far out in the Pacific Ocean his dad could see from his window, whether he could watch battleships practicing maneuvers and cool stuff like that.

By now, though, Aiden was getting really scared that he was never going to hear from him again. Every night after dinner he went up to his room and stayed online, hoping to get an IM; but so far nothing. He had tried sending them out, but every time he did, he just got the message that KCUDYFFAD was not currently logged on, no matter what time of day it was. Once he'd even gotten up at three in the morning and tried, but still nothing.

Tonight it was the same thing: He had surfed the Net awhile, then spent some time on a kind of boring game site. And now he was counting up the number of e-mails he'd gotten from kids who said they were coming to his birthday party.

Thirteen so far. A lot more than he'd expected. The worst thing was that it included that mutant Kyle Lewison—Caitlin had made Aiden invite him because Kyle was his summer homework report buddy.

But Aiden figured it would be okay because his cool camp buddy Nando was also coming. His name was actually Hernando, but everybody called him Nando, and he was taller and weighed a lot more than Kyle. He could kick Kyle's butt if it was necessary.

Aiden was actually starting to get excited about the party. He wondered what presents he'd get, whether anyone would give him Myst—or maybe even Grand Theft Auto, though his mom would never let him keep it. And he'd actually even forgotten to think about his dad when an IM with the screen name KCUDYFFAD popped up.

DUDE!! I KNOW THAT WHEN YOU CHECK OUT THE NAME OF THIS FONT I'M USING YOU'RE GONNA THINK TO YOURSELF "DANG! YOUR OLD DAD IS GETTING COOLER BY THE MINUTE!"

Aiden felt a burst of relief. His dad was back and didn't sound pissed-off at all.

"what's the name of the font?" he typed back.

RAAVI!!!!!

"cool, it's like your name. that's completely awesome!!"

YOU KNOW WHAT'S EVEN MORE AWESOME? I HAVE
DESIGNED A BRAND-NEW FONT CALLED AIDEN AND
I'M IN TOP-SECRET NEGOTIATIONS WITH MICROSOFT
WINDOWS TO LICENSE IT!! YOU KNOW WHAT THAT
MEANS, DON'T YOU?

"no, what?" Aiden typed.

MONEY RIVER, DUDE!! BIG BUCKS!

That meant he'd have enough money to come back to them! Aiden
became hugely excited. He felt an urgent pressure in his bladder.
"wait a minute," he typed, and ran like mad to the bathroom.
Made it just in time before he peed in his pants. Then ran like mad
back to his computer.
"r u still there?" he wrote anxiously.

YOU BET. I WAS AFRAID YOU CUT OUT ON ME AGAIN.

"no!! last time i had to go cos mom came into my room and
wanted to know what i was doing."

/. # (

It was the text message for Hitler—if you turned it sideways, it
looked exactly like him. Aiden laughed.
"yeah, sometimes she acts like hitler," he wrote. "she's out tonight
so it's cool. maria, that's my sitter, is downstairs watching courting
alex. i think that show sucks so i don't watch it."

WHERE DID YOUR MOM GO?

"she's out on a date with this guy Evan."

Aiden waited some moments, but there was no reply. He wrote another message: "dad, r u still there? u don't have to wait for Microsoft for the 500 dollars. u need to come now!"

He tapped on send. He got back the immediate response that KCUDYFFAD was not currently signed on.

It was just what he'd been scared of happening. His mom was going to be hanging with this guy Evan just when he was going to get his dad to come back. But now his dad was going to go disappear again.

Aiden absolutely was not going to let that happen.

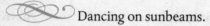 Dancing on sunbeams.

It seemed to be the way Caitlin was feeling much of the time. All the romantic clichés seemed to apply: singing in the rain (not that there was any rain in San Carlino in July); floating in the clouds (ditto for cloudy days); that shivery feeling deep inside (even though the temperature was a consistently balmy seventy-nine degrees) . . .

The reason for this cliché-ridden state of mind was that Evan Kern was giving her a major rush. Dinner at Nashimora, one of those student-frequented sushi bars up by the university. A moody Iranian film at the art theater in the Conquistadora Plaza. Another wander on the shore, this time the rocky Colina Linda beach, which was barely wide enough to walk on at low tide and disappeared entirely at high tide.

They hadn't made love yet, though they almost had after the Iranian movie. Evan had invited her back to the condo he was subletting, and they had snuggled on the couch, sipping brandy, while he showed her his sketchbook for the McArdle Gallery. First, there were just a few quick, scribbly lines; then, with every page, the sketch became more defined, until the award-winning final design emerged.

Caitlin found something amazingly sexy about this—to be able to see right into his mind and follow its creative processes, the mental equivalent of giving birth. She might have pulled him into bed right then and there, except the only sitter she'd been able to round up that night had to leave by ten, leaving no time for even a quickie.

And she definitely didn't want their first time to be a quickie.

In a way, she was glad they hadn't had sex yet. The anticipation of it was so exciting—almost as intense as she could imagine the actual doing would be.

But maybe tonight would be the Big Night. He had invited her to a cocktail party and silent auction to benefit the opening of the new Folk Art Museum—the first time they'd be attending an event in public as a couple. The party would be over by eight—early enough to slip back to his place, maybe for some Thai take-out and a nightcap and then continue to slip right in between the sheets.

And frankly, she couldn't wait!

Evan almost always had to work late, so it had become their practice that she meet him at his makeshift office above an Indonesian import company downtown and he would drive from there.

"My sitter can stay till eleven tonight," she told him as she settled into his Cayenne.

"Oh, hey, sorry, I should've told you," he said. "I've got to cut tonight short. I'm catching a ten-fifteen plane to Seattle."

"You're leaving?" On what was supposed to be their Big Night? She felt crushed.

"Yeah, Corinne's been acting crazy, so I really need to settle things out with her. And I'm dying to see my daughters. It's been nearly a month, and I miss them like mad."

"Oh. Yeah, I'm sure you do."

It occurred to her that they still hadn't had That Conversation— the sticky one in which she pinned down exactly where he stood with his wife. Was it a trial separation? Or were divorce proceedings under way? She knew that Corinne called him constantly; sometimes he'd excuse himself and retreat to someplace private to take the call, and sometimes he'd just turn off the ringer and angrily jam the phone back in his pocket or briefcase. If he *did* take the call, he never revealed what the conversation was about, but he'd be in a distracted and grumpy mood for some time afterward. The first time this had happened, Caitlin had inquired, "Are you okay?" and he'd snapped, "Yeah, fine," so harshly that she'd never mentioned the calls again.

"Are you going to be away long?" she ventured.

"God, I sure hope not. I'd like to get back here as soon as possible."

He shot her a significant look, and that dizzy dancing feeling welled up inside her again.

The Folk Art Museum was housed in a plastered cinder-block building east of the railroad tracks that had once been a women's prison. It was now painted a festive mango color. The bars had been removed from the narrow windows from which fifty years ago the incarcerated ladies—mostly prostitutes, mean drunks, and the occasional husband stabber—would shriek taunts and obscene proposals to the passersby below, and a pyramid-shaped skylight had been erected on the roof.

One of the inevitable retinue of valets hovering at the entrance commandeered the Cayenne, and Caitlin and Evan went into the museum, his arm intimately encircling her shoulder. *We're a couple!* the gesture seemed to blare.

But once inside, he was instantly swarmed. He seemed to have become something of a rock star in Colina Linda social circles: Everybody clamored for his attention. Especially women—they cooed at him from every direction, brushed against him, plucked at his sleeve, pressed powdered cheeks against his. "Evan, I was hoping you'd be here!" "Oh, Evan, love, hello, we were just talking about you!" *Evan! Oh, Evan!*

Caitlin was jostled aside. So much for her triumph in being seen as a couple, she thought dejectedly—she might as well have been invisible.

"Mojito?" A young waiter proffered a tray of tall, mint-garnished drinks.

"You bet." She took one, downed a long gulp, and immediately felt better. She began to wander through the museum. Hard to believe it had ever been a prison. The dormitory cells were now galleries filled with vivid arts and crafts—weather vanes and whirligigs, gilded clay saints and primitive portraiture. The rest of the building had been opened up into one large public space. One wall was covered with a garish mural that looked as if it had been painted by a fifth-grade class; another displayed a psychedelic quilt of blinking and streaming neon signs that had been harvested from old motels and roadhouses.

Caitlin tried to picture the women prisoners brought here in handcuffs, maybe even chains. Being booked, strip-searched, hosed down for lice. Locked into one of the overcrowded cells. What a nightmarish place it must have been for them, and what would they have thought if told that in the future it would be the scene of socialites, and frosty, mint-sprigged rum drinks, and whirligigs?

"Well, hello there," someone said behind her. It was Taller Kern, glorious in a white sports coat matched with a wide turquoise tie hand-painted with tangerine-colored bullfighters. "You'd never guess this was a jail once upon a time, would you?" he added.

"I was just thinking the same thing," Caitlin said. "That such an awful place could be so totally transformed, it's amazing."

"That ugly mural, though—if I had to spend much time looking at it, I'd consider it cruel and unusual punishment." Taller gave an exaggerated shudder. Then his eyes did a quick visual sweep of her outfit. "Sweet dress."

Caitlin flushed. Evan had told her cocktail attire, and, evidently, to most of the women in the room, that meant short rather than long Christian Dior and their second-best diamonds. In just a little skinny-strap Nicole Miller and small gold hoop earrings, Caitlin suddenly felt grotesquely underdressed. She might as well have come in a tracksuit.

"I like your tie," she blurted to Taller. "Vintage, isn't it? Like from the forties?"

"I recognize that tie." Evan suddenly materialized and put his arm around her. Taller raised a you're-together-again? eyebrow.

"It was one of Uncle Walter's, wasn't it? Our mutual great-uncle," Evan explained to Caitlin. "He was famous in the family for forever going off on deep-sea fishing trips down in Baja. Except it turned out he did a little more than fishing. The family found out after he died that he had about a dozen illegitimate niños running around Tijuana."

"But he did have superior taste in neckwear," Taller said with a smirk. He gazed around the crowd. "I've got a date somewhere here, but I seem to have lost her. She went to the powder room and disappeared."

Caitlin glanced at him. It always surprised her to hear that Taller was straight, since he seemed to register about 8.9 on the gaydar scale.

Evan seemed somewhat startled as well. "Who are you with?"

"Are you ready for this? Lally Clemente's black sheep daughter, Sienna. She's been camping out in Lally's old house on Polite Child Lane. I bumped into her at your groundbreaking thing, and she rang me up this morning asking if I'd bring her along tonight. Lally and David are up in Sacramento tonight, dining with the governor, so I figured the coast would be clear." Taller rose on his tiptoes to better scan the crowd. "There she is!" He flapped a hand in the air.

Twice before, Caitlin had had quick glimpses of Sienna—at Lally and David's wedding and at the groundbreaking ceremony—but she still wasn't prepared for the truly stunning creature who shimmered up beside Taller. She was even more underdressed than Caitlin: a clingy acid green tank top, some sort of downtown ripped-black-denim pencil skirt, diamond studs her only jewelry. But it hardly mattered what she had on: With her long pale gold hair that matched her golden skin and half-moon-shaped gold green eyes, she was possibly the most beautiful girl Caitlin had ever seen.

Her sullen expression only accentuated the exquisite natural pout of her lips. "This is so boring," she complained to Taller. "I don't see how Lally stands this kind of thing. I had to sign her name to half the crap in the auction just to keep myself amused. Wait till she finds out she bid five thousand dollars on a lumpy broken pot."

Taller, who was no doubt calculating how unamused Lally was going to be, smiled tightly. "Let me introduce you to some friends. This is Caitlin, um . . . And my cousin Evan Kern."

The half-moon eyes flicked right over Caitlin and fastened with intensity on Evan. "I saw you at that building ceremony. You were the architect."

"I still am." He was staring at her with that ga-ga expression men so often acquired in the presence of gorgeous girls. "I didn't see you there."

"I only stayed for about ten seconds. It was just far too boring."

"I didn't think so," Caitlin said crisply. "I thought it was fascinating."

The girl's gold eyes darted contemptuously to her. "Did you?" she drawled. "I guess you're just more easily amused."

Little snot! Caitlin searched for something clever to say—some brilliant rejoinder to put this awful girl in her place—but her brain was in a fog. She should not have gulped down that mojito.

Sienna's eyes slid back to Evan. "So what did you bid on?"

"Nothing yet."

"Haven't you placed any bids yet?" Taller jumped in. "I'm a trustee of this institution, so it's my duty to make sure everyone bids. No ducking out. There's something for every price range."

"I don't intend to duck out," Evan said.

"You know what you should get?" Sienna said to him. "There's this buckskin jacket, like from Davy Crockett and whatever? It would look so cute on you."

He grinned. "You think so?"

"You ought to try it on. You're not supposed to, but who cares?"

"Well then, hurry up," Taller fussed. "The bidding closes in fifteen minutes." He grabbed Caitlin's arm. "Let's find something for you, too." Before she could react, he began to steer her toward the display of auction exhibits. She glanced helplessly at Evan, who was being steered just as determinedly by Sienna to the other end of the display.

"So now, what catches your fancy?" Taller asked.

Was she expected to bid? She hadn't thought of that! A vision of the electric bill marked "OVERDUE" on her desk at home floated into her mind. But one hint of it to the gossipy Taller Kern would mean instant social death.

A silent auction meant that instead of an auctioneer and bidders raising paddles, you wrote your name and your bid on a sheet beside each item. Each person who signed below you was required to up the bid by a specified increment or more. From a glance, Caitlin could see that most of the stuff had already skyrocketed to over a thousand dollars.

"Got any baby showers to shop for? This little blanket would be ideal," Taller suggested. "Beautiful, isn't it? Hand-crocheted, circa 1900."

The last bid was four thousand three hundred dollars. Eek! "A little out of my price range," she said with a light laugh.

"Okay, then . . . Here's something that's a bargain."

He tugged her over to a bighorn sheep crudely carved in wood. It was an ugly thing, painted a dingy gray, the face wearing a kind of superior scolding expression that reminded Caitlin of Judge Judy chewing out a lying plaintiff.

"A superb example of Okie folk art," Taller proclaimed. "From the Depression, you know."

The last bid was seven hundred and fifty dollars left by someone named Charles F. Greenway. Still way too high. But Caitlin noticed that Mr. Greenway's name appeared five times on the list—every time somebody topped his bid, he jumped back in and topped *theirs*. Caitlin had become something of an expert in auctions—she knew you were almost guaranteed to lose when you were up against a bidder whose heart was set on an item who would go for it no matter what the cost.

Apparently, this Charles F. Greenway really wanted this sheep. Maybe he was a collector of particularly hideous wooden carvings. She presumed he was the man with the bushy white walrus mustache hovering close by the bid sheet.

She bent and scribbled her name, raising the bid by the required hundred-dollar increment to eight fifty.

"Good choice," Taller said.

She glanced back at Mr. Greenway: He'd been suddenly corralled by another of the museum's trustees, Celia Roederer, an octogenarian with a startling taste for miniskirts and patterned leggings. *Stop talking!* Caitlin silently telegraphed to him. *Come back and make another bid!*

She shot a glance in the other direction, searching for Evan. There he was, standing by the exhibits against the adjoining wall, wearing the buckskin jacket. Sienna was buttoning the buttons, and he was leaning in toward her so closely that their foreheads nearly touched.

He's going to kiss her! Caitlin thought with horror.

She stood rooted in confusion, watching them. The crowd shifted, so she could no longer see them. Then suddenly a bell began to clang loudly, and everyone was cheering.

"The bidding's closed," Taller said gleefully. "You won your bid, congratulations."

She stared at him. Oh God! She had just blown most of Aiden's birthday party money on an ugly wooden sheep that looked like Judge Judy. She felt suddenly dizzy.

And then Evan was back at her side, being attentive again, hugging her and laughing about how he'd almost dropped a couple of thousand dollars on a ridiculous buckskin jacket but was saved by the bell. So what she thought she'd seen between him and Sienna—could it have been just her imagination?

She hugged him back, but really she no longer had a clue what to think.

CHAPTER fifteen

Why Did You Have to Go and Flip Out?

A high tea in the dappled shade of the ancient gold cup oak in her garden had been truly an inspiration. Presiding at the head of the long table, Janey congratulated herself on the idea.

Her initial impression of Mr. Martin Drucker at his wedding to her ex-husband Robbie's niece had been of a first-class snob. Some of her friends had sniggered that the primary reason he was marrying Hollis Martinez, who looked like Cruella De Vil's less attractive younger sister, was for her membership in the San Carlino Sailing Club, which was so exclusive that it routinely blackballed gazillionaires if their pedigree didn't go back at least four generations. Janey had therefore suspected that some spuriously upper-crust ritual like an elaborate high tea would knock the socks off him.

She had pulled out all the stops. Had it catered by Cakebread, the shockingly pricey bakery on Little Manzanita: caviar sandwiches, lobster puffs, and fancy fresh-made pastries. She had dusted off the Royal Doulton teaware with the rose damask pattern that had come down to her from her great-great-aunt Dorothea Wickersham; and she'd had her housekeeper meticulously polish the sterling silver service that had been a wedding present from her grammy Kern and had been acquiring tarnish in the dining room sideboard for years. A long table covered with a sprigged linen cloth, wrought iron garden chairs, the Queen Elizabeth and Amazing Grace roses blooming abundantly in their beds—it all completed the illusion of a tea party at a country manor in, say, Herefordshire or Kent.

As for the other guests, Janey had drawn them exclusively from family, on both Robbie's side and her own. The Martinezes from Robbie's side claimed to be descended from Castilian royalty (though Janey suspected at least one branch of the family had hailed from south of the border and had put in some hard time wielding mops and picking strawberries). From her side, Kerns and Wickershams. *Their* pedigree was undeniable: descendants of Michigan robber barons who had been wintering in San Carlino since the nineteenth century before settling here all year round in the early twentieth.

And her instincts were correct. Martin Drucker, sitting on her right, certainly seemed impressed. Hell, he was acting as if he were being presented at the court of King James. He praised everything, from the tea service to the candied apricot scones, with an almost comically exaggerated formality. He practically levitated every time Janey's hatchet-faced aunt Lacey asked him to pass the sugar.

Janey refilled his cup, pouring a thin amber stream of tea to exactly the correct measure.

"By the way, Marty," she said airily, "I've heard through the grapevine that Serenity Waters is looking for a new head of guest services. Have you filled the position yet?"

Martin raised the cup somewhat daintily to his lips. "I'm not sure, but I think the director in charge of hiring has someone in mind."

"But you make the final decision, don't you?"

"Well, yes. I have final approval."

"Well, the reason I'm bringing this up is that I've heard that your people are considering a person named Caitlin Latch, and I just think I ought to warn you. I've headed several benefit committees on which she also served—in a very minor capacity, of course. And she never seemed to have the . . . well, focus would be the word for it. I always thought there was something a little scattered about her. I mean, she'd never be the person I'd rely on if there was something *crucial* that had to be done, if you see what I'm saying."

Martin drew on a look of grave concern. "Well, yes, I think I do. That does sound like a problem."

"Mmm, well, it just was my impression, of course. But I thought that you should know." Janey bit into a plump star-shaped bun. Yum—a cloudburst of almondy whipped cream drifted into her mouth. It would no doubt continue to drift directly to her massive hips. All the Kern women were built heavy in the haunches—they referred to it almost proudly as "the family pear." The last thing in the world Janey wanted to do was add to her own particular pear. But this was a crucial occasion—she needed the bolstering of a high-caloric indulgence. Besides, she could make amends with double sessions of Pilates for the next several days.

"You know what? I think I have the perfect candidate for you!" she exclaimed as if it had just occurred to her. "Marion and Theo Seller's daughter, Cooper. You know the Sellers, don't you? Major contributors to the opera, and they practically keep the zoo afloat."

"Oh yes, of course. Wonderful people."

"Cooper just graduated from Vassar. An extremely attractive girl. Not much experience yet, but she's smart as a whip, and think of the connections she would bring!"

She could see Martin thinking greedily of the connections. "Send her over. I'll have my people interview her right away."

"I will." Smiling with satisfaction, Janey polished off the rest of the cream puff. For the first time in weeks, she experienced a feeling of well-being that didn't come from a vial. The world had been alarmingly off-kilter when atrocious little nobodies like Caitlin were waltzing off with all the prizes; but now some little measure of balance had been restored—the right people were being settled in all the right places, just as it should be.

But then an image of Caitlin Latch sashaying out of the Clemente Foundation groundbreaking with Evan Kern's arm wrapped intimately around her shoulder crept into Janey's mind, and her little bubble of well-being went *pop!*

Why did she have to go and eat that pastry? she lamented. If she could just tone down her hips and revolting thunder thighs, she'd have a figure as fabulous as anybody's. Even Caitlin's. No, even better than Caitlin's.

Under cover of the tablecloth, she gave the bulge of her left hip a furious jab with the heel of her hand.

The family pear was an abomination. It would have to go.

Caitlin had finally rounded up a new car pool—with Nan MacMiller, who at forty-seven had been married for the first time, to a retired aerospace executive, and then at fifty, through some donated eggs/in vitro technology, had given birth to triplets. Her daughters were now nine and attended Sagebrush camp, and though in terms of carpooling they were clearly a threefer, Nan refused to take three times as many turns driving. Her theory was that you had to go to only one home to pick up or deliver them; ergo, they should be counted as one-turn driving. The countertheory was that they took up three valuable car seats—they didn't stack up like Russian nesting dolls in one another's laps—therefore, Nan should take a full three turns.

It was an impasse that had made her a car-pool pariah. But beggars couldn't be choosers, so Caitlin had agreed to pick up the MacMiller triplets every afternoon if Nan would shuttle Aiden in the mornings.

This morning, Nan's black BMW SUV had rolled up when it always did: at precisely nine thirty-one, clockwork timing that no doubt had something to do with her being married to a rocket scientist. After seeing Aiden off, Caitlin waited restlessly another forty-five minutes, until she was sure Amelie Cushing would be in her office. Then she placed a call.

"I just wanted to check about the meeting with Martin Drucker," she said to Amelie when she answered. "I hope you don't think I'm being a pest, but it's just that I'm so very excited about this job."

"And I'm excited that you're excited. Everything's still on track. I just have to interview one more person, but it's just a formality."

"Oh?" Warning bells went off in Caitlin's mind.

"Yeah, you see, Marty's wife has a friend with a daughter who just graduated from Vassar. Just a kid, really, with no experience. I'm interviewing her simply as a favor. So just hang on. I'm still a hundred percent on your side."

"Thank you, Amelie, I appreciate that so very much," Caitlin gushed.

But when she hung up, she felt as if she were going to be sick. Her Martin Drucker meeting was also supposed to be "just a formality." And she could hear something in Amelie's voice—a false tinkle, a rush to finish up the conversation—that hadn't been there before.

The daughter of a family friend. A favor. That was the way things worked, wasn't it?

The job was slipping out of her grasp, and there was nothing she could do about it.

Don't be such a Gloomy Gus. That's what her mother would tell her. *Anything could still happen, you don't know.*

Which was absolutely true. Amelie had assured her things were still on track, and maybe she was telling the truth. Maybe this *was* just an insignificant bump in the process and Caitlin really still did have the job sewed up. Or maybe the daughter of the family friend would turn out to be such a flake that even her precious connections wouldn't get her hired.

She ground some more coffee beans—Trader Joe's house blend—and brewed her fourth cup of the morning. She couldn't help feeling like a Gloomy Gus at the moment. Evan hadn't called her once since he had gone up to Seattle. Caitlin had a creeping fear that he'd reconciled with his wife, the mysterious Corinne who kept ringing his cell phone. She pictured her as a blonde of the Nicole Kidman persuasion: tall and willowy, with a perfect nose and skin so white that you could practically see through it. She imagined the two of them nuzzling on a swing on the deck of their ritzy home on Bainbridge Island. Having a giggle over that pathetic girl back in San Carlino who'd developed such a whopping crush on Evan.

Bounce back!

She sprang up determinedly from the kitchen table and marched upstairs to the cubbyhole of a room she used as an office. It was crammed full of packing stuff—rolls of parcel paper, sealing tape dispensers, sacks of Styrofoam popcorn. Usually it was also littered with items waiting to be listed online. The problem was, Mrs. Butterworth, the Angel of the Thrift Shops, had been stubbornly silent lately. Maybe it was because she'd been repulsed by Caitlin's Gloomy Gus vibes, but for the past week she had refused to whisper in Caitlin's ear. Caitlin had scoured every thrift shop and estate sale within twenty miles and uncovered no hidden treasure, just a few bits of costume jewelry and a Dr. Zhivago–style hat that had shed some of its fake sable.

Almost not even worth the effort of trying to sell.

She wrote them up anyway and posted them on various auction sites. Then she checked an item she had listed on eBay—a rhinestone-and-marcasite Deco bracelet, circa 1930. It was the one thing she still had high expectations for—expectations that were dashed as she stared at the computer screen. Less than three hours left till the close of the auction and nowhere near meeting the reserve.

And tomorrow she had to put down the deposit for JungaZone or lose the reservation.

She flipped her laptop closed, then sat for a moment, elbows on her desk, her throbbing head in her hands.

Okay, there was no other choice: She'd have to borrow some money from her mother.

Her mother, Frances, was brilliant at bouncing back. In a remarkably short time after the death of Caitlin's father, Frances had bounced into a job as a guide at a local wildlife preserve, complete with snappy tan uniform and visored cap. A couple of years after that, she'd bounced into a new marriage with a divorced kitchen appliance company sales manager whom everybody, including his new wife, called by his last name, Dooley. And now the two of them had bounced into a comfortable retirement on Dooley's cushy pension.

As she punched in her mother's phone number, Caitlin steeled herself for a lecture that would hit on her mother's two favorite talking points. Number one: How could Caitlin have walked out on a good-earning husband just because he had a "nervous breakdown," which he certainly would have bounced back from if Caitlin *hadn't* walked out on him?

Number two: Why on earth was Caitlin trying to raise a son on her own in such a wildly expensive place as San Carlino, when she and Aiden could move out there to Albuquerque, where everything was so much more reasonable? My Lord! They could rent a home with a yard and a two-car garage for a fraction of what Caitlin was paying now for that mingy little bungalow!

"Hullo?"

Shoot, it was her brother, Ken. He worked the evening shift at Target, patio and garden department, and so was almost always home during the day. Speaking to him was like wading through oil sludge. "Hi, Kenny, it's me, Cait. Is Mom there?"

"Nope. They're not home." This response was almost eradicated by the sound of energetic chewing. Ken never ate meals, he just perpetually snacked.

"Well, is she going to be back soon, do you think?"

"Don't know. They're at an association meeting."

It figured. Dooley was forever at war with the "Nazis" on the "Gestapo" committee that imposed the regulations in their ticky-tacky gated community. "Tell Mom to give me a call as soon as she comes in, okay?"

"Yeah, okay."

"Hey, Ken?" Caitlin asked suddenly. "Do you ever think much about Dad? I mean, like why he killed himself?"

"I don't know. He was depressed, I guess."

"Do you remember much about him?"

Kenny crunched while he mulled this over. "I remember him smoking a pipe. And the brown chair he used to sit in watching TV. *Starsky and Hutch*. It was a long time ago."

"Yeah, it was," she said. "Don't forget to tell Mom, okay?"

Caitlin hung up. She remembered that chair, too. A La-Z-Boy. It smelled like pipe smoke. She used to climb onto her father's lap when he was sitting on it, and he'd sing "K-K-K-Katie, beautiful Katie . . ."

But she had no time to be moping over all this: She and Juanita Bosco, whom she'd worked with at the Rape Crisis Center, were meeting for lunch at the Carl's Jr. on Packett Road (a far, far cry from Café Cygne); and before that, she needed to get to the hat blocker and then to the Rite Aid to pick up the prescription cream for that grungy stuff between Aidey's toes. She'd better get a move on it.

And she'd need some ready cash.

She went upstairs to the linen cupboard beside the bathroom. On the top shelf was a small stack of boxes of tampons and panty shields. She jimmied out the bottom box—Stayfree Maxi Pads with wings, twenty-four count. She rummaged through it until she found the wrapper that contained a thin wad of folded hundred- and fifty-dollar bills. Always keep some mad money in the house, her mother had advised. Implying that its purpose was to indulge some frivolous impulse—like splurging on a Hermès scarf or flying down to Rio—not making up the co-payment for a tube of foot fungus ointment.

As she tweezed the bills out of the maxipad wrapper, she could tell at once that the wad was thinner than it should be. A wave of that about-to-vomit feeling surged through her.

She counted the money carefully. It was twelve hundred and fifty when it should be fifteen. She guessed it was a hundred-dollar bill and three fifties that were missing.

Could she have taken them out at some point and spent them and forgotten that she had? She racked her memory.

No, she was positive she hadn't touched any of it.

Maybe Maria Reynaldo, while baby-sitting one night, had been searching for a tampon and come across the stash and swiped some of it.

No, Maria was too trustworthy, Caitlin was sure of that. Besides, it wouldn't explain the money that had disappeared from Caitlin's bag at times when Maria wasn't sitting.

There could be no other explanation: It had to be Aiden.

Her stomach went into turmoil as she considered this. Why was he stealing the money? What was he doing with it?

How had he even known it was there?

And how in the world was she going to confront him about it?

She peeled off the two hundred dollars she'd need right away, then rolled up the rest and wadded it into the toe of a three-year-old pair of Uggs that were in the back of her closet. Only a few days before, she'd felt as though she were dancing on air. Now she felt she was trying to slog her way through the bottom of a very deep ocean.

If only she had someone she could talk to about this. Some strong male figure in her life whom Aiden could relate to. She flashed on the nearly effortless way Evan had been able to engage Aiden in the car, drawing him out on his favorite subjects . . . How Evan had known that tricky handshake maneuver . . .

If Evan would be willing to talk to him, maybe he could get Aiden to confide what was going on.

Forget it. She'd probably never hear from Evan Kern again.

She suddenly thought of a day when Aiden was four—a breath-taking afternoon in October, the three of them, she and Ravi and Aiden, strolling through Golden Gate Park, and Ravi scooping Aiden up and carrying him on his shoulders. A happy, normal family.

Damn you, damn you, Ravi Latch! she thought furiously. Why did you have to go and flip out and leave me having to try to muddle through on my own?

"Whatever you did with Sienna worked!" Lally trilled excitedly, poking her head out of the Bentley's backseat window.

"I didn't do anything," Jessica replied. "And please stop following me."

It was a crystalline Sunday morning, with the scent of mountain laurel and honeysuckle perfuming the air. The deep pealing of the mission bells lent a romantic counterpoint to the jangly bells of the modern churches and the somber moan of train whistles. A few hours before, Jessica had kissed Tommy good-bye, and he'd gone back up to his own house to pack for several days down in L.A., leaving her with that bleak little wash of depression she always felt after tearing herself away from him. Then she had taken her mother to mass at Our Lady of Lourdes (popularly referred to as Our Lady of the Lexus, owing to the profusion of luxury cars in its parking lot). Afterward she had ferried Lillian back to the Sycamore Springs Independent Living Village. Now, she had just pulled up outside Michael's house to pick up Rowan and Alex when Lally's Bentley had glided up beside her.

It seemed ludicrous that wherever she went these days she was being tailed by a six-foot-tall billionairess in a two-hundred-thousand-dollar car.

"I'm not following you," Lally said. "I just happened to see you turn off Palmetto, and I told Stefan to swing a U-turn and go after you. Okay, I guess maybe that is following you. But my point is, I didn't start out with the intention to. Though really, Jessica, you are impossible to get on the phone."

Coming from a woman who had three layers of people to screen her calls, that was pretty rich. "So what do you want, Lally?"

"Just to thank you."

"For what? Did Sienna call you?"

"Well, no, not actually. But you broke the ice. Right after she visited you, she called Taller and had him bring her to the Historical Society benefit. She thought David and I would be there, so obviously she's ready to make contact with me. And then the next day after that, she called David."

Jessica felt a twinge of apprehension. "Why did she call *him*? Why not you?"

"Oh, well, she explained that. It was because she still feels that I'm sort of hostile to her and she wants him to be kind of a go-between. He's in Mexico City just now, but he's going to go over to the house and see her as soon as he gets back."

"By himself? You're not going with him?"

"David said she really wanted to talk to him alone first." Lally gave a chuckle. "She even volunteered to make pasta for him. She said you taught her how."

"No. I didn't."

"You didn't? Well, I guess you inspired her, then. Oh, the most wonderful thing is that she confessed to David about taking Chiara back to Rome, so now we know where she is! You really are a miracle worker, darling!"

"Lally, I think I need to tell you something. It may be nothing, but I think I should warn you . . ."

Jessica paused, realizing that Lally's driver, a young, fair-haired man with sharp light eyes, was within earshot. Having to keep things from the servants seemed like a ridiculous, even despicable, nineteenth-century-aristocracy kind of thing; nevertheless, what she needed to tell Lally was definitely not something Lally would care to have shared at large.

"Warn me about what, darling?" Lally prodded.

"I think I ought to tell you in private—"

Jessica was cut off from saying anything more by her car door opening. Rowan slid into the front seat, and Alex bounced into the back. "Hi, Mom," they choroused.

In the doorway of the house, Amanda the Brain stood gaping at the sight of the Bentley idling in the street. Catching Jessica's eye, she retreated quickly back inside.

Jessica turned back to Lally, who had retracted her head into the Bentley and rolled up her window. The Bentley swooshed away.

Jessica's cell phone rang. She answered it.

"Do you know where I go when I want real privacy?" Lally's voice said. "The changing rooms at La Magdalena."

"The lingerie shop?"

"Yeah. The salesgirls there are amazingly discreet. They have to be, you know—buying fancy new lingerie is the number one indication of an affair. Or actually number two. The first is suddenly getting into shape. But anyway, I can arrange to have a fitting there tomorrow morning, and then you can meet me."

A clandestine meeting in a boutique dressing room? This was becoming farcically cloak-and-dagger.

But it was true, Jessica reflected, that privacy was difficult to come by in Lally's circumstances. Anywhere Lally went in Colina Linda, or probably even anywhere in the greater San Carlino area, she'd be recognized, and you never could tell who'd be eavesdropping. Even if Lally came to her house, Jessica couldn't guarantee her privacy: Rowan and Alex and Jessica's housekeeper, Yolanda, would be constantly popping in and out; and Jessica knew from experience that an army of help circulated constantly through the Clemente household.

"Okay, I'll meet you there," she conceded.

"It's a date, darling. Eleven a.m." Lally hung up.

"Mom?" Rowan said as Jessica started the car. "Would you please inform Dad that I'm allowed to meet my friends at the mall? So if he or Amanda could please take me sometimes, then I could maybe still have a life."

"They don't take us anywhere anymore," Alex chimed in. "They just want to spend all their time with the new babies."

"It's like we hardly even exist!" Rowan added. "All they care about is Fox and Fiona."

Why was she even remotely concerned with Lally Clemente's life? Jessica wondered. She had more than enough to handle with her own.

CHAPTER sixteen

Were You Kissing and All Lovey-Dovey?

*A*iden had a Sunday playdate with his camp buddy Hernando, and Caitlin drove him over in the morning. Nando's family lived in a working-class Latino neighborhood a few miles east of the university, in a square little stucco house painted bright yellow with a red pickup truck in the driveway. His mother was a plump, young-looking lady who spoke only about nine words of English but seemed pretty together: The house was tidier than her own, Caitlin had to admit, and Nando was always neatly dressed and cheerful and polite. No sign of a father, but Caitlin was hardly one to criticize that. There were a number of older siblings as well as relatives and neighbors milling around, and dogs and puppies yelping, and Spanish-language hip-hop playing on a boom box, giving it all a festive atmosphere that Caitlin kind of envied.

The more so as she returned to her own silent, empty house. It was a dispiriting mess. She'd fallen behind on housework lately—dust bunnies under the furniture, greasy dishes in the sink, and a thick web in a corner of the living room ceiling spun by a daddy longlegs. She ought to roll up her sleeves and get cracking on it, but after the festive clamor of the Lopez household, she suddenly felt she couldn't stand to be alone.

Maybe she could round up somebody for brunch. She tried several numbers: Hillary Kopp, whom she knew from spinning classes at the Colina Linda Sports Club when she'd still been able to afford membership; spacey Fran Luchessi, who used to be in her car pool; a bossy woman named Merry Harper, who'd been on the steering board of an Arthritis Fund benefit that Caitlin had once volunteered for and who had suggested they "do lunch" sometime.

Nothing but answering machines. It was a sparkling Sunday, and the entire world was out with husbands, lovers, friends, and family. They were skimming over the sea in fiberglass sailboats or splashing in private pools or hiking up sweet-smelling mountain trails in happy groups.

Another name popped into her mind: Jessica DiSantini. They weren't actually friends: They'd never hung out together or anything. But Jessica was invariably friendly when they did happen to meet, and Caitlin had always sensed she was in some ways a kindred spirit. She did have that glamorous composer boyfriend, but he was usually off traveling the world. And she shared custody of her kids with her ex-husband, so it was possible she might be free today.

Maybe, like Caitlin, she was sitting home in an empty house, feeling weighed down by the silence.

Caitlin looked up Jessica's number and dialed. She was almost startled when Jessica answered. "Oh, hi, Jessica," she stumbled, "it's Caitlin, Cait Latch."

A surprised hesitation on Jessica's side. "Oh, hi, Caitlin. How are you?" There was the sound of a squawky voice in the background. "Quiet, Booter!" Jessica yelled. To Caitlin she said, "Sorry, that's Rowan's mynah. He's been extremely talkative today. So what's up?"

"Nothing. Um, the reason I'm calling is, my son's at a playdate, and I was wondering if, well, if you didn't have your kids today, maybe you'd like to have lunch. I mean, if you weren't doing anything else or anything . . ."

"Right now?"

"Yeah. I mean, well, I'm sure you're probably busy."

"Actually, I am. I'm just heading over to the beach with Alex. We're picnicking with the Greenbachers and Bettina Perkins and her daughter, Madison. But listen, why don't you come along? You carpool with Bettina, don't you?"

"Oh, no . . . Um, I mean, yes, I used to carpool with her. But I really don't have enough time for the beach. I mean, I hardly even have time for lunch, so it's probably just as well." She gave a strained laugh.

"Well, some other time, then," Jessica said.

"Yeah, sure, another time."

So much for her fantasy of Jessica DiSantini languishing alone in a silent house. Of course she'd be booked up with that clique of Colina Linda rich bitches. When you got right down to it, she was one of them.

Caitlin suddenly felt even more desolate than ever.

The phone rang. *Evan?* Her heart skipped.

"Cait?" It was her mother's fluty voice. "Kenny said you called. I had to wait till today to call back because you know I get free minutes on Sunday. I hope there's nothing wrong?"

Caitlin gritted her teeth. This was going to be tougher than she'd thought. "No, nothing wrong, Mom. I just wanted to ask you if I could borrow some money. I'll pay you back."

There was a pause. "How much were you thinking about?"

"A thousand, if that's okay."

"Heavens. That's quite a lot. What do you need it for?"

"I just ran a little short this month. But I'm up for this really fabulous job at a five-star resort, and once I get it, I'll be in terrific financial shape."

Her mother gave a sigh. "Well, dear, this is really not the best time for us. Dooley's Impala needs new brake linings, and our community association dues just went up again. And you know we have to keep the air-conditioning up all night because of Dooley's restless leg syndrome, so our bills have zoomed sky-high."

Yeah, yeah, and pretty soon you'll be living on the street, begging with a tin cup.

"Mom, please, I wouldn't ask you if it wasn't really important," Caitlin said. "It doesn't have to be a thousand, it could be seven hundred."

Another barely audible sigh. "I suppose if it's really that necessary . . ."

"It is really. If you could send it right away, that would be great."

"Okay, fine. You're still planning to bring Aidey out for Labor Day, aren't you?"

"Well, it depends on whether I get this job. . . ."

"There's a widower who's just moved in next door. A retired orthodontist from Kalamazoo, Michigan. Kind of a husky build, but he seems like a lovely man. When you're here, I'll invite him to dinner."

Caitlin interpreted that to mean he was a seventy-year-old who tipped the scales at three hundred pounds. "That'll be great, Mom. And thanks for the loan, really. Love you."

"Love you, too, dear."

Having the check secured made Caitlin suddenly hungry. She went to the refrigerator to browse for lunch. Limp lettuce leaves, stale muffins, condiments. Aiden's peanut butter (Jif creamy); her peanut butter (Nut 'N Better organic); half a dozen jars of jams and jellies. She was behind on her food shopping as well.

At least the freezer was well stocked—Hot Pockets was one of her five basic food groups. She opened it: All the food inside—Hot Pockets, Pop-Tarts, chicken thighs, Birds Eye baby sweet peas—was half-thawed and swimming in pools of icy sludge.

Fuckety-fuck.

Everything in the house was either broken, leaking, or emitting dangerous sparks.

The same, it seemed, for everything in her life.

Maybe her mother was right: Maybe she should quit striving to make it in such a rarefied place as San Carlino. Maybe she should pack up and go to a nice, normal place like Albuquerque. Marry somebody nice and normal. It wouldn't have to be a fat retired orthodontist. It could be a skinny retired dentist. Or, if she really lucked out, a medium-build retired periodontist.

No! she thought violently. She wasn't ready to give up yet!

Almost in a panic, she ran upstairs. She changed from the shirt and jeans she was wearing to a sleeveless lavender linen dress—a generic Bloomingdale's label that could pass for a Donna Karan. She kicked off her worn-down Pumas and slipped on the Blahnik sandals. Tamed her hair with a Paul Mitchell gel and made up her face. Then she grabbed her Vuitton knockoff bag, got in her car, and drove up to Colina Linda.

Instead of hunting for a parking space on Silver Creek Road, she pulled directly up to the striped green-and-buff awning of Café Cygne and handed her keys to the valet on attendance.

Inside the bistro, all was just as Caitlin remembered: same dazzle of white and jonquil and peacock blue. Vivid flowers tumbling promiscuously from pure white vases—check. Atmosphere drenched with a frothy burble of laughter and conversation—still present and accounted for.

A hostess with Cleopatra hair glanced up from her station. "Good afternoon," she said with a haughty smirk. "What reservation, please?"

"Um, I don't have a reservation. Do you have a table available?"

"How many in your party?"

"One. Just me."

Cleopatra seemed momentarily taken aback by this. Her eyes flicked quickly over Caitlin, taking her measure from sandals to earrings. Apparently she passed muster: The hostess picked up a leather-bound menu and murmured, "Follow me, please."

She led Caitlin to a minuscule table half-hidden behind her station. Caitlin sat down uneasily. This was a stupid, stupid idea! She'd been dumped in the lousiest table in the restaurant—what Lally Clemente would refer to as Siberia. The other diners—the ones who really belonged here—appeared to be staring at her, obviously wondering, *What's that person doing here?*

I'm glad I'm here, I'm *glad,* she recited to herself. Her lips curved upward and gelled in their pleasant smile. She squared her shoulders, lifted her chin, and relaxed a little.

She realized that if people were looking at her, it was only in the casual, idly interested way people looked at any new arrival on a scene. Most of them had already switched their attention back to their food or their companions.

She felt a comfort come over her as she opened the menu—a soothing feeling that she was exactly where she was meant to be.

She took her time deciding what she would eat. Finally, she ordered the Dungeness crab and mango salad ($26.95) and a glass of the Saintsbury Reserve Chardonnay ($12.50). It was not the wine Evan had ordered, which was something French that she couldn't even pronounce, but at least it was white and pricey.

The wine arrived quickly, pale gold in a tulip-shaped glass lightly filmed with frost. She took a deep sip. It was almost as if he were here with her—she could so intensely picture him, silver-threaded bronze hair falling into those blue, blue eyes. She even imagined she could hear his laugh, so forthright and infectious.

This was so strong an impression that she swiveled to gaze toward the back booth she and Evan had shared. She caught a gleam of bronze hair, and she froze.

It was definitely Evan. She recognized the sleeve of the blue linen blazer that came into sight when he gesticulated. She hadn't imagined she'd heard him laugh—she could now readily distinguish it amid the babble of other voices.

He was with a woman with sleek, short dark hair and the pushed-in face of a Persian cat. Caitlin recognized her as the aging trophy wife of a wheelchair-bound retired tycoon. She had one of those country club nicknames—Muffy, Moo, Pooky; and like a spoiled Persian cat, she oozed the self-satisfied air of getting all the cream she wanted.

Caitlin twisted back in her seat, scarcely able to breathe. She had to leave—summon the waiter, make up some excuse about why she needed the check immediately. . . .

She turned again to search for the waiter. At that moment, Evan and Muffy-Moo-Pooky began emerging from their booth. She swiveled sharply back and averted her face as they began walking toward the exit. Please don't let him see me, she prayed.

For a moment, she thought her prayer had been answered. Muffy-Moo-Pooky swept past her without a glance, and Evan was following her close behind. But then he gave a slight double take and stopped.

"Hey," he said.

She looked up with a pretense of surprise. "Oh, hello!"

"Having lunch?"

"Uh, yeah. You know how I love the food here."

"It's pretty damn sensational." His eyes took in the single place setting. "Are you here by yourself?"

If only the San Andreas fault would choose this moment to rupture and swallow them all in an 8.6 earthquake. . . .

But the earth remained stubbornly intact. "Yes," she admitted. "I was nearby and just dropped in for a quick bite."

Caitlin could see through the glass entrance door that the valet had already procured Muffy-Moo-Pooky's car—an exquisite dark gray convertible, a Rolls-Royce, wouldn't you just know?

"Evan . . . ?" Muffy-Moo called impatiently.

"Well, nice seeing you," he said to Caitlin. "Enjoy your lunch."

"Nice seeing you, too," she said.

She kept a smile fixed on her face until the two were out the door. She couldn't leave now, that would be too obvious. The waiter set a gorgeously arrayed plate in front of her. She ate slowly, as if savoring every bite, buttering bread, sipping wine. She forced herself to finish almost everything on the plate, then leaned back, smiling again as if in sated contentment.

"Can I tempt you with any dessert today?" the waiter asked.

"Oh no, thank you. It was all delicious, and I'm quite full. Just the check, please."

She paid with her one credit card that wasn't maxed out and left a hefty tip. I'm glad I'm here, I'm *glad,* she recited silently as she walked leisurely out of the restaurant and down the block to her car.

The dark red Cayenne was parked outside her house when she returned.

Her heart began beating violently. There was more than one of those in the world, she told herself. It wasn't necessarily his.

But it had Washington State plates.

And as she swung into her driveway, it was Evan who hopped out of the red car's driver's seat. She parked and got out, and he came toward her. She was trembling a little: She hoped he didn't notice.

"I love it when a woman has the guts to eat in a restaurant alone," he said.

"Did you come here just to tell me that?"

"No. I came here to see you."

She looked at him, confused. "I haven't heard from you in over a week."

"Yeah, I know, and I'm sorry. I wanted to call you, but it was psychodrama up there. Corinne was being impossible. She doesn't want to be married to me, but she's not willing to let me go, either, and my kids are caught in the middle. Both girls will be in college in September, and then I can really make a break. But until then, I've got to walk this crazy tightrope. It's insane, but that's the way it is." He moved a little closer toward her. "I hope you can understand."

Was his wife so crazy that she monitored his every move every single moment, so that he couldn't even make a quick call? "So when did you get back?" Caitlin asked in a strained voice.

"Last night. The flight kept getting delayed, so I didn't get in till about two a.m. Then this morning I had to drag myself up for an early lunch with Poppy Winslett. She's about to build a new beach house up in Big Sur, and I've been angling for the commission to design it, so I had to dance attendance on her."

"Oh." There was a pause, and Caitlin suddenly found herself speechless.

"Look," he said abruptly, "I was going to call you right after I got rid of Poppy. I didn't expect to run into you first."

And if he hadn't, would he be standing here right now? Caitlin wondered. Could she believe anything he said? It was all bewildering. But he was so ridiculously good-looking—and with that little-boy-sorry expression on his face, practically impossible to resist.

"Would you like to come in for a cup of coffee?" she said.

His face lit up. "I'd love to."

She unlocked the front door. "Great little bungalow," he said. He tapped one of the thick pillars flanking the porch. "Kind of a modified Craftsman style. Built when? Twenty-eight? Twenty-nine?"

"Early thirties. And I think the plumbing still dates from then."

He chuckled, following her in. It was the first time he'd actually been inside, instead of just picking her up at the door. "Charming," he declared.

She was usually proud of what she had achieved with the décor—nothing expensive in the way of furnishings, but she'd done a lot with fabrics and paint and had scored some pretty good repro stuff on eBay. But right now she was mortified by the clutter and the daddy longlegs cobweb and—oh God! Was that a pair of Aidey's Y-fronts balled up on the sofa?

Steer him to the kitchen—also a mess, but at least no spiderwebs or underpants. "I could make coffee or tea, or would you rather have a drink?"

"Where's Aiden?" he said.

"He's at a playdate. I'm sure he'll be sorry he missed you."

"So we're all alone?" Big Bad Wolf grin.

She grinned back. "Yeah, I guess we are."

He grabbed her roughly, and she fell into his embrace, meeting his mouth greedily. "Upstairs?" he murmured. She nodded, and he swept her up in his arms and began ascending the stairs Rhett and Scarlett style.

Except, she thought vaguely, Scarlett probably hadn't been obsessing over the fact that she hadn't changed her sheets in over a week.

Aiden could hardly believe that his mom let him spend the whole of Sunday hanging with Nando. Nando's family was so cool. He had two big sisters and a little brother, plus a bunch of aunts and uncles and cousins, and there were lots of kids from the other houses on the block who came over all the time. Plus he had a furry brown dog named Lulu who'd just had puppies, and Nando said Aiden could have one if he could convince his mom it was okay.

Nando's mom drove this awesome red pickup truck, and she let them ride in the back when she drove them to the mall downtown to go see the new Adam Sandler movie. What was cool was that it was Nando who went up and bought the movie tickets because his mom didn't speak much English; and also before the movie, when they went to eat pizza at the California Pizza Kitchen, Nando did all the ordering for her because of the same reason. Later, he told Aiden he could get away with doing a lot of stuff like getting into R-rated movies, and his sister Laura could buy cigarettes just by saying it was for their mom who didn't speak English.

When they were having lunch, Nando said he couldn't come to camp anymore because the hardware store where his mom was working went out of business and she had to take a job cleaning in a motel that didn't pay as much.

"That sucks," Aiden said.

"Yeah, it sucks big-time," Nando said.

After the movie, which was awesome, Nando told him they were going to go to the Greyhound bus terminal, which was on the way back to Aiden's house—you went down Navarro Avenue all the way to the end, and then you turned right at the Jack in the Box. They were picking up Nando's *tía* Soledad and her baby, who'd been visiting another *tía* who lived up north in Sacramento. *Tía* meant "aunt"— Aiden had already known that. It was kind of weird they'd taken the bus when you always heard so many train whistles in San Carlino, but Nando said it was a lot cheaper to go by Greyhound bus than to take a train or a plane, and that's why they did.

It seemed like most of the people getting off the buses were Spanish speaking. Tía Soledad and her little baby got in the front of the pickup, and Nando and Aiden rode out in back again, and they drove Aiden back home. It would be really cool, Aiden thought, if any of his neighbors were watching and saw him riding in the back of the pickup. But like most of the time, there was nobody at all out on his street.

They stopped at his curb. "See ya, man," he said to Nando. They slapped five, and then Aiden jumped out of the pickup and it zoomed off.

Aiden headed up to his door and started to unlock it with the key he wore on a cord around his neck. The weird thing was, it was already unlocked. His mom never kept it unlocked, even during the day, because she was a total freak about security.

He went into the front hall and called, "Mom? . . . Mom, I'm back!"

He heard a kind of scampering around upstairs.

"I'll be right down, sweetie," Caitlin called.

"Yeah, okay." He went on into the kitchen. He'd pigged out on pizza with meatballs and a Mountain Dew and an Oreo cookie sundae for dessert, so he wasn't really hungry, but he was still charged up from his day with Nando and just felt he needed to do something. He scrounged around through the cupboard and came up with a box of Cinnamon Toast Crunch.

Caitlin came hurrying into the kitchen. "You're back a little early, aren't you? Did you have a good time? Did you enjoy the movie?" She was wearing the same thing as when she'd driven him over to Nando's, her jeans with the raggedy hems and the purple daisies sewn on the back pockets, and the big white shirt that he liked to think had once belonged to his dad, even though it probably didn't. But her hair looked kind of funny, like it did sometimes in the morning when she just got up, and she was talking way too fast. "Are you hungry? Don't eat too much of that cereal, we're going to have a big dinner. The freezer's broken, and I've got to cook up everything before it gets completely thawed out."

Before Aiden could answer, he heard somebody else come downstairs. And then that guy Evan came walking into the kitchen with a big grin on his face.

"Hey, Aiden," he said. "How's it going, dude?"

Aiden felt like his feet suddenly had gotten nailed to the floor. "Okay."

"Heard you went to catch that new Adam Sandler. What did you think? Any good?"

"It was okay." He stared down at the top of the cereal box—its plastic lining that he'd just started to rip open.

"Evan came over to see us this afternoon," Caitlin said brightly. "You know how that faucet in the tub has been dripping for so long? I took him upstairs to see it, and he says he can fix it for us."

"Easy as pie," Evan said. "If you want, Aiden, I can even show you how to do it yourself. Would you like to learn how to be handy?"

"I guess."

"Good man. I can borrow some tools from one of the guys on the site. Then next time I'll bring them over and we'll do it, okay?"

"Yeah, okay."

Caitlin and Evan went out into the hall. Aiden could hear them talking in quiet voices by the front door. He dumped some cereal into a bowl and stirred it around with a finger.

The door slammed, and Caitlin came back in the kitchen. She was looking really happy, and for some reason he hated that.

"Why was that guy upstairs?" he asked.

"I told you, sweetie. He's going to fix the drip."

"Were you kissing and all lovey-dovey?"

Caitlin glanced at him sharply. "That's an adult thing and really not something I'm going to talk about with you. Are you going to eat that cereal or just play around with it?"

"Eat it." He spooned a few pieces and chewed listlessly. It tasted like eating old newspapers or something.

She stood watching him. "Didn't you get any lunch?"

"Yeah."

"Do you have any change from that twenty dollars?"

"No. We went to the California Pizza Kitchen, and it's like really expensive. I spent it all."

"Oh. Well, okay. I'm glad you had a good time." She came over and kissed him and smoothed back his hair. "And I'm glad you're home. I'm going to go up and take a bath in that drippy old tub, okay?"

He nodded, continuing to make a big show out of shoveling cereal into his mouth until she had left the kitchen. He heard her go skipping up the stairs and then the sound of water rushing in the pipes. She began singing, a song about blue skies from one of her favorite Willie Nelson albums. She used to sing just about all the time, and he used to love it when she did; but now it made him kind of scared. It was like everything was happening way beyond his control.

He put down his cereal bowl and went to the back door. He opened it really quietly like he'd practiced, so it couldn't be heard, and really quietly, he went outside.

It was still pretty much daylight, even though it was almost dinnertime, so it was a lot easier to do this than when it was dark and he'd had to use a flashlight. He pushed through the thick, scraggly hedges that separated their backyard from the Wynnes' next door. The hedges had sharp little thorns that prickled his skin and got stuck to his clothing.

A guy named Otis used to live next door, and he would sometimes come over and sit with Aiden when his mom went out. Otis was kind of a dork, but he could be pretty funny sometimes—he could really crack you up when he did his toon voices, like SpongeBob SquarePants and Mickey Mouse. But then he got into trouble and got arrested, and his brother who used to live there, too, moved away to Idaho, and now their dad, creepy Mr. Wynne, lived here by himself.

Their yard was a real mess, filled with stuff that no one ever used and rotten old junk that Caitlin said was probably crawling with rats and black widow spiders. Aiden was always afraid that Mr. Wynne would be peeking from one of his windows and come out and yell at him, so he had a story made up about how he'd hit a baseball that came over the bushes and he was looking for it. But so far that hadn't happened.

There was a droopy old orange tree in Mr. Wynne's yard that no-body ever picked anymore, and the ground around it was all covered with squishy rotten oranges. Under the tree was this swing set left over from way back, when Mr. Wynne's kids were little. It was made of wood, and it was now all collapsed and toppled in on itself. Aiden pried up one of the old splintery swing seats from the ground. Under-neath it, scrunched into the rotten oranges and dirt, was a metal CD holder box. He searched carefully around for black widow spiders, then he dug the box up out of the ground and flipped it open.

He had lied to his mom: He hadn't spent the two ten-dollar bills she'd given him. Nando's mom, whose name was Graciela, wouldn't let him pay for anything: She had just waved his money away and opened up her big yellow purse and given Nando the money to pay for everything. So Aiden still had the entire twenty dollars left.

Inside the CD box was a stack of other bills. It was an awesome thick stack now. He'd counted it last time, and it came to four hun-dred and thirty-eight dollars, and with the twenty added to it, it would now be four hundred and fifty-eight. Almost five hundred dol-lars—only forty-two left to go.

A lot of it came from what he'd put in last time, a hundred and three fifties. He'd seen his mom take a bunch of money out of her wallet and go upstairs. He'd crept up quietly a little way behind her, and he'd watched her go to the linen closet and hide it. Later that night, when she was down in the kitchen talking on the phone, he'd gone searching for it. It was gross going through the tampons and stuff, but that's where he'd found the money hidden. He'd felt lousy taking some of it, but he really needed it to make things work.

He now placed the two tens on top of the other bills, smoothing them out neatly. He shut the lid and scrunched the box back down in the dirt and mushy oranges and put the swing seat back down on top of it. Then he edged himself back through the prickly hedges and brushed off all the dirt and thorns that had stuck to his clothes.

And then he returned inside to his own kitchen, closing the door gently and silently behind him.

CHAPTER seventeen

Are You Some Kind of Royalty Now?

The lingerie boutique La Magdalena was located in a swanky cul-de-sac off Third Street called Franciscan Mews. It was tucked between Seaver & Drew, a "to the trade only" custom lampshade shop, and Flower Power, the florist of choice to the rich. Jessica had once purchased a staggeringly expensive white linen cymbidium at Flower Power, only to discover afterward that it emitted a scent reminiscent of Raid ant and roach killer; and she'd once priced (and rejected after hearing the quote) pleated parchment shades for her bedside table lamps at Seaver & Drew.

But she'd never before set foot in La Magdalena. Basically, she was not the wispy-little-nothings type: She was the briefs-cut-panties and lace-trimmed-bra-with-sturdy-underwire type. When ultra-low-cut jeans came into style, she'd tried wearing a thong for a while, but the way it kept wedging itself between the cheeks of her distinctly non-boyish behind gave her the constant urge to dig down there and readjust it, so she'd switched back to her regular panty style. Which was just as well, since it turned out she wasn't the ultra-low-cut-jeans type, either.

Like its neighboring boutiques, La Magdalena was not a shop you could just waltz right into. The door was kept locked: You had to ring, then be scrutinized by unseen eyeballs and judged worthy before being allowed to enter. It took Jessica several moments to locate the bell within the tangle of climbing ivy that surrounded the door. She pressed it. A saleswoman, thin, middle-aged, dressed with terrifying chic, opened it with a deferential smile.

"Mrs. DiSantini? Good morning. Mrs. Clemente is already here."

"Oh, good." Jessica entered the shop and peered around. A dazzle of ribbons and lace, of silks and satins and foamy chiffons, but no Lally. "Where is she?"

"In the changing room. Is there anything in particular I may assist you with?" The saleswoman had one of those mid-European accents that reminded Jessica of fancy pastries and weepy violins.

"No thanks. I'll just browse." Somewhat self-consciously, she directed herself to a rack of frothy garments hung on padded blue satin hangers. Amanda the Brain wore underwear like this, she knew. The reason she happened to know was that shortly after Michael moved out, Jessica had opened a Visa bill and discovered a charge for seven hundred and sixty-something dollars from La Magdalena Lingerie & Essentials, and it had definitely not been hers.

Fancy new lingerie is the number one indication of an affair.

As she flicked through the rack, she wondered which particular items Michael had sprung for. Perhaps it had been this scarlet satin bustier that looked as if it canceled circulation to vital areas of the body?

Or had it been some of these bras that were nothing more than pasties attached by a bit of string?

Six months ago, the question would have obsessed her; but now Jessica found the image of Amanda gamely trying to vamp while trussed up in that torturous bustier simply hilarious.

A more important question edged into her mind: Would Tommy prefer it if she wore this sort of lingerie? She examined a sea foam–colored microbikini bra-and-panty set. It was priced at three hundred and ninety-eight dollars for what couldn't be more than ten square inches of transparent silk.

But Tommy never even seemed to notice her bra or panties—his sole interest was always in getting her naked as swiftly and efficiently as possible. She felt a milky weakness at the backs of her knees. Oh Lord, she should absolutely *not* be thinking about Tommy Bramberg and getting naked right now.

Fortunately, her thoughts were diverted by the sudden appearance of Lally from behind a frosted glass door in the back. "Oh, there you are, darling!" Lally was barefoot and wearing a severe white cotton robe, and her hair was obscured beneath some sort of gauzy white cap: The total impression was of a patient emerging from some mild form of chemotherapy. "I told Sasha we'd share a room, so pick out whatever you want and come in."

"I'm not really in the market for anything right now."

"Just for the fun of it. Grab something."

Lally retreated back behind the frosted door. Jessica noticed a selection of bras in pretty pastels whose cups were at least a little more substantial than pasties. She selected her size, 36B.

The chic saleswoman, Sasha, appeared at her elbow. She shook her head and plucked another in the same style from the display. "No, you are a 34C. Try it, please."

It was less a request than an order. Jessica obediently exchanged the garment in her hand for the one the saleswoman thrust at her and then headed to the glass door. It opened into a large mirrored dressing room infused with a soft boudoir light. There were two fuzzy pink armchairs, a cushioned bench, and a wool carpet that pooled like spilled cream over the floor. A basket set on a low ebony table contained more of the gauzy white caps. Another was filled with those stick-on crotch-covering pads that were for trying on panties in a sanitary manner.

Lally stood posed before a mirror, sporting one of the micro-bikini panty-and-bra sets in a delicate lilac trimmed with ivory. Despite copious hooks and hangers in the room, her street clothes were strewn across the carpet, creating a little archipelago of fabric and leather. Jessica stepped over an atoll of crumpled chiffon and an islet of Chanel sandal and took a seat on the bench.

"Won't they think it's peculiar that we're sharing a room?" she asked.

"I really couldn't care less," Lally snapped. "Besides, like I told you, these shopgirls are *maniacally* discreet."

"Yeah, but what about anyone else who comes in to shop?"

"They don't let any other customers in while I'm shopping."

Jessica let out a snort of laughter. "So are you like some kind of royalty now, Lally?"

Lally tilted her head, considering the question seriously. "I guess that in a way I am. I can make or break any of these girls' careers. I'm not bragging about it, it just happens to be a fact. I don't even have to show up here, you know. They'll send anything they have to the house."

Jessica had a sudden image of Lally seated on some kind of throne in her Colina Linda mansion, while trembling courtiers laid their wares—pasties-on-a-string, baby doll negligees, crotchless panties—at her royal feet.

She giggled.

"What's funny?" Lally demanded. "This color? It's kind of pukey, isn't it?"

She unhooked the bra she had on and flung it onto the floor. Her naked breasts bobbled free. Having been in the film business, Jessica reflected, Lally naturally would have no problem taking her clothes off in front of other people. In fact, she'd famously had a brief nude scene in some Charles Bronson action flick back in the eighties.

She glanced at the bra Jessica had brought in. "That's cute," she said. "But is that all you're trying?"

"I don't even think I'll try this one. That saleslady gave me one that's not my size. It's not going to fit."

"You'll be surprised. Sasha is brilliant—she can size you up in a glance, doesn't even need a tape measure. Put it on." Lally began rolling off the panties she was wearing.

Diverting her eyes from Lally's exposed crotch, Jessica began to try on the bra. Not possessing Lally's lack of inhibition, she performed an intricate maneuver involving the unhooking of her own bra, the shimmying off her blouse, and the shrugging on of the new bra, without too much nudity in between. She fastened the front hook, adjusted the cups to her breasts, and turned to the mirror.

"See! Sasha was right," Lally pronounced.

It was true: The garment lifted her breasts and made them look firmer, while simultaneously deepening her cleavage. "You think it looks good?"

"Infinitely better! You've been wearing your tits just a teensy bit too low, darling."

"Really?" Jessica said with dismay.

"Well, not *National Geographic* or anything. But you should immediately throw out all your old bras and take at least a dozen of those. In fact, I'm going to treat you."

"Oh no, I couldn't let you do that."

"Of course you can. You've done more than enough for me."

Lally had now encased herself in a black strapless bra and matching pair of tap pants. She scrutinized herself in the glass. "Look at this bloat! My nutritionist has me taking fistfuls of herbal supplements. They're supposed to cut out hot flashes and all that hideous menopausal stuff, but all they've done is blow me up."

Bloat? All Jessica could perceive was the slightest convexity above the bikini line. The rest of Lally was sleek, tanned, and toned to perfection. I'm the one with the pot, she thought. That little roll above her waistline that Tommy claimed to love. She sucked in her stomach but still couldn't compete with Lally's sleek shape.

"I think you look spectacular," she said to Lally.

"Do you really?" Lally twisted and peered over her shoulder to survey her backside. It was rumored about town that sometime between husbands number three and number four, Lally had had a butt lift, along with a considerable number of other surgical enhancements. Judging by the current appearance of her butt in those clingy black tap pants, Jessica thought, the lift had been a spectacular success.

Lally plopped herself onto one of the fuzzy armchairs and crossed her endless legs fluidly at the knee. "David always tells me I look great. He's such a darling, I'm so fabulously lucky to have him. But as you can probably imagine, a man in his position is constantly besieged with women. Young, gorgeous girls. You wouldn't believe how they throw themselves at him. Sometimes right under my nose."

"Yeah, I would," Jessica said. She flashed on her one sort-of-a-date with David Clemente. It had been at a benefit ball to aid indigent children: Jessica had watched with a certain amusement as, right under *her* nose, a young and gorgeous girl had slipped her phone number into his tuxedo jacket pocket.

She began performing her intricate bra-exchange maneuver in reverse. "Actually, Lally," she said, fitting her arms into the sleeves of her blouse, "that's sort of what I wanted to talk to you about."

"David? I thought it was something about Sienna?"

"It might be. I mean, it might be about them both." She hesitated, wishing Lally would put her robe back on. It was really hard to discuss anything serious with someone when they were stark naked except for a few skimpy patches of silk and a chemotherapy cap. "Look, Lally, I'm probably just imagining things. I'm sure you'll just burst out laughing or tell me I'm out of my mind. In fact, I hope you do."

"For Christ's sake, what *is* it?"

Jessica finished buttoning her blouse. She took a breath. "Could you imagine that your daughter . . . Sienna . . . that she'd ever try to do something like steal your husband away?"

"Steal my husband?"

"You see, it's silly. Idiotic. I've got this insane imagination—"

"No, tell me." Lally picked up her robe and put it on. She took off the cap and shook her burnt sugar–colored hair free. "What makes you think that?"

"Just a few things she was saying the other night."

"Like what? I really want to know."

"Well, I can't remember verbatim—"

"Oh, don't be such a fucking lawyer! I'm not going to make you swear on a Bible or anything. Just tell me approximately what she said."

"I don't know, just some inappropriate things. About your marriage to David and what a job it was going to be for you to hang on to him . . . I mean, I know she likes to be shocking, so I'm sure that's what she was trying to do, shock me. . . ." Jessica shook her head. "I can't believe she was serious."

Lally gave a grunt.

"It's just that . . . well, maybe when David goes over to see her, he shouldn't go by himself. Not that you shouldn't trust him," Jessica added quickly.

"But I shouldn't trust my daughter," Lally said flatly.

"Well, just in case she decides to do something silly. In order to be shocking, I mean."

"God, I should have guessed it before," Lally cried. "The second I found out she was here, I should have figured it out. She's going to go for the big prize. It's so damn obvious!"

"Lally, look. I might be all wrong about this. Tommy thinks I'm crazy for even suspecting it."

"Oh, please. I told you before, Tommy's blind when it comes to Sienna. The thing is, she's pulled stuff like this in the past. It's so perfectly typical of her. And so fucking goddamn obvious that I could just scream."

Lally picked up a basket from the ebony table and hurled it at one of the mirrors. A flurry of panty shields went snowing through the room. Then, with a low shriek, she kicked over the ebony table.

"Good Lord, Lally!" Jessica exclaimed. "Control yourself."

"The fuck with control!" She lashed out with her leg and kicked at the bench. "My God, she's intent on screwing me! I should have guessed it after I found out she signed me up for twenty thousand dollars' worth of crap at that fucking auction!" Another high-pitched "Ee-yop!" and the bench went toppling.

Jessica shrank into a corner. Lally had had karate training while preparing for her role as Bond girl Priscilla Much: If she ran out of inanimate targets to trash, she might start in on the animate ones.

There was a soft knock at the door. "Do you need anything, Mrs. Clemente?" Sasha called.

"No! Yes!"

Sasha opened the door, her face impassive.

Lally scooped up the lilac bra she had been trying on and flung them at Sasha. "This color looks like puke. Like dog fucking vomit! Take it away and get me something I could actually wear!"

"Right away, Mrs. Clemente." Sasha retreated without a flicker of emotion.

Lally plopped herself onto a chair. Her face was red and streaming.

"Are you feeling better now?" Jessica inquired tentatively.

"Yeah, I guess a little. But so much for all that herbal crap. It obviously doesn't do shit for the mood swings." She grabbed a pair of satin-and-lace panties and blotted her streaming face with it. "Or the hot flashes."

Sasha glided in, hung a rainbow of bras—teal blue, salmon, sunset mauve—on a rack, and glided out again.

"You were right about one thing," Jessica remarked. "The salespeople are pretty damn discreet."

Lally gave a dry laugh. "Told you. Look, I'm sorry for the tantrum, but this thing with Sienna has just thrown me for a loop. I think I'm going to need your help on it."

"Forget it. I've already gone way overboard in even mentioning any of this. I'm not getting involved in it anymore."

Lally shot her a calculating look. "You know, I still carry a certain amount of influence with Tommy. If I were to tell him I had serious doubts about your relationship, I think he might listen to me."

Jessica stood up rigidly. "You can go right to hell!"

"Okay, okay, I'm sorry, that was stupid. I didn't mean that. I'm just in such a state." Lally started gathering up her things from the floor. "You're probably right, I'm making far too much of this. I'm sure there's nothing for me to worry about." She gave a breezy little laugh.

But Jessica saw something she had never before seen on Lally Chandler Clemente's face: a look of absolute terror.

Janey was speeding south on the 101 freeway in her fresh-from-the-showroom Mercedes S-Class sedan (over ninety grand and there'd still been a three-month waiting list). She felt totally discombobulated by the news she'd just received. Her cousin Debora (Debba) Louise Kern was engaged to be married to Janey's ex-husband, Robbie!

Debba's mother, Janey's aunt Lavinia, had dropped the bombshell a couple of hours ago over lobster salad at the golf club. The *thwack* of five irons smacking balls had punctuated each of Aunt Lavinia's stupefying statements:

Thwack! Debba had been visiting Robbie at his minimum-security prison upstate in Petaluma ever since he'd been incarcerated three years before, and he'd proposed to her last Valentine's Day.

Thwack! Since Robbie's release a month ago to a halfway house in Pismo Beach, they'd been having conjugal visits.

Thwack! The wedding was scheduled for early next April, immediately following Robbie's parole. Robbie was going to go work for Uncle George, and since Debba had a pile of her own money, they were going to be able to live comfortably right here in Colina Linda. Debba was already scouting suitable houses.

Naturally, Janey had been prompt with her *all best wishes* and *isn't that fabulous!* and *I couldn't be more pleased!* But really, you could have knocked her over with a feather! All this time, that nasty little slut Debba had been sneaking up to Petaluma behind her back and throwing herself at Robbie Martinez—who no doubt was so demoralized by his incarceration that he lacked any resistance to her disgusting wiles. It was all so, well . . .

Infuriating, that's what it was!

Not that Janey wanted Robbie back or anything. Good God in heaven, no! Their marriage had been rocky from the start, based more on family expectations—two dowdy ducklings from fine old San Carlino families, what could be more suitable?—than on any true love or passion. They had divorced while his trial for financial fraud (cooking the books at his stupid and short-lived pet food dot.com) had still been pending. Janey had never visited him in prison: The divorce had been so nasty, so many hurtful words flung at each other, so many wasteful debts she'd ended up having to pay, that she had never really wanted to see him again.

Still . . . that didn't mean she wanted her sneaky, lying cousin to snatch him up. And Debba, of all people. Everyone always figured her for a born spinster. Didn't even bother to tint her going-gray hair; and not only had she inherited the family pear, she'd packed on enough weight to swell it into something more like a pumpkin.

It was all just so staggering!

Janey glanced at the clock on the dashboard. Yikes, she was running late for her appointment with Bru. She pressed her foot on the accelerator, and the Mercedes sprinted effortlessly to eighty.

Twenty minutes later, she was ensconced in the Santa Monica offices of Dr. Bruce (call me Bru) Goodmayer, the genius plastic surgeon who'd performed her breast augmentation. She sat happily sipping a tumbler of apricot nectar in the consultation room, whose modernist furnishings—all boomerang-shaped steel and palomino pony leather—she had come to know and adore.

Bru bounded into the room. He stopped, stared at her, and let out a loud wolf whistle. "My God, you look hot!"

"Yeah?" She giggled.

"Oh yeah, you're a hottie, babe! The real question is, are you happy?"

"Very happy." She preened and tugged at her Valentino shirt to expose more of her darling cleavage.

Bru perched himself on one of the boomerangs, slicked back his streaked blond hair with the palm of his hand, and smiled his dazzling smile. When she had first consulted him nearly a year ago, he'd looked about twenty-three years old, and he hadn't aged a day since. He was wearing his customary outfit of slim-cut black jeans and black Italian T-shirt. Janey had recently caught him on an episode of *Extreme Makeover*—he'd sculpted the chin and cheeks on the face of a woman who'd been born distressfully lacking in either—and except for when in the actual operating room, he'd been dressed exactly the same way.

"So now what's your pleasure today?" he said. "How can we make you even happier?"

Janey was momentarily reminded of the hand-dipped Belgian

chocolate shop called Paradis on Silver Creek Road. Jacques, the elderly proprietor, always said things like "And what is your pleasure today, madame?" Now that she thought of it, Bru's office was a kind of candy shop, offering similar sorts of mouthwatering treats:

Champagne white truffle = a nose identical to Sharon Stone's.

Dark chocolate filled with Cointreau = an ideal keyhole-shaped belly button.

Exotic assortment of tea and spice-flavored semisweets = your toes realigned in perfect descending order, from big toe to pinky.

Like Belgian chocolates, these were treats that were indulgent to the point of sinfulness; but somehow, once you got a taste of them, it seemed as though you could hardly go on living without them.

"Remember last time we talked about doing some lipo?" she ventured. She poked at one side of her gargantuan haunches. "To thin down this stuff down here?"

"The family pear." Bru grinned. "Great expression. A terrific way to describe it. I've used it with other patients to lighten things up while talking about it."

"Yeah, well, I'm ready to do it. I want to say good-bye to the pear."

"As well you should. You're perfect on top, and now you deserve to be perfect on the bottom."

"Will it be hard to do?"

"Shouldn't be. We'll start off with some ultrasound, which will explode the walls of those fat cells and liquefy the fat. Then we just vacuum it out."

Janey could almost hear the popping of those disgusting cells and the satisfying gurgle as they were pumped out. "Let's do it," she said eagerly.

"And what do you say we do a tummy tuck while we're at it? To complete the silhouette."

"Oh yeah, I'd love that!" Janey said. "And could you change my belly button? It's an outy and I've always wanted to have an inny."

"You want it, you got it. We'll just have to decide what shape you'd like it to be. How about a nice flirty little slit? It would be like a little wink right above your bikini."

"No," Janey said firmly. "I want a perfect keyhole."

"You want it," Bru said, "you got it."

CHAPTER eighteen

Divorced Moms Go on Dates with Guys

"Mom, you went right past it!" Aiden said stridently.

"Are you sure?"

"I saw the sign. Now we're going in the total wrong direction!"

"Okay," Caitlin told him, "I'll turn around."

They were on their way to shop for party favors at Party On!, a gift shop on Jacaranda Lane in Colina Linda that sold the kind of trashy tchotchkes you could buy in any drugstore for half the price. But the shiny candy-colored gift bags with the store's name written on them in wiggly gold script had become a must for birthday parties. Aiden had freaked when she'd suggested they shop someplace cheaper. "It's gotta be Party On!" he'd insisted. "Otherwise they're all gonna think I'm a loser!"

She swung a U-turn and headed back north on Jacaranda.

"You went by it *again*!" Aiden's voice hit its highest soprano. "Can't you even see?"

"I know I went by it. I'm looking for a parking space."

Jeez Louise, he was being difficult!

Clearly it had been a mistake for her to jump into bed with Evan like that, knowing it was possible that Aiden might come home early. But she'd been literally swept off her feet; and then the sex had been so phenomenal that she'd lost all sense of time.

But since then, Aiden had become even more furtive and secretive than before. Evan, bless him, had made a real effort to win him over. The next evening, he'd come back and fixed the leaky tub faucet, patiently showing Aiden how to take it apart and change the washer and put it all back together again. Then he'd taken them out to play miniature golf at the Jurassic Jungle course over by the botanical gardens, and Evan had kept missing shots, obviously on purpose, in order to let Aiden win. Afterward, having dinner at P. F. Chang's, which was one of Aiden's favorite places, Evan had worked heroically to get back the rapport he'd established with Aiden last time, peppering him with guy-to-guy-type questions, baseball stuff and what about the latest PlayStation? But Aiden had been whiny and sullen, answering mostly in monosyllables: "Yeah." "No." "Dunno." Sulking when the waiter said they didn't have Sprite. Spending an interminable time in the men's room doing God knew what.

It was almost as if he were punishing her for some reason. But it couldn't be just because of Evan. Aidey had never been the type of kid who was so possessive that he wouldn't let her be involved with anyone else. He'd always seemed to accept the fact that she dated: Divorced moms go on dates with guys—that was just the way life shaped up. He might not have been thrilled about it, but he'd never acted out like this when she'd had other relationships.

Maybe it was because he'd never sensed she'd been in love before.

The thought struck her almost violently. Was she in love? she asked herself. She felt dizzy and dancing and floating on air, sure. She was in lust, definitely. But more than that . . . ?

She suddenly flashed on one night in the early days of her mar-

riage to Ravi. U2 was blasting from the boom box in the kitchen, and
Ravi was twirling and spinning her all through the apartment. She remembered thinking how she was about ready to shatter from happi-
ness and that every time he spun her back into his arms, she'd felt as
if she were returning home.

Would she ever feel that way with Evan? she wondered. Maybe it
was just too soon to tell.

Now, as she and Aiden drove down Jacaranda Lane,
she crossed her fingers that his birthday party would snap him out
of whatever this thing was he was going through. Eighteen kids
had accepted, including some of the popular little snots who'd
never spoken more than three words to him before, unless it was
for a buddy homework assignment. He had to be excited about it—
he just wasn't letting on.

She swung another U-turn and slotted the car into a parking
space across from the shop. Inside the store, Aiden ran through the
aisles, collecting loot for the gift bags: sno-cones, miniature picture
frames, Superballs, glittery pens . . . It turned out the shiny Party On!
bags did not come free with purchase but were an extra dollar thirty-
five each, meaning that by the time Aiden was done, Caitlin had
shelled out ninety bucks.

Back in the Volvo, they drove south down the coast to Mar Verde,
where JungaZone was located on the glass-bubbled upper story of a
strip mall. Its walls were adorned with various beasts of the jungle as
well as a few imported from the Australian Outback, dressed in camouflage fatigues and cheerfully annihilating one another with laser
weapons. The *blurp*ing and *ping*ing of arcade games competed with
the roaring of lions, the *ack-ack-ack*ing of jungle birds, and the trum-
peting of elephants.

Aiden had his pick of killer animal–themed party rooms. He vacillated between Kangaroo and Wolverine, then finally chose Gorilla. They inspected the black-light maze, its walls fashioned to resemble the entanglement of thick rain forest growth. "Awesome!" Aiden pronounced. Then he selected his menu (Junga-dogs and tortilla chips), and Caitlin wrote out a check for five hundred and fifty dollars.

There would still be tips to hand out afterward. And figure about twenty dollars' worth of coins to distribute to the kids to play arcade games before the laser tag . . . Oh, and the cake—she could get one at Costco, but no, it had to be the Cookie Dough Delirium from Cold Stone, and she'd better order it soon. . . .

The bottom line was that the seven-hundred-dollar check she'd received from her mother had just gone up in smoke.

Maybe Amelie Cushing called, she thought as they headed back home. She'd left two messages for Amelie over the last two days and had not yet had a call back. Maybe Amelie was out sick or had an emergency with her son she had to attend to. Or it could be she was just waiting to get back to Caitlin until she could deliver positive news.

At home, she raced to the answering machine. One message, from Evan, confirming their date tonight—seven o'clock, his place. For the past few days, he'd had to squire Poppy Winslett around, and yesterday he'd been up with her at the Big Sur site. The thought of seeing him this evening—making love with him this evening!—gave her an intense rush of pleasure.

But nothing from Amelie Cushing.

Don't call her again, she admonished herself. Amelie would be in touch as soon as she had something to say.

The best way to make the phone ring was to throw yourself into some other activity and forget you're waiting for it to ring. She helped Aiden stuff the gift bags, which consumed half an hour. Then she virtuously tackled the vacuuming on the ground floor and scrubbed the grime off the kitchen counters and tossed an extra-large load of whites into the washing machine in the garage.

Another hour and ten minutes ticked off. It was getting on toward six o'clock, when Amelie would be gone for the day. . . .

She couldn't stand it anymore: She picked up the phone and dialed.

This time it was Amelie herself and not her secretary who answered.

"Amelie, it's Caitlin Latch!" Caitlin said brightly. "I'm sure you think I'm a complete pest, but I just wanted to check in and see if by any chance the meeting with Mr. Drucker has been scheduled yet."

"Oh, ah, Caitlin. I was going to call you this afternoon." Gone was the Sisterhood of the Blahniks warmth from Amelie's voice. Now she sounded chilly almost to the point of hostility. "I'm terribly sorry to have to tell you this, but the position has been filled."

"What?" There was a roaring sound in Caitlin's ears, as if Amelie were speaking from under a waterfall. "I thought everything was on track."

"It was, but then something came up. I'm not sure if you know Jane Martinez, but Marty's wife is related to her in some way, and Jane recommended somebody for the job, a terrific girl, actually. . . . And, well, Marty just felt he'd be more comfortable hiring through people he knows. That's actually how I got my job. Through a friend of a friend." Amelie gave a tinkly laugh. "I'm sorry, but I hope you understand."

Caitlin managed some polite response and hung up. Yeah, she certainly did understand. Janey Martinez had managed to screw her. It couldn't be more obvious.

But how the hell did Janey even find out she was up for the Serenity job?

Tilda Lazenby.

That had to be it. Caitlin hadn't been able to resist bragging to Tilda about her fabulous prospects, and Tilda must have trotted right back and blabbed about it to Janey.

That bitch Janey! That pampered, overprivileged, spiteful, big-assed bitch! Caitlin blinked back tears.

If only there was some way to get back at her.

What would be a suitable revenge? Having Janey lose all her money and get kicked out of her inherited house and her entire stupid family turning their backs on her. And then, homeless and destitute, she would come begging on her knees to Caitlin for any scrap of a job—weeding her garden, scrubbing her floors. And Caitlin would laugh at her and tell her to drop dead.

Or maybe she could start a rumor that Janey had some disgusting and highly contagious fungus, so no guy would ever touch her again, even with a forty-foot stick. Or that she was into some deviant sex practice involving hamsters or high colonics or whatever—

"Mom!" Aiden shouted down from his room. "Did you call about the cake yet?"

She snapped out of this ridiculous fantasy. "I'm going to right now," she shouted back.

It had been insane to count on the Serenity Waters job before it was certain, she told herself. Forget Jane Martinez and the rest of her skanky pals: she needed to bounce back and begin figuring out things from here.

Start hunting for other jobs. Get her butt out to the estate sales and Goodwills and hope Mrs. Butterworth, the Angel of the Thrift Shops, started whispering in her ear again.

She called the Cold Stone on Mission Plaza and ordered a Cookie Dough Delirium large enough for twenty. The washing machine buzzed the end of its cycle. She crammed the clothes into the dryer and tossed in an antistatic cling sheet of Snuggle.

Had Janey Martinez ever done laundry in her life?

Did Tilda Lazenby even know what a clothes dryer looked like?

There was at least one way to get revenge on the likes of Janey

Martinez, Caitlin decided—that was to waltz off into the sunset with Evan Kern. Tonight, she was not going to wear one of her figure-obscuring designer suits. No demure little tailored jacket and pants.

Tonight she was going to flaunt some slinky number that clung to her spectacular curves and emphasized her cleavage. Something on the sleazy side with fuck-me pumps to match.

Mens sana in corpore slutty: A sound mind in a body made for sex—there were few men in the world who could resist a package like that.

Jane Martinez could blow her entire fortune on makeovers, but she'd never even come close.

Aiden was getting pretty scared. His mom was going out on a date with that guy Evan again. She seemed to be pretty happy about it, and whenever she talked to Evan, it was in a voice that sounded kind of whispery instead of like the way she usually talked.

Aiden could hear her getting ready in her bedroom. He was in his own room, surfing the Web. He wished he could IM Nando. Nando had a Dell computer at his house, but he had to share it with his sisters and little brother, so he didn't get that much time to use it. Aiden tried him anyway, but the message came up that Nando wasn't logged on.

Then, just in case, he tried sending an IM to KCUDYFFAD, Daffy Duck backward: "hey dad, its me aiden. r u there?"

To his astonishment, a message popped back up:

hi aiden. I'm here.

Yes! His dad hadn't gone away for good!

But why wasn't he calling him "dude" like he always did? And why wasn't he writing in capital letters?

"dad where have u been? i've been trying to message u for a long time," he wrote.

sorry sorry sorry that i haven't been in touch. been unable to talk much.

just want you to know that i love you very very much. love forever from

your dad

This message scared Aiden even more, though he wasn't sure why. He started typing furiously:

i really really want you to come to my birthday party. it's going to be this saturday afternoon at the jungazone laser tag down here. u can charge the plane ticket on mastercard and i can give u back the money. moms gone out on a date again with that guy evan and i think she's getting all lovey dovey with him so i really think you should come down and stay with us. i know if you come here she'll tell him to go away.

He suddenly heard the *click-clack* of high heels. He hit send, and then the log off button, just as his mother came into his room.

"What are you doing?" she asked sharply.

She was wearing a dress that made her boobs pop out and perfume that smelled like the jasmine that bloomed at night in the backyard. "Nothing," he said.

"I saw the IM screen. Who were you talking to?"

"Nobody. I mean, just, um, Nando. And then he had to go."

His mother looked at him for a long time. "I'm sorry, but I just don't believe you. I'm taking away your computer privileges for the next two weeks."

"That's not fair!"

"Maybe, but that's the way it's going to be."

She unplugged his Mac and carried it off into her own room. So now he didn't know if his dad had gotten his message and was going to show up at his party or not.

CHAPTER nineteen

A Scorpion's Got to Sting

*O*ne of the many things Taller Kern admired about Lally Chandler Clemente was her meticulous attention to detail. Take, for instance, her current project: the Automatic Lid-Dropping Toilet Installation.

It had come to Lally's attention that despite the diligence of her housekeeping staff, the occasional toilet seat remained lifted owing to the carelessness of some male guest—or even darling David, who was sometimes distracted by more important issues. A gaping commode was a jarring note in a household otherwise famed for its dignity, elegance, and grandeur. Lally had hit upon a solution: She was replacing all eleven facilities in the mansion (not counting those in the staff quarters, pool, chauffeur apartment, playhouses, or two-story security gatehouse that straddled the front drive) with Japanese-made toilets—gorgeous, low-slung items made of the finest porcelain. They worked on an electric eye: The lid lifted automatically when you approached, and after you'd finished your business, both lid and seat (if it had been raised) were gently and automatically lowered. Dignity and grandeur restored!

Unfortunately, the clanking, ringing, and grinding sounds of their installation now reverberated throughout the house, even here, in the blue-and-rose breakfast room, where Taller was nibbling a honey brioche, detracting from what was otherwise a marvelous breakfast. Lally had even provided his must-have one percent Kona bean latte.

Details, he thought approvingly.

Lally had summoned him to breakfast for a strategy meeting: Like any good general about to launch a campaign, she needed to consult with her most brilliant aide-de-camp. To the accompaniment of the Plumber's Symphony—clang, blang!—she filled him in on her suspicions regarding Sienna making a play for David.

"But what makes you so sure that's what she's aiming to do?" Taller asked, spooning English-cut marmalade on a flaky hunk of pastry. "Maybe it's just what she says it is—she simply wants him to be the go-between to smooth things out with you."

"No." Lally hesitated oh so slightly, he noticed, before going on. She was more scared than she was letting on, that much was certain. "No, she's pulled something like this before. Believe me, I know her, she's got absolutely no scruples."

Taller kept an impassive face. He knew for a fact that Sienna had once seduced one of Lally's lovers, some rich Italiano with a villa in Porto Ercole. If the girl did it once, she could do it again.

"So how has she been going about it, exactly?" he asked.

"She's been calling David every night and tugging at his heart-strings. Telling him she's so confused and depressed and how she realizes she's made so many mistakes, blah, blah, blah, and how she simply doesn't know what to do. He almost flew back early yesterday from Mexico City to go running to console her."

"Okay, then, what about him? What makes you think you can't trust your husband? Maybe he just thinks of her as a daughter. If Sienna did go all Lolita on him, it would just turn him off."

"Maybe it would, but I don't want to take a chance. David's a wonderful man, the best I've ever met. But still . . . He's a man."

"Yeah, and Sienna is pure sex in high heels."

Lally shot him a hard look. *You're pushing it,* he warned himself. *Pull back on the reins.* "I mean, any of us guys can be tempted to do something on the spur of the moment that we'd regret later on. Especially by a young girl with no scruples."

Lally nodded miserably. "That's what I mean."

"Okay, then. When David does go to see her, why don't you just insist on going with him? She's your daughter—that should be your prerogative."

"If I show up with him and spoil her plans, she'll be furious. And her revenge will be to never let me see my granddaughter again."

So she had to choose between her grandkid and her husband. Taller really didn't see the problem: He'd gladly relinquish any member of his family, from grandpa to newest-born nephew, in order to hang on to a world-class fortune. "So what are you planning to do?" he asked.

"Well, first of all, I need to keep David out of town as long as possible."

"Good idea. Can't you come up with some urgent foundation business that will send him off to Uzbekistan or wherever?"

"Better than that!" Lally leaned forward with a gleam in her eye. "David's been dying to acquire a blue period Picasso. They almost never come on the market."

Listen to you, Taller thought snidely. Six months ago, Lally Chandler, neé Lorraine Doris Siplowsky, would not have known a blue period Picasso from a frozen pizza. "Don't tell me you've sniffed one out?"

"Maybe. I spent all day yesterday and half the night on the phone to every friend of a friend of a friend. There's a dealer in Berlin who's got a lead on one. Some impoverished baron who might be persuaded to sell if the price is right. David's finishing up this conference Wednesday and then flying over. I'll meet him there on Thursday, and we've got an appraiser coming down from London the next day. If the painting is authentic, we'll spend the weekend with this baron and his wife, buttering them up."

"So that buys you a few days. So what?"

"So this is where you come in." Lally took a sip of her tea, made a face, and pressed a button under the table. A maid hurried into the room. "Rosaria, this is cold," Lally said. The maid swiftly vanished with teapot and cup.

"What is that you're drinking? Looks like medicine."

"Black Cohosh tea. It's supposed to work wonders in alleviating mood swings. It *tastes* like medicine though."

Taller pulled a sympathetic face. "But to get back to the subject about where I come in?"

"Here's what I'm thinking," Lally said. "While David and I are gone, I want you to make a play for Sienna."

Taller nearly choked on his latte. "Are you serious?"

"Entirely. My only chance of getting her off of stalking David is if she gets sidetracked by another man. And you were just salivating over her sexual charms, so what's the problem?"

"She kind of scares me, if you want to know the truth. And besides, what makes you think she'd give up pursuing your filthy rich husband for a poor guy like me?"

"You're far from poor, darling. And you're good-looking enough, and you can name-drop as brilliantly as she can. You've got that whole metro thing going, if you see what I mean."

Taller saw exactly what she meant, and he wasn't flattered. He sulked for a moment, fiddling with the butter knife. It had a beaded pattern he didn't recognize. Georg Jensen? He turned it over: Bingo, Georg Jensen it proved to be!

He was suddenly struck with an inspiration. He put down the butter knife and glanced back up at Lally with a cozy grin. "I really don't think I'd stand a ghost of a chance with Sienna," he said. "But I know somebody who definitely would."

"Oh yeah? Who's that?"

"My glamorous cousin J. Evanson Kern. Our local starchitect. It's not widely known yet, but his wife served him with divorce papers last week, so he's now officially free."

"Evan Kern," Lally mused. "You think? He's certainly attractive, if you go for that charm-boy type."

Taller could remember a time in the not so distant past when Lally would have gone for that charm-boy type in a New York second. But he simply nodded, breaking off another morsel of brioche. "I think he's perfect. He and Sienna met at that Folk Art Museum do, and there were definite sparks flying. They practically started licking each other on the spot."

"But isn't Evan being monopolized by Caitlin Latch?" Lally said.

"Evan has never been monopolized by anybody, including his wife," Taller said smoothly. "Which is why, I believe, she's finally cutting him loose."

"Funny, I had always heard he was leaving *her*."

"Corinne is worth forty-five million bucks. You do the math and tell me who's dumping whom?"

Lally sniggered. "Yeah, I see your point."

The maid rematerialized with a fresh teapot and cup and saucer. "Thank you, Rosaria," Lally murmured. She waited till the maid had vanished again before going on. "So look, I think I can stretch Berlin out to about a week. Do you think you could arrange to get them hooked up in the meantime?"

Taller leaned back in his chair and regarded her, his eyelids half-shut like a lizard's. If he understood Lally correctly, she was asking him to pimp his cousin Evan to her daughter, Sienna.

"I can certainly give it a try," he said smoothly.

After Taller had departed, Lally went to check on the progress of her plumbing installation. She was still acutely aware of the danger of letting Taller know too much about her situation. *A scorpion's got to sting!*

But she was desperate. And frankly, she told herself as she headed toward the first and most ornate of the mansion's three powder rooms, he was the best person for this particular job.

It gave Jessica something of the creeps to be back in her ex-husband's office. She had suggested they meet on neutral ground, coffee at the Manzanita Street Starbucks or a drink at some quiet restaurant. But the Lord God Neurosurgeon declared he simply could not spare the time, so she had agreed to drop by his office suite at the Mission Mercy Medical Tower.

It had been a year since she'd been here, but it hadn't changed. The waiting room had the same blah-green walls and blah-gray carpet, and its mauve sofas were still crammed with patients tensely thumbing through old copies of *Art News* and *Outdoor Life*. Michael's consulting room still featured the aquarium that Jessica, Rowan, and Alex had given him for his fortieth birthday, with the elephant-nose fish that Alex had picked out still dominating the smaller fry.

And Michael's desk was the same Second Empire French oak table they'd bought at a Paris flea market, which seemed like a hundred years ago. She recalled how they'd haggled with the dealer in freshman French with much hand gesturing and grimacing until they'd reached a price that made it feasible to ship back home.

It should have been listed in the divorce settlement, she thought as she sat facing Michael across it. It had to be worth a bundle now.

But this meeting wasn't about money or anything to do with the settlement—a first in their postdivorce history.

"Since you're so incredibly busy, I'll get right to the point," she told him. "I'm very concerned that you're neglecting Alex and Rowan in favor of your new children."

"I don't know why you think that," Michael said sharply.

"Because it's what I'm hearing from them. They say they hardly get a speck of your attention anymore. They feel that you and Amanda are so wrapped up in the babies that you hardly even remember they exist."

"For chrissake, Jessica, they're just playing you. As you know perfectly well, babies demand a little more attention than older children, but that doesn't mean I'm neglecting Allie and Row."

"Oh yeah? Well, Alex was almost in tears the other night because he thinks you don't care about him anymore."

Michael picked up a ballpoint pen and began clicking it rapidly. He always used to acquire props to fiddle with during their arguments, Jessica remembered: He'd snap a rubber band or twirl a pair of glasses in his hand. She'd hated it then, and she hated it now.

"I think Alex needs to be a little more mature," he declared. "Maybe I don't spend quite as much time with them as I used to because, yes, it's true, I now have two more kids to care for. But it's absurd to suggest I'm ignoring them. On Saturday, for instance, Alex and I watched most of a Dodgers game together. Didn't he tell you that?"

"He said it was a few innings and then you had to leave."

"That's right, I did. I got a call from the hospital, telling me one of my post-ops developed intracranial bleeding. Maybe you think I should have just ignored *that*? So what if a patient's life is at stake? I'm watching the Dodgers with my kid, and they're up seven to three!"

"You know that's not what I mean," Jessica said. "I'm talking about a pattern of behavior, not just one instance."

"Speaking of patterns, you know what I think? I think what's really happening is that they're trying to get *your* attention. I think they're reacting to the fact that their mother has a new boyfriend and suddenly *she* doesn't have as much time for them."

"Oh sure, throw it back on me," Jessica snapped.

"Well, believe it or not, the kids tell *me* some things, too. And what I've been hearing from them is how you've become all dreamy and ga-ga over this guy. Acting like a teenager with a crush on a pop star." He leaned toward her over the French table, clicking the pen. "Everybody in town is talking about it—how you've turned into some kind of groupie for this guy."

"What?" Jessica gasped. "That's ridiculous!"

"You think so? You better take a look at yourself, babe. You're setting a pretty inappropriate example for them."

"So we're talking about inappropriate? How about a married brain surgeon screwing one of his head cases? It didn't exactly make you the poster boy for the Medical Ethics Society."

He reddened with anger. His intercom buzzed. "Dr. DiSantini? Mr. Westerhof has been waiting in room one for over twenty minutes."

"Coming." Michael rose with evident relief. "Look," he said to Jessica, "I've got a waiting room full of patients, so the last thing I've got time for is to sit here playing the blame game with you. If it makes you feel any better, Amanda is taking the twins to visit her parents in Wichita next weekend, so Rowan and Alex will have my undivided attention."

"Oh wow! One whole weekend. I'm sure they'll be thrilled." Jessica stood up and started to leave.

"Oh, by the way, Jessica," Michael said smoothly. She stopped. "Better lay off the *vino*. You're getting to be fat," he said.

"And you've always been a smug and arrogant bastard," she replied, and continued out the door.

CHAPTER twenty

Aidey the Lady

Aiden had been positive his dad would be there, but so far they'd been at JungaZone for nearly an hour and no sign of him. Now they were all in the laser maze, but maybe when they went back into the Gorilla room for the refreshments, Aiden would find him waiting there.

A bunch of the kids who said they were coming also didn't show up. Some of their moms had called Caitlin beforehand to say they weren't: Rennie Platt and Sara Amesly both had strep throats, and Jennifer Waddell's grandpa had died, and Lily Cavanagh had gotten into a national championship for horse jumping, so she had to fly out to Pennsylvania. But there were three other kids who just didn't bother to show up at all.

The weird thing was that Nando, who always seemed so cool at camp wearing his yellow T-shirt and jeans, now looked kind of dorky. He had on some funny-looking green shirt with tomatoes and leaves on it and these shiny black pants that were just all wrong. What was weird, too, was that before the laser tag, when they were all playing the arcade games and Kyle Lewison was bragging about how awesome his score was and how everybody else's were pussies, Nando didn't tell him to shut up or anything, the way he did at camp when kids acted like turds. Instead he just let Kyle keep bragging his mutant head off. Nando had even looked kind of impressed.

And another weird thing was happening here in the laser jungle maze. At first it had been cool, with the glowing lights and the awesome laser sounds and everything. But then he started to get the feeling that all the other guys were tagging one another, but nobody much was tagging *him*. Like everywhere he was in the maze, suddenly everybody else was in a different place.

Maybe they were just letting him win because it was his birthday. Except at all the other laser tag parties he'd been to, that was never the way it worked.

He swung around as he heard somebody coming around a bend of the maze. It was Jared Young. Aiden aimed at Jared's vest and fired. Direct hit! Jared's sensor lit up bright orange.

But instead of firing back, Jared just ducked back around the corner and disappeared.

Aiden heard footsteps walking quickly somewhere behind him. He turned and went after them with his weapon aimed.

Then suddenly he tripped on something and went sprawling against a wall of the plastic maze. "Aidey the Lady," he heard a guy chant. It was Jared, he was sure of it.

Then another guy that sounded like Kyle started up: "Aidey the Lady!" There was a laugh and then a lot of running footsteps.

"Hey, no running, you guys," he heard the game master yell. "I'm gonna have to red-button you!"

There was another loud burst of laughter.

Aiden had the creepy, awful feeling that one of them had tripped him up on purpose. He felt like he was going to cry. But if he did, he'd really be Aidey the Lady.

And no way was he going to let his dad see that.

~

Caitlin was pretty ticked off about the kids who hadn't shown up. She'd held up sending the ones who were here into the maze while waiting for possible latecomers. Finally, she'd humbled herself and gotten on her cell and called the no-shows. One Latino housekeeper who didn't understand what she was saying. Two voice mails. A nanny home with a toddler who said the rest of the family had gone to another birthday party. And Kevin Murray's skanky mom, Gillian, who sounded stoned and merely breezed, "Oh, I guess we forgot," without a shred of apology or regret.

The stack of presents on the party table looked skimpy and forlorn. The nine leftover gift bags also on the table looked even more forlorn.

Even worse was the fact that Evan wasn't here either. Caitlin had impulsively invited him after an energetic bout of lovemaking in his sublet condominium. "Sure I'll come," he promised. "I wouldn't miss it for the world!"

Apparently something bigger than the world had come up. She'd tried his cell twice with no response. Now she tried it a third time. Still no answer. With a grunt of exasperation, she flipped the phone closed, then went over to the party table and poured herself a lemonade from the dispenser.

The day was a scorcher. Out in the video game arcade, the air-conditioning was so strong that it almost turned you blue, but in here, in the Gorilla party room, it was practically jungle temperature. Two other moms and one dad had chosen to hang out instead of just dropping off their kids: Constance Moody, who was tall and skinny with wavy hair tinted slightly green from swimming in chlorine (she reminded Caitlin of an asparagus); Annie Thornbridge, who'd sold men's robes and slippers at the now defunct I. Magnin in Beverly Hills before snagging a supermarket chain heir; and Jared Young's father, Stephen, a pension fund hotshot who had ignored two previous sets of children and was making up for it by spoiling Jared rotten.

Annie and Constance sat wilting at one end of the room. Annie was fanning the air in front of her face with an impeccably manicured hand. "It's hot as Hades in here," she pronounced.

"I know," Caitlin said with despair. "I told them, but they said the air-conditioning vent is broken in this room, and we can't move because all the others are occupied."

Constance was starting to look like a steamed asparagus. "It's always been so nice and cool when we've been here before." She glared at Caitlin accusingly, as if suspecting Caitlin had specifically ordered the nonfunctioning air-conditioner room.

"Sorry, there's really nothing I can do," Caitlin muttered.

Stephen Young sidled up to her. Pools of sweat were spreading in the armpits of his pink polo shirt. "So you know, Jared was co-captain of his Little League team this year. Did I tell you they made the regional playoffs?"

Only about twenty-six times. Caitlin fixed her smile on him and nodded.

"They should've gone all the way to the state finals. Jared was batting two seventy-six, and their pitcher was outstanding. But they had a couple of losers on the team who should've been dumped in the beginning of the season, and that brought the rest of them down." As he talked, he backed her steadily up against a bank of foil balloons while sneaking glances down her cleavage.

"Excuse me, Stephen," she said, squeezing past him. "I've got to do a few things before the kids get back."

"Oh yeah, sure." He grudgingly let her slip by.

She went back over to the table and put down her glass of lemonade. The Cold Stone cake with eleven candles jammed in it was starting to melt, listing to one side like a sinking ship. She scooped up the unclaimed gift bags and carried them out into the arcade hall, where she found a trash barrel and stuffed them in. She could almost hear her mother gasping in shock: *Good gracious, Cait! That's like pouring good money down the drain!* Maybe—but at least the damn things wouldn't be there to reproach Aiden when he came back from the maze.

She detoured to the ladies' room and patted cold water on her flushed face, then started back to the party room. Constance and Annie had also escaped into the hall. Their backs were turned to her; as she approached, she heard Annie pronounce the name "Poppy Winslett."

"... she says they go at it like mating gerbils every time Louis is out of town. She says she can call him at the drop of a hat and he shoots right over. And they went up to Big Sur, supposedly to check out her property, but Poppy said they never left their room at the Post Ranch Inn the entire time—"

Constance nudged her, suddenly noticing Caitlin. Annie spun, and her grin froze on her face. "Oh, hi. We were just, um ..."

"We were getting some cool air before we died in there," Constance filled in.

Before Caitlin could respond, they were distracted by the kids bursting out from the laser maze. They swarmed back into the sweltering Gorilla room, where a party organizer was setting out the Junga-dogs and chips.

Caitlin lingered out in the hallway a moment, her mind fixated on the conversation she'd overheard. They had to have been talking about Evan. Insinuating he was screwing Poppy Winslett behind her husband's back—which meant behind Caitlin's as well. Of course, both Annie and Constance were vicious gossips—if they'd so much as seen Evan shake Poppy's hand, they'd immediately trumpet it as a torrid affair.

Except Annie seemed to be saying she'd heard it directly from Poppy.

Who could be lying. Probably was. The wish fulfillment fantasy of a dish-faced middle-aged broad.

Then Caitlin flashed on the way Evan had flirted so blatantly with that awful Sienna at the Historical Society.

And where the hell was he now?

She fished out her cell again and hit the redial. Got the same electronic voice-mail message. She shoved the phone back in her purse and then followed the others into the party room.

It was pandemonium: Death Cab for Cutie was blaring on the speakers, and the kids were shouting and jostling one another and grabbing for the food and sodas. She noticed immediately that none of the kids seemed to be jostling or shouting at Aiden. He stood a little apart from the action, and he was peering around the room with a stricken expression as if looking for somebody who wasn't there.

The two biggest boys, the alpha dogs, Kyle and Jared, seemed to have taken over the party—they were at the center of attention, getting big laughs by pelting each other with globs of the Cold Stone ice-cream cake. And laughing loudest of all was Aiden's camp buddy, Nando.

"Oh, fuckety-fuck," she muttered.

Aiden was still glum on the ride home.

"That was a great party," Caitlin said in a hearty voice. "You got some really cool presents."

The opened gifts were stacked on the backseat—great loot, including two of the Xbox games he'd been wanting and, from the wealthy Thornbridges, the latest video iPod.

"Yeah," he said flatly.

"You blew out the candles in one breath." Luckily, she had managed to salvage most of the cake before those two creeps had totally mangled it.

"Big deal. Everybody can do that."

"Is there something wrong, sweetie?" she asked. "Did something happen in the laser tag?"

"*No!*" he said stridently. "Why do you always think that? Nothing went wrong."

She sighed. "I'm sorry. You just seem kind of sad."

"I'm not sad. I'm totally okay."

"Okay, then. Good." She smiled at him, and he looked away.

She turned down Mission Street with its oh-too-cute boutiques and outrageously priced antique shops. Big mistake: The traffic was clogged with Saturday shoppers and cruising tourists. She progressed slowly down the block, past the Sheffield Inn, an "olde English" restaurant whose dim and dark-paneled interior made it popular as a romantic rendezvous. It had a small parking area attached to it. As Caitlin inched past it, she noticed a Porsche Cayenne, dark red with Washington State plates.

And snuggled right next to it was Poppy Winslett's Rolls-Royce convertible.

CHAPTER twenty-one

The Shoes Had Been a Big Mistake

The shoes had been a big mistake: Lally admitted that to herself now.

Since becoming Mrs. David Alderson Clemente, she had prided herself on how suitably she had dressed for the role: a costly wardrobe of too trendy designer duds shipped off to the resale shops and replaced by an even more costly wardrobe of understated designer duds; hemlines dropped to skimming the center of the knee; necklines raised (at least in daywear) to discreetly above the crack of the cleavage.

But since arriving in Berlin, she had seen so many gorgeous, chic women shod in the season's outrageously high platform stilettos that she had weakened and then capitulated. This morning, she had ducked into Gucci on the Fasanenstrasse and snapped up a delicious pair of five-inch peep-toe sandals in ivory suede with a two-inch platform. And she had not been able to resist wearing them right away to go inspect the bankrupt German scion's Picasso.

Why not? She had always felt at ease in four-inch stilettos. She'd sported them even before Carrie Bradshaw. Danced in them. Even been known to run in them. So another couple of inches—it shouldn't have been a big deal.

The first problem: Though David was just a hair under six feet two, these shoes made her an inch and a half taller. Alpha male that he was, he clearly was nonplussed by that. Kept making cracks about how he might recruit her as a point guard for the Wildcats, the women's pro basketball team he owned.

The second problem: Eight months earlier, Lally had suffered a fracture of the fifth metatarsal of her right foot while thwarting a sexual assault with a karate kick to the would-be assailant's head. Contrary to her doctor's orders, she had refused to stay off her feet long enough to let the bone heal properly. The angle that these towering sandals forced her feet into somehow made the injury flare up again. It was difficult enough to keep her balance in them; add pain to the mix, and walking became downright precarious.

And then there was the problem of Herr Kurt Shulmann's villa. It had those uneven, crumbly, tightly winding European stairways that made every step of hers potentially lethal. *If he sells the damn painting, he ought to invest in a few elevators,* she thought testily, making her way up the third winding flight.

Shulmann, a portly middle-aged man with silvery blue eyes and lousy teeth, led the way up, followed by Lally and David. They were trailed by the art dealer, a jittery thirty-five-year-old dressed in some avant-garde outfit that looked made out of Reynolds Wrap, and the Picasso expert David had summoned from London, a serene-looking septuagenarian in a white Savile Row summer suit. On the third landing, Shulmann ushered the group into an enormous salon cluttered with several centuries' worth of furniture, paintings, and bibelots. The drapery was faded, the upholstery frayed, the rugs threadbare: Lally had known more than a few women who'd shelled out hundreds of thousands of dollars to decorators to achieve exactly this look—minus, of course, the leak-blackened ceiling and pervasive layer of grime.

The Picasso was lit and hanging above a formerly crimson sofa. It depicted an anorexic and rather depressed-looking young man sitting at a bar and strumming a guitar. The palette was, unsurprisingly, mostly in shades of blue.

"My grandfather bought it directly from Pablo in 1929, and it's never been cataloged," Shulmann declared. "It is quite spectacular, I think you will all agree."

"Spectacular!" echoed the black-clad dealer.

"It is lovely," David murmured.

"Yes, exquisite," Lally said. Her damn foot was throbbing mercilessly.

The expert in white gave a noncommittal little sniff.

As he took down the painting and began his examination, the rest of them moved discreetly to one of the tall windows at the other end of the room and engaged in polite chitchat. Nobody offered a seat—for all Lally knew, the tattered pieces of furniture were all priceless heirlooms and no longer meant to accommodate human backsides—so she remained balanced precariously on her platforms. To make matters worse, both Germans were only about five feet six. She had always loved being among the tallest in a room, able to see above the heads of most women and many men; but at the moment, it had gone from commanding to freakish. She was beginning to feel like freaking André the Giant!

If she were to kick off her shoes and go barefoot, would it be such a horrifying breach of propriety that the Shulmanns would refuse to sell them their masterpiece?

She was starting not to care. *Screw the Picasso*—she just wanted to get off her feet.

At last, the expert cleared his throat discreetly. Everyone turned anxiously his way.

"I'm sorry, but I'm afraid this is not right."

"What?" spluttered Shulmann. "What do you mean not right?"

"You mean it's a forgery?" David said.

"In my opinion, yes, it is a fake. A very clever fake. The paint and canvas are old. However, there are elements in the picture that are taken from five or six other pictures from the period, and this gives it away as a fake. For example, you'll notice the left hand is identical to that in *Boy Leading a Horse*. The goblet is very similar to that of *Strolling Gymnasts* . . ."

Shulmann's face had turned white. He let out a sound that was like the gurgle of fifty million euros going down the drain. "It's impossible," he croaked. "You must not know what you're talking about."

"I beg your pardon," huffed the expert.

Shulmann gave a lunging step forward as if about to take a swing at the elderly expert, who hopped several steps back in alarm. David intervened smoothly. He thanked Herr Shulmann profusely for his time and hospitality, remarking that he would confer further about this with his people. No sale, Lally interpreted.

Then they were all trooping back down the winding stairways, and the Clementes and the British expert headed briskly into their waiting cars.

On the ride back to the hotel, Lally pondered the situation. Their reason for staying in Berlin had just been abruptly curtailed. Knowing David, she was sure he'd want to leave immediately. Get back home to the tornado of work waiting for him.

And to the postponed visit to Sienna.

Lally felt panic rising in her. She'd been in constant contact with Taller, of course. He was tossing an intimate drinks party at which he would contrive to play matchmaker between Sienna and his cousin, but that wasn't until the evening after next. Somehow she had to stall returning until then.

She frantically shuffled through several options: Sightseeing?

Yeah, right. Shopping? Not a chance. Popping up to the Italian lakes or taking the waters at some Swiss spa? Been there, done it.

Damn it, nothing that would tempt David to put off going home.

The car floated up to the hotel, and a doorman promptly opened her door. *Think!* she exhorted herself as she emerged from the car. *Think of something!*

She stepped fretfully toward the ornate hotel entrance and promptly fell off her shoes.

"Jesus God, Lally! Are you okay?" David exclaimed. He rushed over to where she lay crumpled on the ground.

"Ouch!" A sharp shooting pain in her ankle told her she had probably fractured it. She wriggled it and the pain became excruciating.

People began crowding around her—all of Berlin, swiftly followed by the rest of the world, would soon receive the entertaining news that Lally Clemente had toppled off her Gucci platforms. Too humiliating!

"Don't try to move, sweetheart," David said. "We've got an ambulance on the way."

She had a sudden realization—a broken ankle required a hospital stay; and she certainly wouldn't be up for traveling for . . . oh, at least a week. She gazed with loving helplessness up at darling David.

She couldn't have asked for anything better.

Jessica descended the winding stone stairs to the wine cellar that Michael had constructed at great cost from a storage space in the basement. Oh, the happy hours he had spent down here, tasting, rearranging, reading his *Wine Spectator*. He would herd all guests down here and babble on about "nose" and "finish" and accents of licorice and black raspberry. Jessica had received half the contents of the cellar in the settlement; and for some months after the divorce, she had taken great pleasure in guzzling down Michael's treasured old Bordeauxs and Montrachets as if they were lukewarm bottles of Coke. But after some reckless behavior made her realize she was teetering on the brink of Boozy Divorcée, she had scrupulously avoided coming down here.

But now she needed courage. And she had discovered there was nothing to instill courage like several glasses of a twenty-year-old Chateau Lafitte Rothschild Pauillac. This was the vintage she chose now. She slid two dusty bottles from their niches, wrapped them in towels, and stowed them in a tote.

Michael's comments had reverberated in her head long after she'd left his office. Not about her being fat. He had always taunted her for not being built like a heroin-addicted supermodel. A stick with a vagina seemed to be his ideal; Amanda, prepregnant with twins, had looked practically like a famine victim.

No, what nagged at her was the Tommy-groupie thing. Was he right? Jessica wondered. Had she been flinging herself so obviously at Tom Bramberg that she'd become a laughingstock in town?

She had noticed that she was being asked to join fewer benefit committees, invited to fewer charitable events, skipped over for a number of the usual dinner parties. She had chalked this up to her reduced status as an ex-wife—but what if it was because she'd been making a grade-A fool of herself?

She ran an instant replay of her behavior over the past months. All moony and la-di-da when Tommy was in town. All dragging-her-ass when he was away. Compulsively playing his recordings. Dropping his name into conversations for the sheer pleasure of forming it on her lips.

Neglecting her clients' casework to compose lists of why she and Tom should break up.

And was it true, as Michael said, that Rowan and Alex were becoming ashamed of her?

That was probably an exaggeration. Rowan, at least, would have let her know: *Mom, you're acting like a total head case, and it's like so-o-o embarrassing!*

What was obvious, though, was that she had to reassess her situation with Tommy before she did cause them embarrassment.

She went out to her car. Alex and Rowan were already sitting in it, waiting to be shuttled over to their father's. She stashed the tote bag in the trunk, then drove the four blocks and dropped them off with hugs and kisses. And then she pointed the Saab toward the freeway entrance and headed south to L.A.

Just under two hours later, she made a turn off the Sunset Strip and pulled up to the valet at the Chateau Marmont. She grabbed the tote bag from the trunk, went into the hotel, and crowded into a tiny elevator along with a tattooed rocker type, a craggy-faced B-list actor, and a stunning young black woman in an Armani suit. The elevator ascended creakily. Jessica got out at the third floor, turned down a claustrophobic hallway, and rapped on the door of Tommy's suite.

He opened it immediately. "I'm glad you came," he said, and pulled her inside.

It was a spacious one-bedroom suite with a wraparound balcony: the view was of a gigantic twisting iPod girl looming over the Strip. Jessica set the tote bag on an armchair. A large suitcase lay unfolded beside it. On these trips, Tom literally lived out of his suitcase. Not even a token attempt to unpack.

She turned to him, and he gathered her in his long arms. He began kissing her and unbuttoning her blouse. She made a feeble attempt to resist. It wasn't what she was here for, and she had promised herself she would not give in.

But she couldn't help herself. Maybe she hadn't become addicted to alcohol—but she had become addicted to Tom Bramberg. And she simply couldn't resist her craving for him.

Later, after the lovemaking and after they had finished off one of the bottles of the Lafitte, Jessica sat in the rumpled bed while Tommy smoked a Marlboro out on the balcony. She sipped another glass of the second bottle of soft, luscious wine. It made her feel both heady and bold—exactly what she needed right now.

Tom stepped in and flopped back down on the bed beside her. He held out his wineglass for a refill.

"Tom? Listen . . . ," Jessica began, pouring.

"Yeah, I know, filthy habit. I'm going to kick it when I get back to San Carlino."

"Oh, good. But that's not what I was going to say. I mean . . ." She took a breath. "I need to know what this is about."

"What what is about?"

"Us. What we're doing. Where it's going."

Jessica had once heard Lally complain about the famous Tom Bramberg Look—the one where his eyes narrowed and the corners of his wide mouth tightened in a half smile, and it made you feel he could see right through whatever you were saying and rip open whatever you were trying to hide.

It was the Look he was giving her now.

"Is it just sex?" she went on. "Is it being in love? Is it marriage and forever?"

"Why does it have to be about anything? Why can't it just be?"

"Because we're not a couple of hippies in Haight-Ashbury. I've got kids and a career I'm trying to get back on some kind of track and a house I'm barely hanging on to by the skin of my teeth. I need some sense of the future."

He rolled over on his back and gazed up at the ceiling.

Okay, Jessica thought. If he could see right through what she was saying, then he knew what she wanted to hear: *I love you desperately. I can't live without you. I want to have children with you, and I want our two souls to be joined forever and ever, even after death.*

"I don't know," he said flatly. "I can't tell you what the future will bring."

Jessica felt a numbness replace the heady glow of the wine. She lay still a moment. Then she got up and picked up all her clothes from the floor and carried them into the bathroom. She got dressed, quickly, efficiently, and then came back out. She paused for a second and then, without looking at him, headed for the door.

FINAL REASON TO BREAK UP WITH TOM BRAMBERG:
HE DIDN'T STOP ME FROM WALKING OUT THE DOOR.

Evan had phoned the evening after Aiden's party, just as Caitlin was sure he would. She let the machine pick it up, listening rigidly as he spouted his bullshit message: "Hi, baby. Hey, I'm really sorry I didn't make it this afternoon. Had an emergency with the construction union—a big dust-up over working conditions. I've been shut up with my chief engineer and the union boss all day. But hey, call me. The other night—wow, it was great, I'm still rocking. How about tomorrow? A quiet Sunday evening, just the two of us?"

Yeah, right, Caitlin thought. The emergency was in Poppy Winslett's wanna-build-my-beach-house pants. She'd snapped her fingers, and he had obligingly come running. It was so pathetically obvious that Caitlin nearly laughed.

She called him back in the morning.

"Hey, I feel like crap for missing Aiden's bash," he said, "but there was nothing I could do about it."

"Of course, I understand. It was completely beyond your control."

"I knew you'd understand. So how about tonight? Can you get away?"

"Yeah, as a matter of fact I can. And you know what I'd just love to do? There's a Sting concert at the Corinthian Theater. It's sold out, but there are scalper tickets available. I checked—great seats for five hundred a pair."

Evan hesitated, as she figured he would. She had finally realized something she should have long before—he was cheap! All those walks on the beach and cheapo sushi restaurants and quiet, just-the-two-of-us evenings at home . . . After that first reel-her-in lunch at Café Cygne, he'd scarcely spent a nickel on her. "But you have to let me take *you*," she went on. "I just had a huge windfall—I dug up an old bracelet at a yard sale that turned out to be Cartier and sold it for a bundle. And I always feel that when I get one of these windfalls it's bad luck if I don't share some of it."

"Oh, but I couldn't let you . . ."

"You've got to," she said lightly. "Otherwise I'll be cursed."

He gave a chuckle. "I wouldn't want that to happen."

"Nope. So listen, the scalper office closes at one. It's right near you, on La Presa, so why don't you pick up the tickets, and I'll pay you back? I'll meet you at the entrance to the theater at seven forty-five, okay?"

Another slight hesitation. "Uh, yeah, okay. Great. Can't wait to see you."

"I can't wait to see you, too," she purred.

She hung up and was startled to see Aiden in the doorway. "That was your grandma," she improvised. "We were talking about when the best time would be to go to Magic Mountain."

Aiden nodded.

"Hey, it's hot. Why don't we go to the beach? And later on, how about a movie? Any one you want that's not an R."

"Yeah, okay," he said.

"Good. Go get changed."

He turned and shuffled upstairs. Caitlin sat for a moment, with a hollow sensation in the pit of her stomach.

Good-bye, Evan, she thought. She pictured him tonight pacing anxiously in front of the entrance to the Corinthian. Placing a series of increasingly agitated calls to her cell phone, which she would not answer. Finally realizing that not only had he been stood up, but he was stuck with five hundred bucks' worth of tickets.

The thought cheered her a bit. But it was still going to be a while before she totally bounced back.

Aiden knew his mom was lying about talking to his grandma. It was the voice she used with Evan, and she sounded more lovey-dovey than ever.

He figured his dad never got the IM, which was why he hadn't shown up at the party, and Aiden couldn't go back online until his mom gave him his computer back. So what he was most afraid of was coming true: His mom was going to get married to Evan, and his dad would never be coming back.

He pulled on his bathing trunks and stuck his bare feet into flip-flops. He'd have to go to his other plan now, and he'd have to do it as soon as possible. Tomorrow or the day after. He was really terrified about going through with it. But no way he could punk out, because if he did, he'd just be acting like Aidey the Lady.

So really, he had no other choice.

CHAPTER twenty-two

Oldest Trick in the Book

"Hee-hee." Taller couldn't help chuckling while he listened to his cousin Evan rant on the phone about the goddamn bitch who'd stood him up Sunday night. Taller had to hand it to that sexy little Caitlin Latch—he hadn't realized she possessed such delightfully vindictive gumption.

"Yeah, you certainly got done over," he commiserated to Evan. "But forget it, you'll have a fabulous time tonight. There are a few people I particularly want you to meet."

"Oh yeah? Any potential clients?"

"You bet. These people are all oozing money and itching to build. And of course they already know you by reputation."

"Oh, well, great." Evan sounded immediately cheered. "See ya later, then."

Taller had carefully crafted a sunset drinks-at-poolside soirée with one goal in mind, but it was not to further his cousin's career—it was to bring about his merger with Sienna Bramberg. Taller didn't think it would be an inordinately difficult task: The chemistry between the two had already been established; they were currently the two most fabulous-looking people in town; and even their names seemed to belong together, like fabric choices at the Ralph Lauren Home Store (this couch comes in Hunter, Heather, Evan, or Sienna). It would simply be a question of setting the right snare, then snapping the door shut and (Taller was positive) watching the two hotties start humping like bunnies.

By seven that evening, the snare seemed to be perfectly set: A crescent moon rising in a streaky pink and gold sky; the pool lit to the translucent milky blue of a rare opal; Bellinis made with fresh white peaches and vintage Dom Pérignon.

And to make absolutely certain Evan and Sienna made a beeline for each other, Taller had selected the rest of the guests for their utter and collective lack of sex appeal. Evan, who had arrived early and was now circulating among them, looked like a god in comparison.

Nevertheless, things weren't working quite as Taller had expected.

First of all, no Sienna. He'd dangled a little fib as bait—that David Clemente was returning early from Europe without Lally and would be coming solo to the party—and Sienna had seemed to snap at it. Of course, she was notorious for never being on time, so he still had hopes she'd show.

But other problems had presented themselves. Here was Tabitha Montgomery, invited because she had the face of a rat terrier attached to the body of an overfed beagle. Nobody had informed Taller she'd recently dropped forty pounds at an Oaxacan fat farm and had her features plumped up with massive injections of Restylane and was suddenly fetching enough that Evan had made a beeline to *her*.

And then the Heberlings, who had the look and disposition of a pair of trolls with indigestion, cornered Evan to talk about their plans to knock down their hacienda-style home and replace it with a contemporary château—and so his attention was now focused on *them*.

And Taller's trump card, his cousin Jane, who had always thrown herself shamelessly at Evan, and who looked suitably atrocious tonight, with her thunder thighs and big black circles under her eyes. She had brought a date! An Ichabod Crane look-alike she'd picked up at some trustees of the library blah-blah-blah. She was sticking by his side like gum to the sole of a shoe and not pestering Evan at all.

Taller ran around refilling Bellinis and making cocktail chatter and wondering how he was going to break it to Lally that he had failed miserably. Then at last, just as the last streak of gold faded in the sky, Sienna made her appearance. She looked yummy, long tan legs, protruding nipples beneath a skimpy pink dress, and that slippery silvery blond hair.

He hurried over to greet her.

"So where's David?" she demanded.

"He's not here yet," Taller replied smoothly. "I'm not quite sure he's going to be able to make it."

"You said he was coming!" she said, pouting.

"Yes, and I'm hoping he will."

She lit a cigarette, blew smoke in his face, and flicked the ashes in his pool. *Nasty little skank.* "Who are all these geeks?" she said.

"Some very interesting people, actually. Let me introduce you. My cousin, the prominent architect Evan Kern, I think you've met him . . . ?"

The girl showed a flicker of interest. "He's here?"

"Yes, he is, somewhere." Taller gazed around desperately. Evan was still firmly in the grip of both Heberling trolls. Janey had disappeared, and her Ichabod Crane date was now huddled with Tabitha Montgomery. The rest of this gang really were geeks, he had to admit.

Maybe he had outsmarted himself. Sienna was looking poutier by the second. If he didn't do something fast, she'd probably finish her cigarette, stub it out on his delicate limestone tile, and disappear.

He hated to be unoriginal. Hated even more to be unsubtle. But hell, he was desperate and had no time for niceties.

"Evan!" he shouted out.

As Evan craned his neck from around the Heberlings, Taller expansively threw out his arms as if to summon him and—oldest trick in the book—slapped Sienna efficiently into the pool.

Somehow, Janey had discovered, the real estate agents had become wise to her little reconnaissance missions. At every open house she'd crashed lately, she couldn't move a step without finding one of them glued to her elbow.

In desperation, she'd hit a few of the general-public open houses yesterday, and it was the same story—anytime she tried to sneak a peek into a bedroom drawer or bathroom cabinet, she found some sniffy real estate agent hovering close by.

Maybe it was just coincidence, she reasoned: There were scads of Realtors in San Carlino County—every bored housewife, every *other* gay guy, nearly every over-forty divorcée who was running out of funds and new husband options, scurried out and picked up a real estate license. They couldn't *all* recognize her face, could they? It wasn't as if it had been printed on flyers and circulated around town or published on the front page of the *Courier* real estate section or anything.

The upshot was that she'd been unable to get a decent night's sleep for a week, and she looked and felt like the Wreck of Ages. She'd been rather startled by Taller's invite tonight. He rarely asked her to anything except family gatherings. Didn't consider her chic enough to mingle with the crème de la crème of his friends. Thank God she'd been able to round up an escort, even if it was just Paul Gifferman, who worked in admissions at the university (*Not quite our class, dear*, her mother would say), so at least she wouldn't be left stranded, grinning and clutching a glass in her hand, while Taller's trendoid pals ignored her.

But then horrors! Taller had invited Evan! Janey had been rejoicing at the news that he had dumped Caitlin Latch—but she'd been as-

LINDSAY GRAVES ～ 226

siduously avoiding him until she'd had the lipo and tummy tuck. After that, flaunting her stunning svelte new figure, she'd planned to renew her assault. But how dreadful to run into him now when she still had her hideous pear shape and was all haggard and baggy-eyed from lack of sleep and was on the arm of a loser like Paul Gifferman!

Evan, of course, came bounding right up to them and gave her a just-family-type peck on the cheek. He pumped Paul's hand and boomed, "Good to meet you," with hearty insincerity, then said to her, "So what's this I hear about cousin Debba getting engaged to your ex?"

She forced an insouciant smile. "Isn't it amazing? She was kind enough to visit him in jail—Debba's always had lots of time for things like that. And I suppose he was very grateful to her for it."

"But conjugal visits! The mind boggles!" Evan gave an exuberant laugh.

Janey's laugh was strained. She was relieved when he was commandeered by Tabitha Montgomery, whose forty thousand dollars' worth of body and face reconstruction didn't change the fact that she had the brain of a pea. Still, the conversation had left Janey mortified. She stayed on the opposite end of the pool, watching as Evan floated from Tabby to Gayle and Vic Heberling, who'd been nattering about building some grandiose château for the past ten or fifteen years but never really got around to it.

And then horror of horrors! A late arrival—that ghastly Euro-trash daughter of Lally's.

Enough was enough. Time to get the hell out of here. Janey just needed to make one pit stop first. "Paul, dear, hold my glass, will you?" she murmured. "I'm going to pop into the powder room."

She ducked inside. Taller's house was a single story modern, which he had recently redecorated with a retro-fifties flair—she happened to know he'd paid for the whole thing by blowing the entire wad he inherited from their great-uncle Franklin, who died last

Christmas Eve. She ignored the black-and-aqua-tiled powder room off the front hall and continued to Taller's bedroom in the L-shaped wing at the rear of the house. She slipped into the adjoining bathroom and locked the door behind her.

She began nosing around: cruddy combs; hairs in the tub; glops of mousse in the sink; caps left off toothpaste and jars. Maybe all the people who were convinced Taller was gay would change their minds if they knew he was such a secret slob.

She rummaged through the many artifacts on the edge of the sink. Nothing of interest. She opened the medicine cabinet. It was brimming with stuff, from ancient used razor blades to encrusted tubes—more secret slob evidence.

With some meticulousness, she began delving through it all. Hooray! a prescription vial! But it was just leftover amoxicillin from one of Taller's famous bouts of bronchitis. She stuck it back on the shelf, shoved aside a bottle of cough syrup and an enema bulb, and came across another vial. Tranxene—and about a third filled. Hooray, hooray!

She shook out two of the lovely pale blue pills, twisted them up in toilet paper like a Tootsie Roll, and popped them into her bag.

Then suddenly she heard a loud cry from outside, followed by the sound of a splash. Then a lot of voices raised in commotion. There was a window above the tub that overlooked the patio. Gingerly she stepped into the tub, stood on tippy-toes, and peered out.

That awful Sienna was attempting to climb stark naked out of the pool! No, not naked—her dress, wet and clinging to her body, was now transparent. She was wearing no bra and just a triangle of see-through panties. "Help me out!" she was yelling.

Evan and Taller hauled her out of the water like a flopping pale fish. "It's cold out here!" she bawled. "I'm fucking freezing!"

The air was in fact a caressing seventy-five degrees, but the dryness of the Southern California climate made water evaporate quickly, taking body heat with it. So, yeah, she must be freezing her exposed buns off. Janey would have found this amusing—except that it seemed to prompt Evan to scramble over and chivalrously drape his jacket around her, like Walter Raleigh or somebody. Janey knew that jacket of his. Paul Smith cream linen. He'd been wearing it once when she was with him, and he'd nearly had fits when it got sprinkled by a few drops of water from a leaky air conditioner. Observe him now, please, enfolding the sopping wet Sienna in it as tenderly as if wrapping an expensive present.

She could hear Taller, bossy as usual, murmuring some directive to him, and then Evan was solicitously leading the dreadful girl away.

Janey watched them pass out of sight. She stepped out of the tub and went back to the vial of Tranxene and helped herself to three more pills.

What the hell, she told herself—she deserved it.

Taller relaxed on a pool recliner, savoring a silky Montecristo cigar that his nephew Jonas had smuggled back from Cuba. Not a bad night's work. He had suggested to Evan that he escort Sienna back to her house (Lally's house!) to change out of her wet clothes— and if he knew his Evan Kerns, a beautiful, wet, and practically naked girl would be too much to resist. He'd pounce; and given the way she'd been rather melting into his embrace, Sienna would pounce right back.

It was certainly an excellent sign they hadn't returned to the drinks party. Taller was almost positive he'd be able to report to Lally that the mission was accomplished.

His thoughts drifted leisurely to his other cousin, dear old Janey. He'd been certain that at some point she'd concoct an excuse to sneak up to his medicine cabinet—last time she'd been at his house, she'd copped half a bottle of Ativan and a couple of Fiorinal.

This time, he was prepared for her pilfering. He had some Viagra left over from a short-lived affair with an extremely well-preserved divorcée who'd rented the Eisenbergs' place last winter. This evening, he'd substituted the blue Viagras for the blue Tranxenes in the vial. The pills were slightly different shapes, but he figured Jane wouldn't really know the difference.

He chortled, thinking about it. If Janey had swiped any—and he'd bet money that she had—they were not going to mellow her out.

But they'd sure give her a hell of an erection.

CHAPTER twenty-three

My Mom Doesn't Speak English

A horn tooted outside. Aiden peeked from the window and saw the MacMillers' black SUV at the curb come to pick him up for camp.

He had to do it now. The last couple of days his mom had walked him out to the car, but now she was upstairs taking one of her long steamy showers. He was so petrified, he almost changed his mind. But he didn't: He hurried upstairs and rapped at the door of the bathroom.

"Mom? Car pool's here."

The shower water turned off. "I'll be right out."

"You don't have to. I'll see you later, okay?"

He raced downstairs before she could come out, feeling really lousy about fooling her. But he didn't have any choice. And he'd already checked to make sure he had everything he needed—his iPod and his backpack with an extra sweater in it in case it got chilly and the cap that he'd figured would be a good idea—so he guessed it would all turn out to be okay.

He went out to the MacMillers' SUV, but instead of squeezing into the back with the triplets, Juney and Lisa and Courtney, he walked around to Nan's window.

"I can't go with you this morning," he told her. "I've got to go see my allergy doctor because I've had a flare-up. My mom is going to take me up to camp after that."

Nan pressed her lips tight together like she was really annoyed. "I hope she's still planning to pick up you and the girls this afternoon."

"Yeah," he said quickly, "she's still gonna do that."

"Well, okay then, Aidey. I hope your allergy gets better."

As soon as Nan started to drive away, Aiden rushed back to his house. But instead of going in the front door, he made a detour around the side and edged himself through the prickly thorn hedges into the Wynnes' backyard. As fast as he could, he went to the rotten swing and yanked it up and dug out the CD box. He grabbed all the money out of it and stuffed it into his backpack with the rest of the stuff.

This time he didn't have to bother burying the box again. He just went back through the hedges, getting a little scratched up because he was moving so fast.

He hurried to the side of the garage where he kept his bike out all summer when there was no chance it would get rained on. His heart was jumping around like crazy. If his mom came outside right now, everything would be ruined. But he knew that after her shower it usually took her a pretty long time to get dressed and dry her hair, so he was pretty sure she wouldn't.

As quietly as he could, he slid off his helmet from where it dangled from the handlebars and put it on. Then he released the kick and swung himself onto the bike and pedaled like crazy off onto the street. His mom didn't come out, and like always, none of the neighbors were hanging around outside, so nobody saw him go.

But it took a lot longer to get to the Greyhound bus terminal than it seemed like it was going to when he was riding in Nando's mom's pickup truck. Navarro Avenue was only three streets over from where he lived, but it went on practically forever, and it was jam-packed with traffic that honked at him whenever he swerved too far from the edge of the road.

But then finally he saw the Jack in the Box! He turned right, and there was the sign he remembered with the running greyhound dog on it. He pedaled into the parking lot that was next door. He only had a cheap lock that would be easy to break, but he figured nobody would steal his bike because it was so beat-up looking.

He locked it to one of the parking meters. Then he took the cap he'd brought out of his backpack and stuck his bike helmet into the backpack. The cap said "VOTE FOR PEDRO." If somebody looked at it and didn't know it was from *Napoleon Dynamite,* they might think he was a Mexican kid, which was what he wanted.

He put it on and pulled the brim down low to his eyebrows, and then he walked into the building. Just like he remembered, there were mostly Spanish-speaking people waiting for buses.

He got in the line to the ticket window. He had already looked up the bus schedule on the Internet. There was one that left at ten thirty-five that he could get on if this line wasn't too slow. If he missed that one, he'd have to wait until eleven forty-eight. But the line moved pretty fast, and he only had to wait a few minutes before it was his turn at the window. A lady with pitch-black hair and wearing glasses attached to a silvery chain was sitting behind it, waiting to take his order.

"I need to buy one ticket for me and one ticket for my mom to San Francisco," he told her. "My mom doesn't speak English."

She looked out her little window. There were a couple of Spanish-speaking ladies sitting on the benches, and Aiden nodded his head in their direction. "She's right over there."

"One-way or round-trip?" the ticket lady asked.

"One-way. My *tía* Soledad is going to drive us back."

"Are you under twelve?"

For a minute, he got scared that she was suspicious of him and going to call the police. But then he remembered that the bus ticket was less money if you were under twelve. "I'm eleven."

"One adult, one child, no return. Sixty-eight dollars and forty cents."

He gave her two fifties from his money, pushing them under the bars of the window. She pushed back his change, and there was a clatter as the tickets were printed out. Then she told him where to go to get the right bus, talking slowly and clearly like she thought *he* didn't understand much English.

He knew it was going to be a long ride. The bus made stops in other cities and didn't end up in San Francisco until seven nineteen in the evening. Luckily it was summer, so it would still be daylight out when he got there. But he figured he'd probably get good and hungry during the ride, so he found some vending machines and stocked up with a bag of apple chips, a Heath bar, some Twizzlers, and two cans of Mountain Dew.

Then he went to where the ticket window lady told him the bus would be waiting. There it was, with the names of all the places it was going zipping across an electronic sign on its front, like the way they showed scores on the bottom of the TV screen on ESPN.

People were already starting to climb on board. Aiden picked out a group of Mexican-looking people, a couple of ladies and a man and a whole bunch of kids who were all together. Holding on to his child's-fare ticket, he stayed close by them as they all climbed onto the bus, so that anybody looking at him, with his "VOTE FOR PEDRO" hat on, would just think he belonged with them.

He chose a seat where they did, squinching himself over to the window so that two of the kids could sit next to him. They stared at him, and he smiled, and they smiled back. Then he put on his iPod, and nobody bothered him after that.

~

Three acquaintances had called Caitlin so far to share the latest gossip—that Evan Kern had run off with Lally Clemente's estranged daughter, Sienna. The two of them had just flown to New York, presumably so Sienna could introduce him to all her Eurotrashy connections and get him scads of commissions and also so they could get away from the glare of local scrutiny.

All the callers sounded as though they expected Caitlin to be on the verge of suicide or something. Of course, she was still depressed: It had been marvelous to think herself even a little in love for a while. That dizzy dancing feeling . . .

But what had she really felt for him?

She'd been bowled over by his looks and charm, certainly. And grateful for his little attentions to Aiden. And it had been a kick to fantasize becoming Mrs. Glam Society Architect . . .

But it seemed that the survival instincts she'd developed since her divorce had been working full force. Subconsciously, she'd been aware of his bullshit: The wife he claimed wouldn't let him go. The glib excuses for disappearing and not calling. Using his sketchbooks as a seduction routine—kind of like the old joke: *Would you like to come up and see my etchings, my dear?*

So, yeah, she was hurt and humiliated—but nowhere near what she'd be if she'd allowed her emotions to run unchecked. It had been a final slap in the face to find out how quickly he had replaced her with Sienna, but she was hardly about to slit her wrists over it.

The last of these pseudosympathy calls had come in just as Caitlin was leaving to pick up Aiden and the MacMiller girls, and she was still mulling it over as she pulled into the trailhead parking lot. Kids from both camps, yellow shirters and green shirters, poured into the lot and filtered into the fleet of cars waiting for them. The MacMiller triplets appeared, squabbling shrilly among themselves.

They slid into the two rear seats of the Volvo wagon and strapped themselves in, as Caitlin searched the diminishing swarm for Aiden. He'd probably had to pee. She couldn't help feeling a twinge of annoyance as she glanced toward the brown cement cubicle that housed the toilets.

But if that's what he was doing, he was sure taking his sweet time. One by one, the other cars pulled away; and now the army of campers had dwindled to three Sagebrush kids huddled in a droopy little knot around one of their counselors. Caitlin recognized Jessica DiSantini's son, Alex, among them.

She stopped another Sagebrush counselor, a boy with Howdy-Doody-ish orange hair and freckles. "Excuse me, I think my son is in the restroom. Could you go check for me?"

"No problem. What's his name?"

"Aiden."

The boy gave a thumbs-up and loped off toward the cubicle.

A midnight blue Saab suddenly came racing into the parking lot, and a disheveled-looking Jessica leapt out. The remaining Sagebrush campers perked up and came scampering toward her.

"Guys, I am so sorry!" Jessica exclaimed. She gave her son a penitent squeeze. "Your dad had to go into emergency surgery and couldn't come. I got here as fast as I could."

As the kids climbed into her car, Jessica turned and noticed Caitlin. "Cait? You're still waiting?"

"Yeah. I think Aiden must have gone to the john. I sent a counselor to go get him."

Jessica nodded. "Michael was supposed to pick up my gang. When he couldn't, I had to cut short a deposition with an extremely difficult witness to come racing up here."

Caitlin glanced toward the cubicle and saw the Howdy-Doody kid striding back. He shook his head. "Not there," he called.

She felt a stab of fear. "You sure? What about the other side?"

"The girls' section? I checked there, too. Nada."

Caitlin exchanged a look of alarm with Jessica.

"Maybe he's still down at the campsite," Jessica suggested. "Why don't you ask one of the Cottonwood counselors to go check?"

Caitlin spotted one she recognized heading toward the administration bungalow—a dark-haired girl named Rebecca whom Aiden had once pointed out as his favorite. Caitlin jogged toward her, shouting her name. "Rebecca! Hello, I'm Aiden Latch's mom. I'm still waiting for him. Do you think he might have gotten left behind at the campsite?"

"Aiden?" The girl scrunched her forehead. "I didn't see him at all today. I don't think he was here."

"Are you sure?" Jessica had appeared behind Caitlin. "You sure you know the boy we're talking about?"

"Yeah, Aiden. Dark hair, pretty eyes, about yea tall . . . ?" The counselor held out a hand shoulder level. "He used to be buddies with that big Latino kid, Nando, before he had to drop out? I know Aiden wasn't here this afternoon, 'cause we were short one guy on the Badger team."

Caitlin felt a terror seize her. She stared out over the wide expanse of the canyon. Why had she never realized it was so filled with dangers? Steep rocky ledges to tumble off of; acres of wild pine forest to get lost in; rattlesnakes and maybe even mountain lions; and—*oh God!*—human predators . . .

Her legs started shaking, and her throat constricted. "You mean he never showed up at all today?"

"I don't know about that," the girl admitted.

"Let's ask the MacMiller girls," Jessica suggested. "He rode with them this morning, right? See what they say."

"Yes, good idea!" Caitlin raced back to the Volvo and yanked open the back door. "Guys, when Aiden got out of the car this morning, did you see if he actually went down to Cottonwood?"

The triplets shot her screwy looks. "Aiden didn't come in our car this morning," Courtney declared.

"He had to go to the allergy doctor," said Juney.

"Yeah, he said you were taking him there, and then you were going to drive him to camp afterwards," added Lisa.

"Oh my God!" Caitlin whispered.

"Okay, look, he's probably just playing hooky," Jessica told her. "Maybe he snuck off to meet a friend and go to the movies or something. He might even be home by now."

"Do you think so?" Caitlin felt a surge of hope.

"Do you have the numbers of his friends? Call and see if he's with any of them."

Friends? Caitlin's mind was suddenly in a fog. All she could think of was that one boy Jonathan Lazaris. But Jonathan had moved away to Arizona, she didn't even know which city. . . .

Nando! That's who he could be with! Aiden hadn't mentioned him at all since his laser tag party, and Caitlin had guessed that Aiden didn't want to see him anymore. But who knows? Maybe they had made up and were friends again.

"There's one boy," she said. "I know where he lives, but I don't have the number with me. I can drive over there and see, it's not that far from here."

She started to get into her car and realized the triplets were still strapped in back, fixing her with three identical stares. She froze. Everything suddenly seemed to be in a swirl of terrifying confusion.

"I'll squeeze the girls into my car and run them home," Jessica told her. "Go check Aiden's friend. If he's not there, then see if he's gone back to your house."

Caitlin nodded mutely.

"And I'll call the police," Jessica added. "Just as a precaution."

Faced with the reality of calling the police Caitlin was seized with another spasm of dread.

"Girls, you're coming with me," Jessica said to the triplets.

"We're *all* supposed to get in your car?" Lisa demanded.

"I don't think that many is allowed!" Courtney stated.

"It's okay just this once," Jessica told them. She directed them firmly into her Saab.

Caitlin slid behind the driver's seat and with trembling hands took the wheel. She drove at a frenetic speed down the mountain and shot across town, weaving frantically through the rush-hour traffic to Nando's neighborhood. She'd thought she could easily find the house, but in her panic she kept turning down wrong streets and wasted fifteen minutes searching for it. Finally she recognized the red pickup truck; she stamped on her brakes, parked, and raced up to the house.

Nando was home but insisted he hadn't seen Aiden today. "Not since his party," he said.

His mother hovered nervously behind him. He said something in rapid Spanish to her. "Aiden no is here," she said to Caitlin.

"Okay, thank you," Caitlin managed. She jumped back into her car and sped home. Please be there, she prayed.

There was a police cruiser at her curb and two uniformed cops, one male, one female, standing at the door. They've found him and he's dead! was her wild thought. She got out of her car, hardly able to walk.

But they were just responding to Jessica DiSantini's call. The male cop, Officer Landers, was someone Caitlin had worked with from time to time back at her job at the Rape Crisis Center—a soft-spoken African American with a reassuring air of competence.

"Let's make absolutely sure he's not hanging out inside," he said. "Nine times out of ten, kids make it back home before we get here."

Please be here! Caitlin ran inside and raced into all the rooms, up-stairs and down, loudly yelling Aiden's name. Her own voice just seemed to echo horribly back at her. She led the officers down into the yard and continued shouting for him.

"He's not here!" she said, suppressing a sob.

"Okay," Officer Landers said calmly. "Does he have a skateboard or a bike?"

"Both."

"Let's see if either one is missing."

"He keeps his bike on the side of the garage." They walked quickly around to the side. "It's gone!"

"Okay, then he's probably on his bike. Did he have any money?"

Caitlin felt a shock of guilt. "Yeah, probably. He's been stealing money lately. From my purse and other places. I didn't say anything, I thought it was just a phase he was going through. . . . I stopped leaving any where he could find it."

"About how much would you say he's got?" asked the female cop—Officer Perez, according to her badge.

"I don't know. Several hundred dollars, if he hasn't spent any. Maybe even more."

The cops exchanged glances. Probably marveling at her abominable stupidity. As they should be, she reflected. She was overwhelmed by it herself.

They headed back into the house, and the officers had her describe Aiden, his bike, and what he'd been wearing in the morning. Officer Landers called in the description and told Caitlin that units would be checking the malls, movie theaters, and video arcades.

"Caitlin?" Jessica appeared in the living room. "The door was half-open so I let myself in. Any news?"

"We think he might have gone off on his bike, but God knows where. Anything could have happened, he could've been hit by a car or something."

"There've been no reports of any accident involving a child," Perez said.

Caitlin could no longer help herself: She burst into tears. She was dimly aware of Jessica's arms wrapping around her, and Jessica soothing, "It's going to be okay. I'm sure it is. Just try to stay strong."

Caitlin nodded. But if anything happened to Aiden, she wouldn't be able to stand it. It was the one thing she could never bounce back from . . . no, not ever.

CHAPTER twenty-four

Child Molesters, Kidnappers, Escaped Psychotics

The whole Mexican family got off the bus in the city of Oakland, and Aiden was left sitting by himself. He huddled down in his seat, really scared the bus driver or one of the other passengers would ask him how come he didn't get off with the rest of them, wasn't that his family? But it didn't happen. The bus finally started up again with a loud grinding of its gears, and the driver announced on the crackly loudspeaker that the next stop would be San Francisco Transbay Terminal.

It was still going to be a pretty long ride, though—almost another hour to go. Aiden had eaten up all the snacks he'd bought and was really starving. Except the bus had started to get kind of a funky smell, like eggs and perfume together, so at the same time as being hungry, he also felt like he was going to hurl.

And then he must have fallen asleep for a little while, because all of a sudden everybody was lining up in the aisle waiting to get off, so he figured they must have arrived in San Francisco.

He climbed out with everybody else and followed them into the terminal station. It was filled with a lot of wooden benches, but nobody seemed to be waiting on them except homeless people with shopping carts piled up with junk. He scooted really fast past the homeless people and went out the doors to the street. It was all cloudy and gray outside and a whole lot chillier than it ever was in San Carlino in the summertime. He removed his sweater from his backpack and yanked it on over his head, wishing he had brought one of his jackets with him. He sure could use one now.

The bus terminal was located under a steel bridge. He walked from underneath the bridge to a street corner where the sign said "Mission St." That was the same name as a street in San Carlino, except this Mission Street had lots of extremely high buildings, and a bus that went by was painted green instead of red and had a weird wire shooting up from it that was attached to the electric lines overhead. He wondered if it was running on electricity, which for a bus would be kind of cool.

He looked up and down the street as far as he could. The pictures of the Transamerica Building online made it look like you could see it sticking up anywhere you were in San Francisco, since it was the tallest building in the entire city. But all of these buildings looked just as tall, and none of them were shaped like a pyramid.

He didn't have a clue which way to go.

It was starting to feel like a dream. At the suggestion of the police, Caitlin had begun contacting everyone she could think of who had any relation to Aiden. All of it—walking into the kitchen, taking the St. Mattie's telephone tree down from where it was tacked on the corkboard next to the phone, dividing up the numbers with Jessica, who had volunteered to help with the calls—all of it felt utterly unreal. Caitlin seemed to be dialing number after number, somehow speaking to the voices that answered or leaving messages after the beeps, but none of it was real: It was all taking place in an endless nightmare.

She suddenly realized Officer Landers was hovering beside her. "Okay, we've located the bike." His voice came tinnily from some remote land of wakefulness. "It's in the parking lot of the Greyhound bus terminal."

"The bus terminal?" Caitlin's heart jumped with new terror.

Jessica, who had been about to dial a number, put down her phone. "So you think he got on a bus?"

"We're not sure. None of the ticket sellers who were working this morning remember selling a ticket to a boy traveling alone. But he might have been with an adult. We're contacting the drivers now."

"Oh God!" Caitlin pictured child molesters, kidnappers, escaped psychotics. Her blood turned to ice.

"What we need to do now is to search his e-mail," Landers went on. "To see if he's been in contact with anyone. We've got a cyber expert on the way, he should be here in a few minutes. He'll look for things that might have been erased."

Caitlin suppressed a shriek.

"It would be a help if you could go pull up his account," said Officer Perez.

"Yeah, okay."

Still in a dream state, she floated upstairs to Aiden's room. She felt as if she were seeing it for the first time after a long absence. All the artifacts of his past and present enthusiasms: Harry Potter and Transformers and T.rex dinosaurs and Pokemon and his neglected clarinet . . . everything seemed both familiar and strange at the same time.

Or maybe this was what it was like to go out of your mind.

She forced herself to his Mac, turned it on, logged in his password. No new mail. She pulled up his buddy list and raced through it. No new names had been added, she was positive.

Then she gave a start as a message blinked into the instant message box.

dude, there you are! sorry for the silence. your old dad was going through some rough stuff for a while but I'm okay now. I'd really love to talk to you dude. ☺

Caitlin stared rigidly at the screen for several moments, scarcely able to breathe. Was she dreaming or not? It had become impossible to tell.

She drew a deep breath and steadied her fingers enough to type.

"ravi?" she wrote. "is that you?"

Aiden pulled his sweater tighter around himself. There was a lot of cold, damp wind blowing, especially when he got to street corners. He'd been walking for what seemed like a long time, hoping the Transamerica Building would show up; but every time he came to a new street, he just saw more buildings that weren't it.

He started up a hilly street, and the buildings became nowhere near so tall. And then suddenly they had Chinese writing on them instead of English, and there were things that looked like pagodas attached to some of the windows. The Transamerica Building didn't look very Chinese, so he was probably heading in totally the wrong direction.

He wished he could ask somebody directions, but his mom and his teachers were always saying how it was too dangerous to talk to strangers. If you ever got lost, you were supposed to find a policeman. But then he'd have to explain why he was walking around here all by himself, and he'd probably end up getting in a lot of trouble; so he couldn't do that, either.

"Hey, man, that's me!" somebody hollered at him. "Vote for me, man!"

Aiden looked up with a startled jerk of his head. The guy talking to him was like a homeless guy—he had raggedy black hair and a beard like a pirate, and he was wearing a bunch of really bright-colored clothes that didn't match. He was pointing to Aiden's "VOTE FOR PEDRO" cap like he was going to snatch it right off his head. "That's me, Pedro, man, and I appreciate it, man, I appreciate the campaign promise. Vote for me and I'll make it good, man. Free gas-o-leen for everybody and all the prisoners go free."

The guy was a stranger and probably a crazy. If he thought a *Napoleon Dynamite* cap was about him, he *had* to be a crazy.

But Aiden suddenly had a kind of fuzzy memory from back when he was about six years old—back before his dad got sick and had to go away to get cured and was still living with them here in San Francisco. He remembered his dad had a buddy who had a beard and dressed in bright-colored clothes. He was a pretty cool guy who used to take him out on walks sometimes, holding his hand and not walking too fast, because Aiden was just a little kid and otherwise couldn't keep up.

Not that he thought this guy Pedro was the same guy or anything lame like that. It was just that remembering about his dad's old buddy made Aiden feel kind of friendly toward him.

"Do you know where the Transamerica Building is?" he asked.

Pedro looked at him in the weirdest way, like he was going to burst out laughing or something. "For sure, man. For sure I know where the Transam is."

Aiden brightened. "Can you tell me how to get there?"

"Hey, vote for Pedro, man, vote for me, and I will me-myself-and-I escort you personally to the Transam-of-America Pyramid building."

He turned and then made a signal for Aiden to follow him. "Vote for Pedro!" he hollered loudly.

Aiden hesitated, but only for a second. Going with him just seemed like the totally right thing to do.

"You crazy goddamn stupid son of a bitch!" Caitlin screamed at Ravi. He had called as soon as she had identified herself, and for a full five minutes she'd vented her rage at him: How dared he contact Aiden behind her back? Thanks to his insane recklessness, their eleven-year-old son had run away from home and was wandering around by himself . . . or, God, *worse,* he might have been abducted by some pedophile or some deranged criminal . . .

"You're right, I take full responsibility," Ravi admitted. "I slipped off my meds. If anything happens to him, I'll never forgive myself."

"If anything happens to him, I'll kill you, Ravi, I swear to God I will. Where are you, anyway?"

"Back in San Francisco. I've been here since last month."

"Are you with your parents? Why didn't they tell me?"

"They don't know—I haven't spoken to them yet. I was really off my rocker for a while. Remember my old Stanford roommate, Winston Rudd? I'm staying at his house on Russian Hill. He's been helping me get back into shape."

"Jesus," Caitlin muttered.

She glanced up from the phone as Officer Landers came into the room. "One of the bus drivers ID'd your son. He disembarked at Transbay Terminal in San Francisco. The driver had thought he was with a Mexican group that got off in Oakland—said he was surprised to see him getting off at Transbay. Figured he was with one of the other adults and had just wanted to sit on his own, like kids sometimes want to do. We've got the SFPD on alert."

"Ravi, he's in San Francisco!" Caitlin shouted into the phone. "Does he know where you are?"

"No. At least I don't think so. I wasn't being rational. I told him all sorts of crap, I don't remember most of it."

"I'm coming up there! I'm getting on the next plane." She scribbled down his address and gave him her cell phone number and slammed down the phone.

Jessica had followed the policeman into the room. "I heard he was seen getting off the bus."

"Can you take me to the airport?" Caitlin asked. "I need to get on the next plane to San Francisco."

"Yeah, of course," Jessica said. "But wait—I might have a better idea."

They had walked almost forever up this one steep hill, and now they were going down another one. Aiden was so tired, he thought he was going to drop. Pedro didn't talk much to him again but sometimes kind of talked to himself in a way that reminded Aiden of the weird message his dad had sent that time—the one about 1999 and the tree in India that ate bats.

Then Pedro bumped into a guy he knew—another homeless person wearing a hat with a bunch of feathers in it like an Indian, except he had greasy blond hair and a fat stomach and didn't look much like an Indian. The two of them started talking together and laughing a lot in a totally weird way and kind of slapping each other on the arms. Aiden thought maybe Pedro had forgotten all about him, and so now what was he supposed to do?

But then all of a sudden Pedro shouted out, "Transam Pyramid, man, here we come, man!" and started walking away from the blond Indian guy. Aiden figured he was still supposed to follow him and rushed to keep up.

The sidewalks were getting more crowded with people, and the streets had more cars on them, but there was also more fog, so it was harder to see. They passed a Jamba Juice store: Aiden wished he could get a Strawberry Whirl smoothie, but Pedro was walking superfast now and didn't seem like he wanted to stop.

A cable car came rattling by, clanging its bell. Once at Christmas when Aiden had been visiting his grandma and grandpa in Walnut Creek, they'd taken him into the city to see the *Nutcracker*, and afterward they'd all jumped on a cable car. It was awesome! He wondered if Pedro was going to take him on one now, but he just let it go right by, so Aiden guessed not.

And then suddenly Pedro did stop. "Vote for Pedro, man!" he said, and flashed a big V with his fingers.

Aiden realized he'd been so tired and sore and starving that for a long time he'd forgotten to keep looking up. But now he did. And he could see it right through the fog—a pyramid soaring high up into the sky! It looked kind of ghostly—like a huge, tall angel guarding over the city.

And that's where his dad was, he thought excitedly. At the top of the angel, seeing all.

But then suddenly they weren't walking in the direction of the pyramid anymore, they were heading in completely the opposite way. "Why are we going this way?" Aiden said. "I can see the Transamerica Building. It's back over there."

But Pedro just kind of ignored him and headed into this deserted alleyway that went between some other streets. It was filled with cruddy old newspapers and broken glass and big Dumpsters that smelled like garbage. Aiden felt nervous about following Pedro into the alley since nobody else was there. And it was already getting kind of dark because of all the clouds and fog seeping in.

Pedro went over and parked himself between two of the Dumpsters and started fiddling with his pants zipper, which made Aiden really get scared. But then he realized Pedro was just unzipping in order to pee, so he relaxed again. Plus he realized he had to go right now, too. He went to the other side of one of the Dumpsters, took a quick look around to make sure no one was looking, and then took a whiz on the broken glass and garbage on the ground.

He zipped up. Pedro was finished, too, and started walking out of the alleyway, talking about Transam-here-we-come again; and this time he headed back in the right direction.

And then suddenly it looked like the pyramid was almost right on top of them! Aiden rolled his head way back to try to see the pointy top, but there was too much fog.

But he knew it was up there; and he'd never felt so excited in his life.

CHAPTER twenty-five

You're Sure Lucky You're Not Flying Commercial

*L*ally had long ago learned that if you've made a fool of yourself, the best way to head off ridicule was to laugh at yourself about it first.

So she had immediately made a huge joke of her "falling off her peep-toe platforms in Berlin" incident. No sooner had her ankle been set and she was cozily established in a private and sleekly modern hospital room than she was on the phone to friends around the world, describing her klutzy misadventure with the highest humor: *You'd have laughed yourself silly, darling, if you'd seen me take the dive! I should have been awarded at least a silver.*

And ten days later, back home in Colina Linda, she had brilliantly extended the joke by making her broken ankle the grounds for a fund-raiser: Those several dozen of her closest acquaintances who could pony up ten grand a couple were invited for champagne, hors d'oeuvres, and the privilege of signing Lally's cast—proceeds to benefit Doctors Without Borders (or, as Lally pronounced it, Médecins Sans Frontières).

Lally now lay semireclined on a neoclassical day bed that had been shifted from one of the six guest bedrooms into the orangery, where the party was taking place. In a salute to the scene of her mishap, the theme was Weimar Republic Berlin: remastered recordings of Lotte Lenya belting Kurt Weill, vintage 2000 Krug champagne, and the Otto Dix painting moved from the library to preside over the event. Lally wore a purple-and-silver kimono-style robe, very twenties, that stopped just short of (and was color-coordinated with) her pink fiberglass cast. A lumpy papier-mâché tray fashioned by Noah Clemente at age eight sat on an ottoman beside the day bed, holding a selection of colored felt-tip pens; and for the past hour, people had been scribbling their names and anything else that moved them on the cast.

Lally was in high spirits. Things had turned out so satisfactorily—at least for the short run. Sienna had decamped to New York with her glamorous new fling. Lally had finally spoken to her, naturally never breathing a word about her daughter's designs on David. As a peace offering, she'd sent Sienna a little running-around money (a check for a hundred and fifty grand); and in return, Sienna had granted her a visit with Chiara as soon as Lally was rid of her cast. Lally had already booked a suite at the Palace Hotel in Rome for the middle two weeks of September.

Of course, she knew Sienna would grow bored with Evan, just as she'd grown bored with her Polish film director and ersatz Italian count and Greek financier and every other guy she'd ever hooked up with. And when she did give Evan Kern his walking papers, she might well revert to her plan to go after David again.

But if she did, this time Lally would be prepared.

Lally toasted herself with a frothy sip of Krug.

She had another reason to rejoice: The hot flashes and most of the other ghastly symptoms of menopause were gone. One of the doctors who'd attended her in Berlin (a hunky, golden-haired osteopath who had reminded her of her second husband, Helmut, though presumably the doc wasn't a psychotic wife-beating megalomaniac) had convinced her she should try taking hormones to relieve the symptoms. So now she was, and it was making a *universe* of difference. She felt almost like her normal old springy self.

Kiki and Stu Morrison had just trooped over to sign her ankle. They picked out green and fuchsia pens and scrawled their signatures with lots of ostentatious loops and swirls. Kiki remarked that she would never even *attempt* to wear those skyscraper platforms, and Lally said, "That's so wise of you, darling! After I get out of this beastly cast, I'm sticking to last year's Jimmy Choos." The Morrisons were supplanted by Doug Steenken, who planted a slobbery kiss on the corner of her lips and scribbled something, probably obscene, on the heel of her cast where she couldn't see it. He was followed by the Miottas, a shy, elderly couple, who diffidently printed their names and then scurried back into the camouflage of the crowd.

Then, over the rim of her champagne flute, Lally spied Jessica DiSantini bearing down on her. This was a surprise—she didn't recall seeing Jessica on the guest list. She'd have thought this event was a bit too rich for Jessica's blood these days. And irksomely, Jessica didn't seem quite dressed for the event—a sloppy T-shirt and clam diggers and scuffed turquoise-colored Dr. Scholl's on her feet. Lally wondered if it was Tommy's influence—that I-don't-give-a-crap-about-conventions pose. Fine if you were a brooding world-prominent composer; a little iffy for a forty-something divorcée.

"Really, darling," she scolded Jessica, "you might have put a little more thought into your attire. We're informal tonight, but not quite *that* informal."

Jessica was acutely aware that she was still in her grungy carpool-mom outfit: Everybody in the room was gawking at her. Self-consciously, she folded her arms across her chest. "I'm not here for your party, Lally. I'm here because I couldn't get you on your goddamn phone. Where's David?"

"He's over in the office wing on an international conference call. He should be out very soon. Why?"

"I need you to ask him for a favor."

Lally stiffened. She had been a billionaire's wife for only several months, but that was decidedly long enough to become hardened to people clamoring for favors. "What kind of favor?"

"I need to borrow his plane to get somebody up to San Francisco right away."

Lally gave a dry laugh. "Do you know how much it costs to run that jet even for short hops?"

"Oh please," Jessica scoffed. "It's about ten seconds' worth of David's income. And I happen to know the corporation keeps a flight crew standing by, so they're already being paid."

"But really, Jessica, I can't go lending the plane to any of our acquaintance that ask for it."

"No, but you owe me, Lally. You said so yourself."

"Yes, and I'd be glad to take you to a marvelous lunch."

Jessica smiled thinly. "You're so right, Lally, I shouldn't be asking you for this. I should go directly to David. I haven't spoken to him in so long, and there's so much we could catch up on. I could fill him in on some of the conversations you and I have been having lately."

"You wouldn't!" Lally gasped. "That would be betraying attorney-client privilege."

"You're not my client. And if you don't think I'd tell him anything, why don't you just try me?"

Lally's face darkened and her body tensed. For a moment, Jessica was afraid she was going to spring up and go into one of her Jackie Chan routines. Then she realized that with Lally's foot in a cast, her martial arts abilities would be somewhat compromised.

Lally seemed to realize it, too, and settled back down. "Okay," she conceded. "I'll ask David. But at least tell me what you need the plane for."

"Caitlin Latch's son has run away from home. We think he got on a bus and made it to San Francisco. He's only twelve."

"My God!" Lally exclaimed. "Why didn't you say so to begin with?"

Caitlin had been waiting in Jessica's car at the portico of the Clemente mansion for what seemed like ages. Jessica had gotten through the copious security by insisting to the guards that she was supposed to be on the guest list. Finally, the guards had called Lally's assistant—Perla, was that her name?—who was acquainted with Jessica and seemed to conclude that she should be allowed to pass. But maybe now they were having her arrested for crashing the party.

To her relief, Jessica finally reappeared and got back into the car. "It's all set," she said, starting up the engine. "We can go directly to the airfield."

"Really? I can go on their plane?"

"Yep. You know how Lally loves to play the hero. Once she found out that it was to rescue a lost kid, she was on it like a shot. If it wasn't for her broken ankle, she'd probably be coming with you. And bringing along a crew of photographers."

"Oh God! That would be the last thing I could deal with right now."

"Yeah, I can imagine. But anyway, you should be in San Francisco in not much more than an hour from now." Jessica directed the car back down the long crushed-stone drive.

It was twenty minutes to the private airfield tucked between the Coast Highway and the ocean just south of Colina Linda. Caitlin had been here only once before, but she felt a strong jolt of recognition as they pulled up to the gray Quonset hut terminal.

"I better get back to my kids," Jessica told her. "I left Rowan in charge, and she's usually fine, but it's getting a little late. Are you going to be okay?"

Caitlin gave a shaky nod. "Yeah, I think so. Thanks so much for everything."

They hugged each other tightly. Then Caitlin slid out of the car and headed into the Quonset hut.

A perky young woman in a marine blue uniform greeted her: "Good evening, Ms. Latch. The pilot is just filing his flight plan—as soon as he's done, you're good to go."

Through the plate glass wall at the other end of the room, Caitlin could see the white Gulfstream idling on the runway. The terminal door behind her suddenly opened and David Clemente came striding in.

"Everything's all set," he said to her crisply. He was wearing those square-framed black glasses she remembered so vividly, the ones that made him look sort of like Elvis Costello. "Your flight time will be approximately forty-eight minutes. I've arranged for a car to meet you and take you wherever you need to go in town. I also have people coordinating with the Bay Area police, and we'll keep you closely informed."

"Thank you," she breathed. "I can't tell you how much—"

He cut her off gruffly. "You don't have to. I can only imagine what you're going through. Anything more I can do, anything at all, just have the flight crew call."

They stood silently a second. She wondered if he would say anything about their brief affair, how he had once sent this plane to pick her up in Arizona so she could attend a dinner party with him in Colina Linda. . . .

"You're good for takeoff, Ms. Latch," the perky young woman announced to her.

David gave her arm an avuncular squeeze. "Don't worry. We'll find him."

She nodded tensely, then walked out onto the tarmac and climbed the little stairway into the jet.

Another jolt of recognition. The chocolate-and-mint colors of the interior. The luxurious leather seats that molded like soft wax to your body. The pilot and copilot who introduced themselves by their first names, and the boyish-looking steward who peppered you with offers of drinks, sandwiches, cookies the second you sat down.

The way the jet shot down the runway and leapt almost straight up in the air was less like a plane, it seemed to Caitlin, than like Superman.

"You're sure lucky you're not flying commercial tonight," the steward said, pressing a crystal tumbler into her hand. "The fog has them stacked up like poker chips at SFO—you wouldn't be landing until way after midnight."

She leaned back in the leather seat and took a sip of the cognac she hoped would steady her nerves. *All this could have been yours.* . . . The thought stabbed sharply into her mind.

But she didn't want all this. Or any of it. She just wanted Aiden back safe and sound.

Pedro wanted the "VOTE FOR PEDRO" hat. Aiden didn't really want to give it up, because it was so cold and foggy and the wind was so chilly, and at least the cap kept his head warm. But Pedro looked like he might start yelling or something, so Aiden gave it to him. Pedro stuck it on his head and grinned and shot him another big V sign. Then he turned and started to shuffle off across the street.

"Bye, Pedro!" Aiden called. "Thanks for showing me the way!"

But Pedro didn't turn around again.

Aiden began to search for the door to go inside the building. He tried one, but it was locked up and dark. He walked around a corner of the building to a big revolving door and pushed at it, but it was also locked, and he couldn't see anything that looked like a doorbell or a buzzer to ring. He kept on walking around the building. A big gust of cold wind came howling through, so hard that it almost blew him right over.

He kept walking, past some large, round-shaped things that made the wind cut into him even sharper. He came to another revolving door and inside he could see a guy in a uniform jacket sitting at a desk and talking on a phone.

Aiden immediately cheered up. He shoved at the door, but it was locked.

The guy looked up. "It's closed," he shouted. "The building's closed."

What about the people who lived there? Aiden knocked on the glass and pushed at it, but the guy went back to talking on the phone and wouldn't look up again.

Aiden started walking back toward the first revolving door, figuring he'd try it again, but he was so freezing and tired, he just sat down on a bench that was there and wrapped his arms around himself to try to stop shivering. He wished he could go home. It was really getting dark now, and the fog made everything spooky and pretty weird. He felt like he was going to start to cry.

Aidey the Lady.

He swiped the tears away with the sleeve of his sweater and made himself stop. No way he was going to cry.

Then he saw two guys coming from around the corner of the building. "Hey, there's a kid," one of them said. "Is that him?"

The other guy started running right toward him. Aiden jumped to his feet, feeling like maybe he should run away.

But then he heard a voice that even after so long a time was still totally familiar to him.

"It's okay, dude," his dad was saying. "You're okay now. I've got you. I'm here."

CHAPTER twenty-six

That Dreamlike Feeling Again

Caitlin had given a start when she heard her cell phone ring in the middle of the flight; and when she'd seen that it was Ravi's number, her stomach had clenched with fear. But then she'd let out a scream of joy, and the steward was congratulating her, and the copilot had come back and nearly smothered her in a big bear hug.

After that it was a blur: the details that Ravi related over the phone about how he'd finally remembered telling Aiden that he lived at the Transamerica Building, and how he and Winston had gone to look there and found him sitting on a bench, nearly blue with cold and crying, and something about how a man named Pedro had befriended him . . .

And then the jet was touching down, and a town car was rushing her into the city, and it was gliding up hilly Jones Street while she searched for the right house number; and she almost stumbled as she scrambled up the steps of an enormous Victorian house.

But then suddenly she had Aiden in her arms, and she was crying and laughing and squeezing him so tightly that he had to gasp for air. She was hearing the entire story of his journey, and though it made her hair stand on end, she was also secretly proud. She *knew* he was smart!

"I guess you must be really mad at me," he said.

"Oh no, sweetie, I'm mad at *me*. I haven't been paying much attention to you, have I? But I'm just so glad you're okay. So really, really glad." She hugged him again, feeling as though she would never let him go.

Eventually, she became aware of her surroundings—a large, decorator-furnished living room with tall ceilings and a graceful bay window. Ravi was perched on the window seat. He was thinner than last time she had seen him, but he looked far calmer and more focused: He was not wearing a saffron robe but was dressed in a regular slouchy sweater and Levi's. Nor was his head shaved now: His hair had grown back thick and dark and flopping over the tips of his ears, the way he'd worn it when they'd first met. She'd almost forgotten how extremely handsome he was.

He now looked like the adorable, sweet-natured, normal guy she had fallen head over heels with.

And so much like Aiden, it gave her the shivers.

There were several policemen also milling around the room; they seemed to be operating on the suspicion that Ravi had been responsible for snatching Aiden. After some time extensively questioning all three of them, they were finally convinced otherwise, and they left with a stamping of feet and crackling of walkie-talkies.

"I can't tell you how incredibly sorry I am," Ravi said to Caitlin. "I really blame myself for everything."

"Yeah, I blame you, too," she said. "I just thank God you found him."

"Mom, can I stay here with Dad for a little while?" Aiden asked excitedly. "He can show me where we used to live, and we can go see Grandma and Grandpa and do a lot of cool stuff. So please, can I?"

"I told him it was up to you," Ravi said.

Not on your life! Caitlin was about to say. She had almost died of fear due to his insane, irresponsible, flipped-out behavior. . . .

But then she looked at Aiden. He was wearing one of Ravi's Stanford sweatshirts, and he was beaming and bouncing with excitement on the balls of his feet. He was happy, she realized—maybe happier than she'd ever seen him.

"Hey, Aidey, why don't you go in and see how Winston's doing in the kitchen," Ravi said.

"He's making five-alarm chili!" Aiden piped excitedly. "And cornbread, and he's got like a zillion kinds of Ben and Jerry's to pick from for dessert."

"That sounds great, sweetheart," Caitlin said.

He darted out of the room.

Ravi came up to her, his hands sheepishly jammed in the pockets of his jeans. "Okay, here's the deal. I'm back on all medications. I'm seeing a shrink twice a week, and I've got résumés out to a number of brokerage houses. Win says I can stay here as long as I need to. He owns this entire house. Five bedrooms, four baths. Aiden can have his own room. You, too, if you want to stay for a few days."

Caitlin was stirred by a strong emotion: Could it be true that Ravi was really better? She still felt like throttling him; she still didn't really trust him and maybe never entirely would. Except she had a crazy urge to float over to him and wrap herself in his arms and maybe get back that heavenly feeling that she was returning home.

The memories she'd had of him before his crack-up—they were coming back in floods. Maybe she had never stopped being in love with him, she thought with a jolt—she'd only stopped letting herself admit it.

"So what do you say?" Ravi pursued. "Can Aiden stay for a while? He's already bonded with Winston. They're crazy about each other."

"Looks like Winston's gotten rich." Caitlin had only a dim memory of Winston Rudd from their wedding—a techno-geek who'd been living in Austin, Texas, back then. He was shy—had hardly spoken a word to anyone at the reception and then vanished from their lives immediately afterward.

"Loaded. He jumped from Internet programming to cable broadcasting. Started a network of home shopping shows on local channels, and he's been cleaning up. Come on in and say hello. He's rustling up some dinner for us—he loves to cook."

Ravi led her down a hallway hung with black-and-white photographs of moonlit western plains. They entered a large kitchen that was a pleasing mixture of old-fashioned white cabinetry and high-tech stainless steel appliances.

A small chubby man with wiry red hair was pulling a fragrant pan out of a gleaming Viking range. He straightened up and grinned shyly at Caitlin. "Hello there," he said. "I hope you like cornbread."

She was struck with that dreamlike feeling again. The last five hours had been so surreal: the shock of Aiden missing from the campsite; the horror of cops talking about strangers and buses; the flight in a billionaire's Gulfstream.

And now suddenly, miraculously, finding herself in a swanky Russian Hill Victorian, with her ex-husband whom she hadn't seen in over five years and a rich, wiry-haired guy asking her about cornbread.

For equilibrium, she recited her silent mantra: *I'm glad I'm here, I'm glad.* Her lips turned up and set in the I'm-glad-to-be-here smile, and she assumed a voice to match, assured, sincere, slightly amused.

"I adore cornbread," she said. "It's actually one of my favorite things in the world."

Winston's eyes, which were slightly protuberant, seemed to pop out a little further. "Whoa, that's perfect. I mean, your look and your voice, awesome. Ravi said you were into jewelry, like, you sold it on the Internet, right? So have you ever been on camera?"

"Actually, some," she said. "I majored in communications in college."

"Whoa," Winston said, setting the hot pan down on the stove. "That's excellent."

Janey's liposuction and tummy tuck were scheduled for six thirty a.m., and she dutifully checked herself into Santa Monica General at a bleary-eyed five fifteen. She hadn't told a soul she was doing this procedure. She planned to simply present herself back in circulation with her svelte new waist and hipline and let people draw their own conclusions—that she'd discovered a fabulous new trainer or stumbled on a miraculous new diet or whatever. Lally would probably guess, she being the all-time prom queen of cosmetic procedures.

But so what? Janey hardly cared what Lally Chandler Clemente thought of her anymore.

Janey had spent the night at the Briarcliff, a boutique hotel off Montana Avenue that specialized in cosmetic surgery recovery and to which she would be returning after her procedure for another three nights. She hadn't been able to sleep much. She'd thumbed through a stack of style magazines, *Vogue, Elle, Harper's Bazaar,* earmarking all the delectable stovepipe jeans and slinky tube skirts she'd finally be able to wear, but it had failed to soothe her. Finally, sometime after midnight, she had popped one of the Tranxene tabs she had filched from Taller. Hadn't knocked her out, though. If anything, she had felt even more jazzed up. After a couple of hours more, she'd popped another one but still hadn't managed more than a fitful hour or so of sleep.

And now at the hospital, she still felt jumpy and tense—certainly much more than she recalled feeling before getting her breast augmentation. And this wasn't even as drastic a procedure.

The admitting nurse asked if she'd had anything to eat or drink after midnight, and Janey fibbed just a little—told her one Tranxene at around one, one-thirty a.m. It didn't seem like a big deal to the nurse, so Janey figured having actually taken two over the past six hours couldn't be much of a problem either.

Then she was being prepped and transferred to the gurney and wheeled into the futuristic white glare of the operating room. And here was Bru Goodmayer's grinning Doogie Howser face swimming in huge close-up right over her.

"Do you have any idea how ravishing you are going to look?" he told her. "Jessica Alba, watch out!"

The anesthesiologist was hovering close, about to insert the needle into the back of her hand.

"Say good night, Gracie," Bru said.

"Good night, Gracie," Janey replied.

CHAPTER twenty-seven

That Little Cadre of Four Ex-Wives

All of San Carlino was stunned by the news that Janey Kern Martinez had succumbed to cardiac arrest on the table while undergoing minor liposuction and a routine tummy tuck.

Even more stunning was the rumor rapidly following the news that the autopsy had revealed a large quantity of Viagra in her system, which may or may not have been the cause of the heart failure. But this was quickly discounted. Everyone knew that Janey had a bit of a prescription drug problem, but it was in the nature of sedatives, sleeping aids, mother's little helpers. If you'd heard she'd been pumped to the gills with Nembutal or Librium or that Xanax had been running riot in her blood—well, that would have made you nod and go "Mm-hmm," and mutter "Yes, poor dear Jane, her addiction finally did her in."

But Viagra? Made no sense at all. The rumor mill must have got it wrong.

But everyone did agree that the requiem high mass at Our Lady of

Lourdes (for once no one snidely referred to it as Our Lady of the Lexus) was an exquisitely perfect send-off. The bishop presided, assisted by the monsignor and two parish priests, all wearing vestments of deepest purple, such a striking contrast to the profusion of pure white roses that covered the altar. Selections from Bach and Purcell and "As the Hart Longs" by Felix Mendelssohn performed by a full choir and orchestra, and *the* most beautiful readings from Psalms and Corinthians and (as a special favor during the homily) Deepak Chopra, who had been Janey's favorite author.

By the end of the service, there wasn't a dry eye in the congregation.

Even though she'd arrived early, Lally discovered that the first ten pews were already filled with the enormous extended families of Kerns and Martinezes, so she slipped into an aisle spot in the eleventh. She was wearing a sugar plum–colored Balenciaga suit, which was, believe it or not, the most somber item in her summer wardrobe. She'd briefly considered a quick purchase of something black, but nobody was showing it this season; and frankly, black had never been her color—it brought out something sickly greenish in her skin—and she felt she owed it to Janey to look her absolute best. And obviously the old rules didn't apply anymore: Gazing around the church, she saw scarcely a soul under the age of seventy wearing any color gloomier than navy blue.

Lally was not quite prepared for the sight of Janey's casket on display right below the altar. Closed, thank heavens—nevertheless, that was Janey's dead body, right in there! Too gruesome and strange even to contemplate.

It was a gorgeous casket, though, all rich walnut and polished brass and snowed under with great drifts of white roses and calla lilies. Back in Lally's early acting days, her most successful audition scene had been from *Stage Door*, Katharine Hepburn's speech about the calla lilies: "Such a strange flower—suitable to any occasion . . ." The rest of it had slipped Lally's mind, something about carrying them at a wedding and now bringing them for something that had died. . . .

Janey was dead! Too strange! For a time last year, Janey had been her protégée: Lally had guided her from frumpy duckling to society chic. It had been an oddly satisfying endeavor, like becoming a sculptor, Pygmalion or whoever, effecting the transformation.

But then Janey had gone too far. True, it was Lally who had suggested she augment her flat-to-the-point-of-concave chest and set her up with Bru Goodmayer, who had done Lally's own nips and tucks. But Janey, all on her own, had opted for those humongous double D hooters. Lally had been appalled! Seeing her creation disfigured like that . . . well, it was worse than having it destroyed.

And when Lally had reacted to such monstrosities with a little burst of laughter—a restrained reaction, really, considering—well, Janey had turned on her viciously. Had played that nasty trick on Lally that had almost prevented her from becoming Mrs. David Clemente.

Janey might be dead and gone, but Lally suddenly had an urge to slap her silly.

She gave a start as someone tapped her on the shoulder. She wiped the snarl off her face, replaced it with an expression of beautifully composed sorrow, and swiveled to find Jessica DiSantini in the pew directly behind her.

"It's astonishing, isn't it?" Jessica whispered. "Who could imagine?"

"I'm still in shock. I mean, for a while, Janey and I were *like that*." Lally crossed her index and middle finger. "I can't believe she's suddenly just blinked out of existence."

Jessica nodded. She'd never been *like that* with Janey Martinez, but they had socialized regularly: They had donated to each other's

causes and invited each other to their holiday drinks parties and occasionally shot a few holes together at the golf club, even though
Janey had been a par golfer and Jessica's handicap sucked. Of course,
Janey'd had that infuriating habit of snickering whenever Jessica
flubbed a putt. And she'd never coughed up half as much to Jessica's
causes as Jessica had to hers.

And it had been Janey who had bounced Tommy from the music
festival, causing him to leave town instead of staying for the summer,
where maybe, just maybe, he and Jessica might have worked things
out. . . .

She let out a low growl of fury, remembering how she felt she
could have just murdered Janey. She probably should be sorry for the
thought now that Janey actually was deceased.

Eventually she probably would be. But not quite yet.

Lally glanced back at her. "Poor Jane!" Jessica said, hoping Lally
would think her growl had been a sob caught in her throat. She fished
out a packet of Kleenex and slit it open.

"Hand me a few of those, would you?" Lally said. "Silly of me not
to have brought any."

Jessica gave her the packet. "Keep it, I've got more. Where's
David?"

"World malnutrition conference in Singapore. He would have
flown back to attend this, but the most crucial day of it was today, so
I told him not to. I hear Tom's doing the music on the new Scorsese?
Maybe he'll win another Oscar!"

"Maybe he will," Jessica said. She hadn't spoken to him since her
dramatic exit from his hotel room, but she hadn't told anyone, not
even Rowan and Alex, that they were split. Suddenly she actually did
feel like sobbing. Tears brimmed in her eyes, and she blotted them
with a tissue.

She was grateful for the distraction of Caitlin Latch sliding into
the pew beside her. They hugged, and Lally mouthed an air kiss.

"This is staggering, isn't it?" Caitlin said.

The other two nodded solemnly.

"Do either of you believe the Viagra thing?" Caitlin pursued.

"Not in the least," Lally declared. "Janey was into pills, that was no secret, but Viagra makes no sense at all."

"Maybe a pharmacist got it wrong," Jessica suggested. "You wouldn't believe how many lawsuits are filed over pharmacy error."

"Or maybe somebody slipped it to her, like as a joke," Caitlin put in.

"Some joke," Lally said. "Who would do such a thing?"

Only about nine thousand people, Caitlin thought acidly.

She had to admit that when she'd heard the news that Janey Martinez had bitten the dust, her first thought was: It served her right. Janey could no longer go around screwing up other people's lives anymore. Caitlin flashed on her little revenge fantasy of being able to tell Janey to drop dead. How amazing that Janey had been so obliging as to actually go ahead and do it!

Don't be so hard-hearted, Caitlin chastised herself. Things had been working out so remarkably well—you could almost say Janey had done her a favor by stabbing her in the back over the Serenity Waters job. Caitlin had not only recovered, but she had bounced back onto one of those brilliant peaks she had often dreamed about; and now that Janey was no longer around to try to push her off of it, Caitlin could afford to feel sorry for her.

At least just a tiny bit sorry.

"Hey, I saw you on TV on Saturday!" Jessica whispered to her. "You looked terrific!"

"Oh no, I was a horror! They keep making my hair too puffy, like it's Grand Ole Opry or something."

"No, I thought you looked gorgeous. You've become a real TV star!"

Lally, overhearing this, smiled stiffly. Caitlin Latch a television star? Really, did being hostess of a local cable channel home shopping show qualify as a *star*? Lally had been a Bond girl and had co-starred in four other feature films (B movies, but features nevertheless) and had had guest shots in many of the hottest shows of the eighties and early nineties (*Falcon Crest! The A-Team! Miami Vice!*); so it was disconcerting, to say the least, to hear Caitlin being touted as the star.

But then Lally reminded herself that whatever acting aspirations she'd once had were now well eclipsed by her present role—international philanthropist and billionaire's wife. Wouldn't it be petty of her not to applaud the minor successes of others?

"I'm sure you're terrific, darling," she whispered to Caitlin. "I haven't seen the show yet, but I'll be sure to tune in."

Caitlin's response was stifled by an elaborate Baroque cascade from the grand organ. The congregation rose to its feet as the procession of celebrants began moving up the aisle.

Lally swiveled again to Jessica and Caitlin. "I wonder what outfit they buried her in?" she hissed. "I hope it wasn't the lilac Chanel. It was her favorite, I know, but it really made her look so bottom-heavy—"

She stopped, remembering that bottom-heavy was exactly the defect that Janey, fatally, had tried to rectify. A tear trickled down Lally's cheek, tracing a minute contrail through her custom-blended foundation.

Taller Kern, ensconced in the midst of the Kern-Martinez family thicket several rows in front, caught a glimpse of Lally dabbing her eyes. So Lally was all broken up? She and Jane had had quite a huge falling-out last year, so perhaps it was more guilt than sorrow she was feeling.

And in fact Taller was burdened by a fair amount of guilt himself. It was a sensation that he was not enormously familiar with. But he'd been the one to switch the Tranxene with Viagra—so in a sense, *he* was the one who had killed poor dear old Janey. One could say it was all his fault!

The liturgical procession marched slowly by, circumnavigating the flower-strewn casket as it made its way to the altar. Of course, Taller reasoned to himself, he'd had no way of knowing she'd load up on the drugs before undergoing surgery.

What kind of crazy fool takes *any* kind of drug before going under anesthesia? Certainly common sense should dictate otherwise. Not that Jane had ever been the quintessence of any kind of sense . . . but really, she should have known better.

Plus, he reasoned further, it wasn't even certain that the Viagra had caused her heart failure. More likely, she'd had some sort of underlying condition to begin with—at least that was the prevailing theory among his doctor pals at Mission Mercy.

The swelling of the ornate music seemed to relieve him of his guilt like a priest's absolution. It really wasn't his fault, he told himself: It had just been an unfortunate accident. Terribly sad and tragic, of course, but surely beyond anyone's control.

As the last of the procession passed him by, he glanced again at Lally and noticed that Jessica DiSantini and Caitlin Latch were right behind her. That little cadre of four ex-wives in whose romantic lives he had taken an interest—Lally and Jessica and Caitlin and Janey . . .

The thought wafted through his mind that now there were only three.

Caitlin did not join the others in going on to the graveside—the sycamore-shaded Kern family plot in the picturesque Colina Linda cemetery—since she had to get to the set location of the Constant Shoppers Network, for the taping of her show, *Golden Moments.*

Three times a week, she made the hour-and-a-half trip southeast to Santa Clarita, where the bare-bones warehouse studio was located. She knew that Winston had hired her mostly as a favor to Ravi, and her first week of hosting the show, she'd been dreadful: her smile too frozen, her body language awkward, her chatter totally inane. She'd expected to be sacked at any moment.

But then, miraculously, in the middle of her second week, while she was fielding a call-in from a dental receptionist who was considering the purchase of an eighteen-karat-gold-mesh necklace with hand-blown Murano glass beading (only three left in stock!), something clicked. Almost literally, like the click you hear when a chiropractor does one of those twisting-back-in-place things with your neck. One minute Caitlin was tense and hesitating, and the next minute she was having fun.

That's exactly what it had become—fun! Fun to be fussed over in makeup and hair. Fun to preside on a set with all the lights and cameras trained on *you*. Fun to have the little mike hidden in your clothes, and to shoot the breeze with the models, and to exchange wisecracks with the director, and even to deflect the smutty innuendos of her somewhat spooky co-host, Gordon Blaine.

It didn't pay big bucks: She wasn't about to trade in her Volvo for a Rolls or anything. But it was enough—more than enough—to take away the grinding worry of paying her everyday bills. The producer, Marilyn Copek, was already talking about expanding the show to a fourth afternoon and hinting that she might slot Caitlin in as substitute host for the Saturday morning *Accent on Accessories!*

And who knew?—it could be her foot in the door to bigger things in broadcasting.

Now, as she cruised down the Coast Highway, the dazzle of the Pacific on her right reminding her of a simulated sapphire bracelet that had sold briskly the day before, she thought of Aiden: the change that had come over him since he'd been with Ravi. The kid who had whined and dragged his butt and never seemed to be happy about anything ever now chatted nonstop about all the things he did with his dad and all the stuff they were going to do. Particularly now that Ravi was going to come stay with them.

She was still a little uneasy about this last development. It was Ravi who'd suggested it. He didn't want to be separated from Aiden anymore. Had decided he'd look for a brokerage job in San Carlino or a town within commuting distance—he'd already had a few substantial leads.

"But one slip off your meds and you die," she'd warned him.

He was arriving Sunday. How strange it was going to be to have him back. Sleeping on the couch, of course—she'd made that crystal clear. But there would be his familiar presence: That floppy dark hair and those beautiful caramel-colored eyes . . . His teasing Ravi laugh and dazzling Ravi smile . . . All the things she used to love about him and probably still did . . . Okay, yeah, it made her nervous, but she couldn't deny she was excited by it as well.

They'd be sort of a family again! How amazing was that?

She slipped on a pair of sunglasses to diminish the glitter of the sea and sang along to "Like a Virgin" on the rock classics station, bouncing a little in her seat.

Acknowledgments

To all suspects, usual and unusual: Charlotte Herscher, Signe Pike, Allison Dickens, Barbara Lowenstein, Susan Wald, Cameron Ramos, R. J. Fein. All my thanks.

READ ON FOR A SNEAK PREVIEW OF
LINDSAY GRAVES'S NEXT EX-WIVES NOVEL,

To
KILL
a Husband

Coming Soon!

PUBLISHED BY BALLANTINE BOOKS

The ghastly New Girls had all been invited to the Frost and Fire Ball!

Lally Chandler Clemente received the news while having her eyelashes dyed and extended at the luxurious Colina Linda salon called La Rocha, and it caused a jolt of alarm that ran down to the soles of her Dior suede boots. A clique of pushy nobodies were crashing the most exclusive gates of San Carlino society!

The Frost and Fire Ball was the most important event of the winter social season in San Carlino, a city that, by reason of being located in Southern California, knew very little of frost but had a regrettably close familiarity with fire. It was a lavish dinner dance to benefit

Huntington's disease, held every alternate year on the evening of Valentine's Day under an Arabian tent in the Botanical Gardens. Tradition demanded that women wear only gowns of flame red or frost white and adorn themselves with fire and ice—the most spectacular of those diamond and ruby necklaces, bracelets, and even tiaras that were kept most of the year locked away in bank vaults and safes.

But not just anyone who could afford the thousand bucks for a ticket could attend. Absolutely not! You had to receive one of the exquisite pale green embossed envelopes containing not only an invitation to purchase tickets, but also specifying how many you were permitted to buy. For this reason, the ball had become an indicator of Who Was In and Who Was Out in San Carlino circles, particularly among the residents of the city's exclusive neighboring village, Colina Linda.

Lally Chandler Clemente, who was the wife of the billionaire David Clemente, never had any doubts that she'd be invited: even before becoming Mrs. Clemente, she'd been the undisputed Queen Bee of local society, her name attached to every benefit committee that counted—including that of the Frost and Fire Ball. And indeed, the envelope had arrived punctually that morning; and, just as promptly, Lally's social secretary, Perla, had whipped off a check to purchase an entire table of ten. Lally's only dilemma was deciding which of her lucky acquaintance she would bestow her extra tickets on.

Since marrying David, Lally had become executive director of the Clemente philanthropic foundation and subsequently spent much of her time traveling on its behalf. Meeting a Minister of Health here, conferring with disaster-relief people there, inspecting preschools and midwifery projects and AIDS facilities everywhere.

Thrilling, yes. But to be perfectly honest, on the world stage, Lally had found herself to be . . . well, not exactly insignificant, but not at the pinnacle, either. She had to face it: she'd had a little flurry of fame as an actress back in the eighties (she'd been a Bond girl, opposite Roger Moore in *A Good Day to Die*), but it didn't count for squat next to Angelina Jolie.

Wouldn't it be better to be Queen Bee of San Carlino society than a bit player internationally?

Lately, though, she'd had the unsettling suspicion that even here on the San Carlino stage, her position was slipping. A dazzling appearance at the Frost and Fire Ball would be a giant step to reestablishing it.

And now, as Lally reclined on one of La Rocha's padded raspberry-colored loungers waiting for her eyelashes to set, she placed her first call: to her closest friend and confidant Taller Kern. Taller was a member of one of the oldest and most socially-prominent families in San Carlino—the Kerns had been here, God!, practically before the dinosaurs, and were so exclusive they tended to marry only their second cousins.

She reached him at the little rare-books shop, Ex Libris, that he dabbled in as a cachet occupation.

"I'm so sorry, Lally, but I'm already going," he said. That purry voice he affected when he was delivering unpleasant news. "I've agreed to escort Gilly Fogler. Her husband is having heart surgery next week, so he's not going to be up and boogying for some time to come."

"Who the hell invited Gilly Fogler?" Lally snapped.

"Her whole gang has been invited. The benefit committee thought the New Girls would jazz things up a bit. You've got to admit, our old crowd has gotten a little stodgy. We *could* use some jazzing up."

The New Girls had all been invited! If Lally hadn't already been horizontal, she would have keeled over.

"Why wasn't I consulted? I'm on the committee."

"Just a guess, but maybe because you weren't in town? If you're going to be globe-hopping instead of showing up at benefit meetings, you've got to expect to be out of the loop."

"Speaking of our old crowd," Taller purred on, "I'm giving a little lunch at the golf club for the Neilings on Friday. Can you make it? I haven't seen you in ages."

"Sorry, I can't, I'll be interviewing butlers all day Friday. We've been in chaos since Eduardo left us for the Costners. Another time, darling."

She hung up with agitation. This set of New Girls had been creeping into town like a fungus. They all seemed to be exactly thirty-eight years old, and they all had scads of money: some were divorced, with huge alimony checks; others got their income came from daddy. The rest were *married* to daddy—the fourth or fifth wives of rich octogenarians or barely-breathing film stars whose careers had peaked back in the fifties. The New Girls were noisy and crass; they dressed like Hollywood Boulevard hookers and wore their hair in post-punk styles, dyed platinum blond tresses with roots or crimson spikes. And now here was Taller Kern, scion of old society, escorting one of these deplorable creatures to the Frost and Fire Ball!

It was like a Jedi knight going over to the Dark Side!

And given that kind of betrayal, Lally was damned if she would grace his grubby little lunch with the honor of her presence.

Chiba the esthetician padded back in, removed the compress and began applying false lashes, one by one, to fill out the sable-dyed ones. The process took another thirty minutes, during which Lally continued to squirm with agitation. When it was finally completed, she bolted off the lounger and marched quickly into the changing room, shrugging off the unisex purple kimono that La Rocha issued to its patrons and efficiently getting back into her Chanel dress. It was a knee-skimming, almost severe black knit she'd purchased last October on the Avenue Montaigne during a whirlwind week in Paris.

She surveyed herself in the mirror. Maybe a little pulling around the hips, but knits always clung, she rationalized. She sucked in her stomach, which made things better, and headed out to the salon's coffee room.

The coffee room at La Rocha was the center of buzz in Colina

Linda: it was where gossip was exchanged and visiting celebrities often sighted, and Lally definitely felt the need to reconnect to the buzz.

Lally made a quick survey of the occupants: Lilly Hawkins—she'd be having the accordion pleats in her forehead filled in with Restylane. . . .

And Jessica DiSantini, settled in a corner, barefoot, with white explosions of cotton wool separating her freshly pedicured toes.

Jessica was on the Frost and Fire Ball committee, Lally recalled suddenly, and so she made a beeline toward her.

PHOTO: PETER D. GRAVES

LINDSAY GRAVES has worked as a journalist, scriptwriter, and a television producer. She lives in the Hollywood Hills and is currently not an ex-wife.